Suburban Dangers

Megan Whitson Lee

Publishing History
First Watershed Edition, 2017
Paperback Edition ISBN 9781611168945
Electronic Edition ISBN 9781611168921
Published in the United States of America

Dedication

To Stephen, who always believed in me and in our marriage. I thank God for you every day.

Acknowledgements

The horror and enslavement of sex trafficking and its counterpart, pornography, has long burdened my heart. Prostitution in all of its forms is not a victimless crime, despite what society says.

I am thankful to all who have helped with the formation of this novel. This was not an easy one to write. In many ways, it was harder than my first novel, Captives, which was about the same subject. So much has changed within the public schools, technology, and trafficking practices, that I really needed as much input as possible.

To Alycia Morales who read my original manuscript and made so many great suggestions to help me improve the scope and focus, I am so grateful.

To Officer Brad Wrobel and Onzlow Williamson for lending their time to discuss their roles as Security Resource Officer and School Security Guard, respectively, and for giving me an honest idea of the day-to-day experiences and difficulties of "policing" and interacting with kids in a school environment. I know I've had to take some liberties for the sake of the story, but I hope I have at least honored the hard jobs you both have.

To readers of my first draft: Deborah Harris, Cheryl Breeding, Bethany Harar, Debra Metzler, and Misha Chernov. Your comments on my very rough draft guided so much of what it became. Thanks for letting me know what was interesting and what wasn't.

To everyone at Pelican Book Group. I am so honored to be a part of this team. Thank you, Nicola

Martinez, for understanding the importance of this subject and for creating such a fabulous cover. Thank you, M. Jamie West, for your stellar editing. There is a lot of intuition, wisdom, and talent in this group.

To Lisa Thompson, for always being my touchstone and cutting edge information on this tough subject matter. You work in the trenches every day and see the worst of the worst. I pray for this story to be an homage to the women who have come through these horrible experiences.

To my family, for always supporting me and standing with me through this quest to write tough, gritty, sometimes dark topics. You guys have always been my biggest fans and my cheerleaders.

To my husband, Stephen, for always encouraging and motivating me. You've cheered with me in my victories and grieved with me in my losses. Your support and love means the world to me.

Finally, to my Lord and Savior, Jesus Christ. I write stories about and for those who need You in their lives. Thank You for allowing me the honor to serve You.

Have mercy on me, O God,
according to your unfailing love;
according to your great compassion
blot out my transgressions.
Wash away all my iniquity
and cleanse me from my sin.

~Psalm 51: 1-2

1

Kaki
Tuesday, September 15

Kaki was sixteen when she met Sydney Diaz.

The school year had just started, and Sydney was new to Runnymede Secondary. With her long, straight, black hair that hung down to her waist and a lot of piercings, Sydney was one of those girls who stood out. She was in Kaki's algebra and gym class, but right away Kaki could tell Sydney didn't want to be in school. Her face was tight and hard, and she put her feet up on the desk until the teacher told her to take them off.

In gym, Kaki was flattered when Sydney started talking to her. They stood out by the track, waiting their turn to run. Kaki stretched, pulling her ankles behind her. She liked running. She was thin and willowy with long legs that carried her along with speed and agility. "Granddaddy-Long-Legs" her father used to call her. She'd hated that. It made her feel as if her legs were too long, too thin. Weird-looking, somehow.

Sydney looked as if she could be pretty fast, too, but she was just leaning up against the chain-link fence with a slack-faced and bored expression. Kaki could almost envision her with a cigarette in hand, blowing smoke into the autumn haze—if they'd been allowed to do that.

"So like, what do people do around here?" Sydney stared off at the other runners circling the track.

Because Kaki was surprised that this interesting, probably super-cool girl was talking to her, she did a double-take to make sure she was the one being addressed. She didn't really have a lot of friends. On those ridiculous surveys that the school made them take every year—the ones that asked questions like: *How would you describe yourself?*—she always answered the same. *Shy. I like to read, run track, and sometimes hang out with the girls on the track team.* But she couldn't really say she was great friends with any of those kids. Kaki looked at Sydney and shrugged. She couldn't think of how to answer her. "Um…I don't know."

"I mean, like, what's fun to do around here? It seems like this school's pretty lame."

Kaki laughed out of politeness. "I guess it depends on what you think is fun. Everyone around here does the normal kind of stuff."

Sydney yawned, bending her leg back to brace herself against the chain-link. "What do you like to do?"

Kaki's face warmed. People didn't usually ask her that. "I don't know. I'm kind of boring, I guess. I run track, and, well, that's about it, really."

"Girls, you're up!" At the sound of Coach Plant's voice, they moved toward the starting line.

Sydney pushed herself off the fence as though it took an enormous amount of effort and stood beside her at the line.

"Go!" the coach called as he clicked his stopwatch. They began to jog. Sydney was much slower, and she kept motioning with her hand for Kaki to hang back. Finally, Kaki slowed her pace as much as she could.

"You got a job?" she asked, already starting to pant a little, even though she was barely running.

"No," Kaki said. "I just turned sixteen." She didn't know anyone who had a job.

"So? I know a lot of sixteen-year-olds who make a lot of money."

"Really? Doing what?"

Sydney pointed her thumb at herself. "Like me—I mean, I'm sixteen, but with what I'm doing now, I'm making so much money, I'll be able to retire by the age of twenty-two."

Kaki wondered if she was lying. Sometimes kids just said stuff to seem cool. She focused on the finish line ahead. "Wow. That's amazing. What are you doing to make so much money?"

Sydney looked over, and Kaki got the feeling Sydney was trying to read her—trying to see if she could trust her.

"I don't know if I should tell you right now."

"OK." It didn't really matter to her whether Sydney told her or not. If she was selling drugs or something, Kaki didn't want to know anyway.

"Maybe later."

As they crossed the finish line, Coach Plant said,

"That's the slowest I've ever seen you run, Kaki. What's going on with you today? Let's pick up the pace!"

~*~

At home that night while Kaki checked her social media sites, she was surprised to see that Sydney had followed her. @HotSydGirl was Sydney's handle, but Kaki immediately recognized Sydney's picture—a close-up shot of her posing for the camera with puckered lips. Later, Sydney's picture and name popped up on another one of Kaki's accounts. *Sydney Diaz has just followed you.*

Kaki was excited. She'd figured Sydney would think she was a total loser after their conversation on the track. "Maybe I'm just one of the only people she knows at school," she said out loud as she clicked to confirm. She scanned Sydney's page for her statuses, pictures, and people she knew. Sydney had over 2,000 followers on one account and over a thousand on her other accounts.

Inferiority crept over Kaki. She only had around 160 followers, and most of those were family members, distant cousins, and a few friends. Her other social networking accounts were just as pathetic, and she wondered how it felt to be someone like Sydney Diaz—obviously popular, especially with the guys. Most of the posts to her page were messages from them:

hey syd. where u been girl?
heard you moved schools. Ill still c u this weekend rite?
got some peeps for u to meet.

There were a lot of posted selfies from guys and a few girls dressed up in short-short skirts, high-high heels, and tight-tight tops. Sydney definitely moved in different social circles.

Pictures on Kaki's page were of friends making faces in the camera, a few family photos, and a lot of shared dorky sayings: *Only you can make it happen* and *Just because someone doesn't like you doesn't mean you're not likeable*. Kaki felt too intimated to even send Sydney a private message. And she resolved not to be clingy at school either. The quickest way to drive a cool girl away from you was to be too needy.

But over the next few weeks, Sydney hung out with her as though they'd been friends forever. That was when she was in school. Sydney was absent a lot, and Kaki could tell she had a lot of boyfriends, both inside and outside of school.

~*~

"How did you get kicked out of your old school?" Kaki asked Sydney one day in the cafeteria.

"One of the guys I was dating asked me to, like, hold some weed for him. I mean, like, it wasn't even mine. Anyway, someone ratted, and the next thing I knew security guards were doing the big shake-down on me. So I got expelled 'cause it was like the third time I'd gotten caught with something. And I had a lot of money on me, so they figured I was selling it."

"Were you?"

"Nah. I already had that money."

The noisy cafeteria was usually where Sydney relayed the details of her social media life and the guys she met there. Often the story involved the guy spending a lot of money on her. Sydney seemed to love that. She always had a story, and Kaki was a willing listener, although sometimes she felt more like a fan or a follower than a friend.

"So there was this guy I met last night at the club. You would have loved him. He was exactly your type." Sydney crumpled up her napkin and threw it down the length of the table where it bounced off of someone else's tray.

Her type. Did she have a type? If so, what was it? She'd only looked at boys in her classes with a safely removed longing. The idea of approaching them or talking to them was terrifying.

"We were out all night. I got home at like three this morning," Sydney said.

Kaki noticed Sydney's slightly smeared makeup. She'd probably slept in it, if she'd slept at all. "What about your parents? Don't they care you were out all night?" As busy and self-absorbed as her own parents were, they would not be OK with her staying out all night.

Sydney's face darkened. That was the best way Kaki could describe it. She'd read that line in a book once, but she'd never really understood its meaning until then.

"It's just me and my mom. And her boyfriends."

"*Boyfriends*? Like…multiple ones?" Kaki laughed.

"Yeah, they come and go."

"So, you're kind of like her." Kaki meant it innocently enough, but Sydney turned on her with the quickest mood swing she'd ever seen.

"I'm nothing like her. Nothing. *Nothing*. You understand? Guys never get something for nothing from me. Not like my mom…"

"OK." Kaki raised her eyebrows and turned away. Wow. That wasn't the reaction she had expected.

Sydney looked as if she could sprout fangs.

The bell rang and everyone began filing out of the cafeteria.

But Kaki could only focus on how she'd offended Sydney. Sydney would probably unfriend her or something.

In algebra class later that day, as if nothing had happened, Sydney held up her phone, showing Kaki a picture of a smiling guy in a white T-shirt. He had dark hair and tanned skin. "This is Damien," she said in a voice slightly louder than a whisper. "He's really into you."

Kaki racked her brain. Damien, Damien. Did she know a Damien? She didn't think so. Anyway, that guy looked older than anyone she went to school with. "How does he know me?" Kaki whispered back.

Sydney looked down at her phone, texting something. "He saw you at the track the other day. He likes your legs. He said they're like, long and sexy."

Kaki's heart drummed. It must be a joke. Guys didn't like her like that. "Yeah, right."

"Serious. He told me. Look, he's texting me about you right now."

Sydney held up the phone to Kaki's face again, and she saw the text in the green bubble. *Did u talk to ur friend about me?*

"Girls!" Mrs. Moss called out, her voice punctuated with irritation. "Put the cell phone away."

"Yeah, in just a sec," Sydney said, obviously determined to finish her text response to Damien.

Mrs. Moss's face flared. "No, now, Sydney!"

Sydney paid her no attention. Still smiling, she completed her text.

Everyone knew that teachers couldn't do anything

about cell phones. They could ask students to put them away, but they weren't allowed to take them.

Triumphantly, Sydney smiled at Kaki and put her phone down on her desk even as it buzzed against the wood. "I just said to meet us after school. Then you can meet him in person."

Truthfully, Kaki didn't want to meet him—well, she did, but she didn't. Like any other girl, she wanted a guy to like her, but she didn't want to have to come up with conversation and try to be as cool as Sydney. It required too much energy.

~*~

Sydney pulled Kaki into the bathroom after the bell rang and forced some of her red lipstick onto her lips. "You never wear any makeup, and you really should. You've got great lips." Sydney made a smacking sound as she demonstrated how to pop her lips together so that the color spread across the top and the bottom.

When Kaki looked in the mirror, she thought she looked OK, although the bright red was a brash contrast with her pale hair and skin. It would take some getting used to.

"Let's go!" Sydney grabbed Kaki's hand and pulled her down the back steps toward the parking lot by the football field. "He said he'd wait for us out here."

"But I'll miss my bus!" Kaki protested.

"He'll drive us home."

2

Tyler
Saturday, September 19

Tyler didn't know what was wrong with his wife. She'd been sullen and non-communicative since they'd left their friends' house. Lifting his eyes from the illuminated yellow lines in the road, he stole a glance at her pale profile etched against the dark background outside the passenger window.

The gentle slope of her nose gave way to naturally pouty lips and a proportionally prominent chin—a profile as familiar as his own face after ten years of marriage. The downward turn of her mouth and the creases tugging at the corners had always been an endearing part of her facial features, but over the past few years the lines had deepened with discontentment.

"What's wrong?" he asked.

"Nothing."

He sighed. Her response signified this would be one of those conversations where he asked and pleaded for information, and she punished him with silence for some offense he'd committed and knew nothing about.

"I know it's not nothing, so you might as well tell me what I did. Things were fine back at Hilary and Drew's house. Now what?"

She shook her head, crossed her arms, and turned her body toward the window where the outside scenery blew by in a mask of neons, car lights, and darkened landscape.

"I did what you wanted, didn't I? I told them how great everything looked. What else did you want me to do? Did I not act envious enough or something?"

"This has nothing to do with you, Tyler," Lana said, her voice muffled and trembling, the way it always sounded just before she burst into tears.

"If it's not me, then what is it?"

"The world doesn't revolve around you." She sounded just like her mother.

He ground his teeth. "Man, and don't I know it."

These days, Lana never missed an opportunity to remind him that not only did the world not revolve around him, but he was on a priority list in a galaxy somewhere outside of her solar system. He was lucky to get a civil word out of her unless they were going out to eat or doing something extraordinary.

"What's that supposed to mean?" she snipped.

Tyler shrugged. "I never know what's going on with you, Lana. You asked me to come with you to this thing tonight, and I agreed—even though I really don't care that their house was remodeled by some television network and they're going to be on that home show. And really, I don't know why you're so impressed with that either. We have a nice house, too."

"Yeah, right. I'd be embarrassed to ask Hilary and Drew over."

Tyler shook his head. He refused to respond to her goad. Now she was just picking a fight.

Lana sniffed, turning her face toward the window. "Between your mess—the golf clubs, the computer stuff—and the kids' junk all over the place, some days I feel like checking into a hotel."

"Fine," Tyler said. "You need me to do more around the house? Is that what you're saying? 'Cause I can do that. Just let me know."

But it was obvious this offer wasn't enough for her. Oh no. She was looking for a proper battle tonight, and nothing he said would cool Lana's belligerent state of mind. Her ice-blue eyes—the ones he'd fallen in love with so long ago—bored into the side of his face.

"Did you see the storage units they put in their basement? And the size of their master bath? It would be great to have some updated hardware in our bathrooms, instead of the builder's special from fifteen years ago."

"Well, maybe we can look into that," Tyler said as anger circled his emotional periphery, banging at the outskirts of his brain with all of the clumsiness of an off-kilter washing machine. "We'll see what we can do, Lana. We don't have the budget a TV network has, though."

"Or the Newell's budget," Lana reminded him.

They'd had this conversation more than a few times recently—ever since Hilary and Drew Newell, friends from church, had been contacted by Remodel, Inc., Television and were told they'd been chosen from thousands of applicants to appear on one of the reality shows.

"After the new year, we'll contact The DIY Outlet, OK? I'll see if I can have someone come in and give us a quote on our master bathroom, but we can't go crazy and do an entire remodel like they did. We don't have that kind of cash."

Lana turned on him. "I know that. Why do you

keep saying that? What do you want me to do? Go back to work? Put the kids in daycare?"

"No, Lana, I'd just like you to be satisfied for once in your life. It doesn't matter how much we have, you always want more. We could live in a mansion in Great Falls and you'd want us to live in Newport, Rhode Island, instead. You are never, never happy!" The rage came on suddenly, leaving him no space to talk himself down from it. He'd been reading a book on controlling his anger, and he was working on redirecting it, channeling it into his workouts at the gym, or finding ways to deflect or control it before it flared. But tonight, the techniques weren't working.

Lana went silent.

He sighed heavily as the adrenaline subsided, and he propped his elbow against the window, leaning his head upon his hand as he drove. "I'm sorry," he breathed, as much to himself as to his wife.

At least he had dinner with the Wolfs to look forward to. He and Lana had gone early to the Newells' open house so they could still meet Josh and Molly for drinks and dinner. Plus, tonight they were trying out the new restaurant on the corner of Elden Street and Herndon Parkway. That was secretly the only reason he'd gone to this thing anyway. That and the chance for a night away from the kids. "You might text Molly and Josh and let them know we'll be a few minutes late," Tyler suggested.

"Oh, I'm not going. Text and tell them to forget it."

A tight knot developed in the pit of Tyler's stomach. He knew that tone all too well, and it usually meant she would dig in her heels. Some of their worst fights had ended that way, and in the last few years, the fights were more frequent. Embarrassing premature exits from church events and Bible studies, feeble excuses as to why they couldn't attend birthday parties, sheepish phone calls to his parents asking if the kids could stay the night with them because of some emergency or other...Tyler knew they never really fooled anyone. "Come on, Lana. I've been looking forward to this all week."

"Why? So you can stare across the table at Molly all night?"

"What?" Tyler shot her a glare. "What are you talking about?"

"Never mind."

"No. That's ridiculous. And you know it."

"Is it?" she sneered.

"Yes, it is. Now you're acting like some crazy person. Let's just go and have a nice meal and forget about this."

"No." She crossed her arms. "I'm not going. I'll jump out of this car right now."

"Molly and Josh are our friends, Lana. It's not like you don't know them. Anyway, they're probably already there."

"You want to call them or you want me to do it?"

"Come on, Lana." He really did want to go. He wanted to sit down with friends and talk and laugh. He wanted to pretend like they were in love—as they used to be.

"Nope. I'm not going."

"What do you want to tell them?"

"I don't care. Tell them there's an emergency with the kids or the babysitter."

"You mean lie."

"I don't care what you tell them. Tell them the truth, for all I care."

Tyler's shoulders slumped with defeat. The clicking of the car's signal light reminded him of the *tsking* noise his father sometimes made—the one he'd made ten years ago when Tyler had told him he was going to marry Lana. His father hadn't liked Lana from the start. And Tyler's father had never been wrong about anything.

Tyler shook his head as he jerked the steering wheel to the right and onto the street that would take them home rather than to dinner. "Fine. Go ahead and call them. Tell them whatever you want."

3

Kaki
September

Damien was a hot guy and everything, but to Kaki, he looked a little older than she'd expected. Way older-than-high-school old. Not dad-old, but definitely twenties.

"Hey pretty ladies!" he called out as they approached.

Kaki lagged behind a little as Sydney walk up to him. She really knew how to strut with confidence. Shoulders back, head held high, hips swaying everywhere. She had the clothes, too. The skinny jeans, the figure-enhancing top, the high-heeled pumps.

Kaki wore the same jeans she always did, straight-legged and plain. Her favorite button-down hung like a shapeless sack over her T-shirt. Her slip-ons were like house slippers. Sensible, comfortable, sometimes sporty, never sexy.

"Hey-hey!" Sydney swaggered up to him, throwing her arms around his neck.

Kaki could hardly look at him. He had sharp eyes that pierced her skin like arrows. Hot, prickly things raked over her insides as his gaze moved up and down her body.

"I saw you at the track the other day. Girl, you can run," he said.

Standing beside her, Sydney was beaming, her eyes searching his for approval at her lucky find. "She's good at *everything*."

"No, I'm not," Kaki protested, hating the flirty way Sydney said the words. Red blotches flamed over Kaki's neck and cheeks like they always did when she was embarrassed or nervous.

"You ladies wanna take a little ride?" Damien asked. "I was thinking we could drive out to Sterling. Hang with a buddy of mine."

"Sure!" Sydney responded.

Something panged in Kaki's chest—something telling her she shouldn't go. Yeah, he was hot, but his eyes kind of scared her. And how would her mom react to her riding home with some strange, older guy?

"I need to get home," she said.

"Why?" Sydney sneered.

"I—I have homework, and my mom doesn't like me to go anywhere after school." *Yeah, there we go. Use Mom as an excuse.*

"You really want your mom controlling you like that?" Damien's eyes stared right over her head. It seemed he was already losing what little interest he'd had in her. She was too much of a baby.

Kaki shrugged. "I don't know."

Sydney gripped her arm, forcefully pulling her toward Damien's car. Her tone was practical. "Come on. We'll just stay for a little while. Then Damien can drive us both home. Right, Damien?"

"Yeah," he said, settling into the driver's seat.

Sydney opened the passenger door of the blue Mustang, and pulled the lever to slide the seat forward as she motioned Kaki into the back.

With a sick feeling in the pit of her stomach, Kaki

crossed over the threshold of her old life and into the backseat of Damien's car, a place which would forever after remain a symbol of the mode of transportation into her new, secret life.

~*~

That first afternoon when she rode with Damien and Sydney to meet his friends, it really wasn't that bad. She was scared at first, but the neighborhood seemed OK, and that made it all seem a little less scary.

As they walked up to the house behind Damien, Sydney pulled her back and spoke quietly. "So, these two guys are really good friends of Damien's. Spider and Jak. They're cool. But they're also like, really intense. So don't say anything to them unless they talk to you, OK?"

"Spider?" Kaki wrinkled her nose. "What kind of name is that?"

Sydney shushed her. "Seriously. They're super-cool. Be good."

Kaki's heart beat so hard it felt like there were extra vibrations to its rhythm. Like the time she went to a concert with her dad, and the music was so loud and the drum so strong it was kind of hard to breathe—like the drum was changing the rhythm of her heart or something.

And the way these guys looked at them, staring them up and down, licking their lips, and saying words in Spanish. Even the guy who spoke English used so many curse words Kaki had a hard time understanding him. Both guys were marked with blue and black tattoos that swirled and slithered up their necks and down their arms. Kaki wasn't introduced to either of them.

"New girl?" One guy asked Damien.

"Yeah. Hopefully," he said.

Kaki wondered if by "new girl" Damien meant he hoped she'd be his new girlfriend.

It was obvious Sydney knew these guys well. She talked to them in Spanish using flirty tones, touching one guy on the arm and smiling up into his face. Damien made strange hand motions to the other guy.

It was like she was in a foreign country where everyone knew the language but her.

But they didn't stay there very long. Damien and the guy who had *Masters of Sin* tattooed on his forearm exchanged another weird hand motion along with a bag of something, and then they left.

She was supposed to stay at her dad's house that night, so she directed Damien where to drive and drop her off. Damien got out of the car, popping the seat forward so she could crawl out. Sydney stayed in the car, fixated on her phone as though they weren't even there.

"So, you gonna hang out with us or what?" Damien leaned against the door of his car and held her hands in his.

Something like electricity radiated up and down her arms, and it was really hard to look at him. "I don't know." She could barely hear her own voice.

"Why don't you know? Don't you want to hang out with me?"

She shrugged and giggled. She didn't know what to say. *Awkward.* "I don't know. Maybe. Don't you care I'm only sixteen?"

He tugged at her arms, pulling her so close her midsection touched his. "I like sixteen." His eyes narrowed and didn't look directly into hers. "You wanna come out with me this weekend?"

"Umm…" She stalled for time. She wanted to, of course. She didn't know if she was staying at her dad's or her mom's house that weekend, but neither of them would agree to let her go out with this guy. "How old are you?"

"Does it matter?"

"Not to me. But it'll matter to my parents."

"So don't tell them. Haven't you ever heard of sneaking out?"

He moved in closer. Was he going to kiss her? Her stepmother might see from the window of the house. She was always at home. "Don't." She pushed him away with another giggle. "Someone might see."

"Let them see." He pulled her forcefully to him and mashed his lips against hers. She'd never been kissed before, and it sent her heart into a frantic beat, not unlike when she ran track. As he pulled away from her, she imagined her face looked like a goofy kid with a weird smile and half-closed eyes.

"So what time should I pick you up Friday?" he asked.

Sydney answered from the car without even looking up from her phone. "Ten o'clock."

"That's early," he said. "But OK. I'll pick you up at ten. Meet me out front. I'll pick you up on the curb. Be ready. Don't make me wait."

There was the slightest hint of warning in his words—just enough to send a current of fear through her chest. She didn't want to disappoint him. She'd be there.

But ten o'clock was getting close to her weekend curfew, and it would definitely send up red flags with whichever parent she was staying with that night. She'd have to figure a way to get out of the house without them knowing.

~*~

Kaki's mom and dad, Tyler and Christina, divorced when she was very young. She never remembered them living together. Her life, and that of her younger brother's, had been a split screen—the one they lived with their single mother, and the one they lived with her father, stepmother, and half-siblings. Two days a week they lived with her dad; the other days of the week were at her mother's with alternating weekends at either place. It was the only life she and Brandon had known and they were used to it, but sometimes it was a series of confusing and annoying schedule shuffles and mishaps.

"Oh no! This is my A-day book bag!" Kaki squalled. It was Friday morning and as she rummaged through her notebooks in preparation for first period, she realized with a sense of dread that it was a B day.

Sitting next to her, Riley Donaldson laughed. "Let me guess. Left it at your mom's?"

"Yes." Kaki slammed her hands against the top of the desk. "I can't believe I mixed them up again. I did this Monday too. All of my homework is in my B-day bag."

Riley pulled out a plastic bag full of orange slices. She took one out of the bag and offered another one to Kaki. "Want one?"

Kaki shook her head. "No. What am I going to do?"

Chewing, Riley shrugged. "Just tell Ms. Kempton what happened. She'll understand. Tell her you'll turn it in tomorrow."

It wasn't so much Ms. Kempton wouldn't understand, it was more the frustration she had with herself. She was doing this all the time now. Ever since she'd started high school the previous year, it had been harder and harder to keep her schedules straight.

"Did you remember your running shoes?" Riley asked.

Kaki nodded. "Yeah, I keep those in a separate bag and it goes with me to both houses."

"At least you remembered those."

Riley and Kaki had known each other since elementary school, but it had only been last year when they became friends. Running cross country together, the two girls were matched in their sprinting and cross-country abilities, and they ran with similar times. A friendly competition had sprung up between them, each one driving the other to work harder to be the fastest.

As though another thought occurred to her, Riley held up a finger. "Mm. The most important thing is," she sputtered with her mouth full of orange, "did you remember to tell your mom to pick you up after track today?"

Kaki clutched at her hair. "Argh! No, I forgot. I'll text and tell her right now." She pulled her cell phone out of her bag and clicked it on. There was already a text waiting for her on the screen.

Ready for tonight?

Her heart surged. Damien.

Yes.

"Who's that?" Riley asked.

Kaki immediately blackened the screen of the phone and stuffed it back into her bag. "No one."

"Your mom?"

Oh, yeah. She still needed to text her mom. "Yeah, it was just my mom."

~*~

Kaki's mom dropped her off at her dad's and stepmom's house late that afternoon.

Lana, her stepmother, was vacuuming, and she was already drunk. Lana kept tripping over the cord and banging the vacuum into the wall. Her eyes were red and watery, too. Lana drank vodka. Straight up. So what if it was only three o'clock in the afternoon?

Lana probably didn't think anyone knew about it.

She kept a bottle in the kitchen cabinet, tucked behind some tumblers, and another one behind the cleansers in the downstairs bathroom.

Kaki even knew Lana's drinking schedule. Most days, drink number three came right around the same time—in between the kids coming home from school. The youngest, Celia, was home by noon, but napping by two-thirty. Micah, the eight-year-old, never arrived before four o'clock. Last year, Kaki'd had a stomach bug and stayed home from school for nearly a week. She got to know Lana's habits well simply by observing how long she stayed in the downstairs bathroom and noting how fast the clear liquid in the bottle behind the tumblers evaporated.

Lana continued to vacuum but waved to Kaki.

Kaki made her way into the kitchen where the appetizers were assembled on trays. Oh, that's right. Lana had told her earlier in the week that the Wolfs were coming over that night. She only hoped Molly and Josh were gone by ten, as she had to figure out some way to sneak out after that. Anxiety clenched her stomach that she could be late for her first date with Damien.

First date. A thrill ran through her. It was her first date *ever*. And the fact that it would be with a gorgeous and much older guy doubled the electric charge coursing through her body.

Lana had gone to some trouble stringing assorted cheese cubes on red and green toothpicks, topping them off with a perfect square of ham at the end. She'd also made a spinach and artichoke dip, and a steak was marinating in the refrigerator.

Kaki popped a cheese cube into her mouth.

Lana was a good cook—much better than her mother—and Kaki loved eating at their house. Lana said cooking was the only creative outlet she had anymore. Numerous times she'd told Kaki, "I never expected that at thirty-eight, I'd be living in suburbia as a housewife with a bunch of kids. I figured I'd be in California with an acting career. That was what I studied in school, you know. But...it's been eight years since I've even auditioned for anything. Once all the babies came...well, the actress in me died as the children grew in my womb."

Dramatic. But then, Lana was a drama queen. Kaki didn't know how many times she'd heard her tell the same story. Usually after Lana's third vodka.

Moving back into the living room, Kaki caught a glimpse of Lana storing her drink behind some books. "Hey, Katherine—oh, there you are." A smile—like one that a little kid would give when found stealing a finger full of icing from a fresh-baked cake—slinked over her lips. She probably wondered if Kaki had seen her hide the drink. "Hey, would you mind gathering up the laundry upstairs and throwing it in the washer for me? Grab it out of Celia's room, too. She's napping, but you know she sleeps like the dead."

"Sure." She lumbered upstairs, going first into Celia's room where the little girl's form was completely covered by a mound of blankets.

Celia's clothing was in her pink princess hamper. Kaki reached in and pulled out her clothing, laughing softly as Barbie dolls, stuffed animals, and plastic figurines spilled out onto the floor along with the dirty clothes. Kaki picked out the extraneous items and threw the clothes into the plastic bin she carried.

She left the room as quietly as possible and moved to Brandon's room. Brandon was her full brother, three years younger than her. He was a pretty angry kid these days, and she didn't know if that was because he was thirteen, or because her dad and Lana had laid down the law with him. No video games unless the grades improved. Kaki was a straight A student, but in the past year, Brandon's grades had tanked, sliding from As and Bs to Ds and Fs.

A mound of dirty jeans, T-shirts, and socks were all piled carelessly at the end of his bed. This was a typical teenage boy's room strewn with video games, graphic novels, and sport jerseys—a cluttered mess covering most of the floor and furniture. On Brandon's desk, just next to his computer, a pile of notebooks towered. Crumpled papers poked out from between them—no doubt homework he'd never turned in.

Shaking her head at the disarray, Kaki bent over to gather the dirty clothes, her elbow grazing the edge of the desk, shifting the computer's mouse enough to disturb the screen saver. Waking from its sleep, the computer clicked and whirred. As Kaki stood up, her arms and nose wrinkled with disgust at the smell of pungent and musky teenage boy castoffs. She scanned the room and her gaze locked on the computer screen. Graphic images of naked women slapped her in the eyes with the same force as if someone had thrown a bucket of ice water into her face.

She stood frozen, her mouth dropping open as she attempted to adjust to the grotesque pictures. She'd seen pictures of naked people before, but nothing so intense. "Ew!" Closing her eyes momentarily, she opened them again to marvel that those pictures really were there. She grabbed the mouse and closed out of the images. Pausing for a moment, she stared at the screen, now returned to the desktop, still trying to process what she'd seen. Kaki turned away and hurried out of the room, closing the door behind her.

Now what? She threw clothes haphazardly into the washer. Should she tell her dad and Lana? To do so would cause World War III in the house. Anyway, she guessed all teenage boys looked at that kind of stuff.

~*~

Kaki watched the clock on the wall of the living room as she joined the adults for their pre-dinner drinks and appetizers. She couldn't eat anything. She was too nervous about what was to come later that night.

"You should have seen the house!" Lana was telling Josh and Molly Wolf. "I mean, they have an entertainment room with a popcorn machine and everything!"

Molly and Josh listened politely, nodding and smiling.

"It sounds beautiful," Molly said.

"I think they said the show will be broadcast sometime in February. *Renovation Reload*. Have you seen it?" Lana swigged from her glass. She was on drink six, at least.

"I'd be especially happy for the people from HGTV to visit some of our neighbors' homes," her dad interjected while using his teeth to rake cheese cubes off the toothpick and into his mouth. "I mean, let's face it. The last few years the neighborhood has been going downhill. Have you seen the neighbor's house two doors down? Broken windows they've never bothered to fix. Trash all over the front yard. I was glad there was no HOA when we first moved here. Now, I see why people have them."

"I'm worried about the gangs," Josh said. "This town is becoming a breeding ground for them. Body found just last week in the park. Gang related. Unfortunately, we're starting to see activity at the school, too." Josh was the security resource officer at her school. He was a big guy—really tall with broad shoulders—and very good looking. Tonight, he wore a light blue button-down that made the blue of his eyes really stand out. It was always really weird for Kaki to see him out of his uniform.

"Makes me want to pull Katherine and Brandon out of there and enroll them in a Christian school or something," her dad said, tossing her a glance.

Lana laughed and looked over at Kaki. "Yeah, right. Christina would never let you do that. For that matter, Brandon and Katherine probably wouldn't either."

"No, I wouldn't." That would be the last thing she'd ever agree to do.

Kaki couldn't help but stare at Josh and Molly

Wolf. Molly, an English teacher at her school, had really exotic features—a heart-shaped face, high cheekbones, and huge, dark eyes. Molly was in her late thirties and Josh was in his early forties, but both of them looked years younger.

"Katherine," Lana said, waving to her stepdaughter to get her attention. "Could you go in and get us some drink refills?"

Kaki hurried into the kitchen with the tray full of empty glasses.

Molly followed, her black, heeled boots snugly fitting against her thin and toned calves. She click-clacked down the hall. "Do you need any help in here?"

"No, I got it. Thanks."

Suddenly Lana rushed into the kitchen—hot on their heels. "I forgot to put the roast in the oven to warm it up."

Oh, no. How long would that take? At this rate, they wouldn't get to eat dinner until eight. She glanced nervously at the digital clock on the microwave. Kaki refilled glasses of water for Molly and Josh and a martini glass for Lana.

Molly leaned against the counter, watching Lana throw some salt over the meat before putting it into the oven. "Josh and I haven't seen you and Tyler at church lately."

Lana sighed. "There's been a lot going on. It seems like every Sunday there's something else."

Just as Kaki started to pour Lana's drink from the martini shaker, she fumbled and spilled the rest of its contents across the granite countertop.

"Katherine!" Lana scolded.

"Sorry."

"Oh, here. Let me help you with that." Molly reached for a paper towel.

"No, no. It's fine. I got it."

Molly righted the shaker and began scooping up the spilled ice from the floor. As they cleaned water from the floor, Lana kept talking. "Actually, I'll be honest, Molly. My decision not to go to church anymore is a conscious one. The whole faith thing is Tyler's arena, not mine. I mean, I always had a marginal belief in God, and when I married Tyler, I knew it was important to him and his parents, but over the years, it's just been something I do for the kids, not because I truly believe what the pastor's saying. You know? I'm not really sure what I believe anymore."

Molly remained silent. She stood up straight beside the kitchen island and wadded up the vodka-soaked paper towels.

"Thanks for helping me," Kaki said. She liked Molly. She had never had her as a teacher, but she had never heard any of the kids say anything bad about her. She just seemed really nice.

"Are you sure I can't get you something to drink?" Lana asked Molly, her words slurring together a little.

"No, thanks. Just water. That's about all I get to drink anymore. One cup of coffee in the morning, and then water, water, water. No sodas, no sugar, no carbs even though I'm supposed to gain five pounds. It's ridiculous."

Lana snorted. "Gain five pounds. I'd be happy to give you ten of my own pounds."

Molly smiled. "It's supposed to help the conception process."

Molly and Josh had been trying unsuccessfully to have a baby. They'd had a bunch of miscarriages, but there hadn't been any babies born.

Kaki followed Lana as she carried the drinks back into the den where the men sat talking about teenagers and high school and the problem with public education. All topics that didn't interest her in the least.

"I don't know what's going on with Brandon these days—thank you, honey," Dad said, lifting the martini from Lana's hand.

"You're welcome," Lana frowned.

Kaki laughed. Her dad thought the drink was for him. He had no idea how much Lana drank, and Kaki wasn't about to tell him. That wasn't her business. It was just one of the many ways she felt like an outsider in their house. Sometimes she thought of herself as a ghost. She observed, but she didn't intervene.

"Yeah," her dad continued without missing a beat. "He's so angry. He has a lot of his mother's personality anyway—very combative and sullen. But these days *everything* is a battle. His grades have plummeted, and all he wants to do is play video games."

Josh nodded. "Where is Brandon tonight?"

Kaki was wondering the same thing. Hadn't her mom said he would be walking over from a friend's house, and that was why she didn't drop him off? Oh, whatever. Her mom talked all the time anyway. Sometimes it was hard to keep it all straight.

Lana jumped in. "Oh, I forgot to tell you, Tyler. Brandon texted me earlier and said his mom set up some appointment for him early in the morning. He decided just to stay with her tonight."

"What kind of appointment is he going to on a Saturday?" her dad asked.

Lana shrugged. "I don't know. He didn't tell me. I

figured it was another doctor's appointment or something."

Her dad shook his head. "Brandon's mother...get this—she thinks he's *depressed*." He stressed the word with mock sympathetic tones. "He's just so depressed he has trouble getting out of bed in the mornings to go to school. You know what my dad would've done if I'd pulled that kind of stuff?"

"Dragged you out of the bed?" Josh's smile suggested his dad would have done the same.

"Absolutely. They would've cracked me on the head and yanked me out by the hair. And if they'd really needed to, they would've stuck me in a wheelchair and rolled me into the school."

Josh laughed. "Yeah, mine, too. What about when Brandon stays here? How do you get him out of bed to go to school?"

"Oh, believe me. There's no problem when he's here. I don't know how his mother handles stuff, but Brandon knows he's at school on time when he stays with us."

"Which isn't very often anymore," Lana added with a taut smile. "He's pretty much at his mom's during the week now."

"Yeah, kind of funny, huh? It's too hard to stay here where we actually make him—oh, I don't know— *do* something. He's just a little too comfortable for my taste."

"Suburban dangers," Lana said. "And it's not just the kids. We're all so comfortable and complacent here. We're all lulled into this false sense of security. This is what we strive for, right? Marriage, big houses in the suburbs, great jobs, children. And then what? Does it make any of us happy?"

An uncomfortable silence followed Lana's words. Everyone sipped from their drinks as they struggled for something to say.

Kaki looked from Josh to Molly to her dad—who was glaring at Lana. Kaki wasn't sure what Lana was talking about or what she had said that was so wrong, but, obviously, something was bugging him.

Molly broke the silence. "I think you're right, Lana. Isn't that the nature of the human heart, though? We always want more. We're never content with what we have. There's always something else out there that will make us happy."

"Yes," Josh agreed. "That whole God-shaped-hole thing."

That phrase—*God-shaped hole*—always made Kaki cringe. What did that really mean? She wasn't sure she understood a lot of the lingo tossed around in the church. A few years before, she used to go to church with her dad and Lana, but her dad didn't go much anymore, and Lana almost never went.

Eight o'clock. Two more hours. She hoped the roast hurried up and cooked so Molly and Josh could eat it and get out of there. As their conversation continued on, she went to the staircase and began walking up and down it. Some of the steps creaked as her foot pressed them down. She practiced placing her feet on the outer edges. Yes. Much less creaking there.

Molly and Josh left at 9:30. By then Kaki was ready to push them out the door. Would her dad and Lana go to bed soon? If not, she'd have to start thinking about her bedroom window's possibilities. To her relief, within fifteen minutes, they were in the bedroom with the door shut, their raised voices on the other side of it.

"What was that all about?" Her dad's sharp tone

suggested he was hot about something.

"What?"

"That whole speech about 'suburban dangers' and how none of us are happy. Talk about embarrassing. And what's all that supposed to mean, anyway? You're not happy again? What do you need now, Lana? Do we really need to have Remodel, Inc. come in and renovate our house to make you happy?"

"Are *you* happy, Tyler?"

"I'm happy enough."

"Well then, I guess that's all that matters."

After that, their voices died down, and she breathed a sigh of relief. Lana was probably passed out, and her dad slept soundly anyway. Nine fifty. Ten minutes until show time. She looked down at her phone as it buzzed with a text from Sydney.

Good luck tonight. Don't let me down, K?

Let you down? What?

Damien is a good catch. Don't blow it.

With her heart pounding against her rib cage, she quickly changed into a borrowed pair of Sydney's skinny jeans and a black sweater she usually wore for fancy dinners out with her parents. Pulling the rubber band out of her hair, she fanned the yellow strands over her shoulders and assessed herself in the mirror. She still looked really young. Reaching into her purse, she grabbed the red lipstick Sydney had given her and ran it over her lips as Sydney had shown her. Popping her lips together, she evaluated the effect. It was a little better. The lipstick did make her seem a bit older.

As she had rehearsed earlier, she descended the steps, her feet positioned on the outer edges, and managed to keep the creaks to a minimum. She paused at the bottom and listened for any sound from her parents' bedroom. When there wasn't any, she quietly turned the lock on the door, then the knob, and finally she was free. Locking the door, she turned to see Damien in his car, already waiting for her at the curb. As she approached the dark blue car, a sense of panic jolted her. Not enough to keep her from getting in, but enough to dry out her throat and cause her hands to sweat.

Damien hardly looked at her as she climbed in. "Turn off your phone."

"Why?" She grasped at her phone nestled in the little silk purse her grandmother had hand-sewn for her.

"Because." He looked over at her and smiled as he placed his hand on her leg. "I want to have you all to myself. I don't want there to be any interruptions."

Kaki laughed. She didn't know how else she should respond.

"I'm serious," he said. "Before we go anywhere, I want to see you turn off your phone. That'll be your first test—the first chance to show me how much you really care about me."

Not wanting to disappoint him, she switched off her phone. In response, he floored the car, and they peeled out of the cul-de-sac. Within minutes they were speeding east on the Dulles Toll Road toward DC.

"Where are we going?" She yelled over the blaring rap music.

"To a club. Do you like to dance?"

She couldn't remember having done any dancing except the ballet classes her mother had forced her to take as a kid. She shrugged. "I don't know."

The rest of the car ride, Damien didn't talk to her, and even if she'd wanted to talk to him, she couldn't.

The music was too loud. Occasionally she glanced over, but his face was completely unreadable—blank and emotionless. What he was thinking? Did he really like her? It was so hard to tell.

In the city, they entered the club through a back alley littered with trash, beer bottles, and cardboard boxes that looked as if they'd been out there for years—blackened with mildew and partially pulverized into the wet pavement. Something smelled funny, too. Was that beer or urine? Whatever it was, it reeked.

The man standing at the door reminded her of the Incredible Hulk—right down to the green cast onto his skin by a neon light shining over his head. The Hulk nodded in acknowledgement of Damien. They obviously knew each other since Damien didn't flash so much as a driver's license to get them into the club.

It took her eyes several minutes to adjust to the darkness of the place, and the same foul smell was inside as well. Damien grabbed her hand, pulling her through crowds of people blocking the back hallway—men in T-shirts and tattoos, women wearing what looked like bathing suits, all of them drunk, some of them staggering, cackling. Everyone knew Damien.

"Hey, man! How's it going?" the question came from everywhere and everyone they passed. "Damien—been trying to get in touch with you this week. Got a little something for you. Damien! I need to talk to you. Damien! Damien!"

What if someone checked her bed and found her gone? What if something went really wrong and they ended up in a car wreck or something? It was obvious Damien would be drinking. As soon as they walked into the room with the dance floor—its dark floors, walls and ceilings lit only by the strobes and colored stars projected onto the floor—Damien pulled her along. He parted the crowds as they moved until he finally positioned them in front of the bar.

"Whiskey for me." Damien ordered his drink from a stern-looking, black-haired girl wearing very red lipstick. "What'll you have?"

Kaki's mind froze. She didn't know anything about drinks. She'd never had anything other than a sip of beer, which had tasted terrible. "Um…" She stalled. "I—I don't know. A Coke?"

He nodded to the girl. "Yeah, and spruce that up with a little rum, OK?"

The bartender nodded and went off to fill their orders.

"Really?" Kaki's hand flew to her mouth. "Won't we get in trouble?"

"Nope." Damien looked at her, laughed, and shook his head. "You come into a bar and order a Coke?"

"I don't drink. I don't know what to order."

Damien turned toward her, his dark eyes flashing a strange mixture of sexy and sinister. She was beginning to understand the appeal of the bad boy as her skin ignited with attraction for him. At the same time, she was scared, too. This was not the sort of guy who would take her to prom.

"You really *do* need me," Damien said. "Did you grow up Mormon or something?"

"No." A wave of embarrassment swept over her. She must seem really inexperienced and ignorant to him—a mature, sophisticated guy.

A sea of bodies on the dance floor moved like soulless robots, their faces blank and expressionless as they gyrated and jerked and salivated all over each other. *Dark. This is a dark place and not just because it's not well-lit. And no one knows I'm here.* That thought sent a strange shiver up her spine, and she couldn't tell if it was excitement or fear.

Once their drinks arrived, Damien took her hand again and led her down a hallway, into a room just across from the bathrooms. The room was cold, probably because it was positioned so close to the doors, but there were a couple of tables in the room littered with empty Chinese take-out containers and ashtrays full of cigarette butts. Damien motioned her toward a couch on the far side of the room, flanked on either side by posters of bands and scantily clad women. She sat down on the couch. The other end of the room was papered in advertisements for strip joints and several more posters of naked women.

"It's a little quieter in here." Damien fell onto the cushion beside her and nearly spilled his drink. "I thought this would be a good place to talk, get to know one another."

He had to take her all the way into DC to a noisy, crowded bar to talk in a quiet place? He probably had his reasons.

"What is this place?" She finally took a sip from her drink. It was sweet and pretty much tasted just like Coke. "Do you come here a lot or something?"

Damien laughed. "Yeah, I guess you could say that. Me and a buddy own this place."

"You own it?" She was impressed.

"Yeah. For a couple of years now."

"So it's just like…a dance club? You make a lot of money from owning it?"

"Yeah, I make a lot of money. Plenty of money to

take care of the both of us."

Kaki's heart rate sped a little, thrilled at his words. Did he want to take care of her? They hadn't known each other all that long, but her mind started to churn with ideas and dreams and plans.

Damien pulled her close to him, leaning down and kissing her. She tried to respond as best she could with her limited experience. She felt awkward and stupid. Was her mouth doing the right things? And what was she supposed to do with her hands?

As much as Kaki enjoyed the kissing, she involuntarily shrank away when Damien's hands began to move toward the front of her shirt. She gasped. "I'm sorry."

Damien sat back on the couch, fumbling in his pocket for something. He produced a small, clear, plastic bag filled with blue pills. He held them up in front of her face. "Ever tried these?" Before she could shake her head in response, Damien answered his own question. "What am I talking about? Of course you haven't." He opened the bag and pulled out two pills, quickly downing one of them and holding the other out to her. "For you."

"What is it?"

"Oh, come on, baby. Don't ask a bunch of questions. Just try it. You'll like it. I promise."

But Kaki really didn't want to swallow something that she didn't know about. Once a pill was down the hatch there was no getting it back. "What will it do?"

"It'll just relax you. That's all. It'll make you feel a little like you're floating on a cloud."

She didn't want to do it. But she also didn't want to disappoint him. She took the pill from his fingers and popped it into her mouth, washing it down with a generous gulp of her drink.

She didn't feel anything for a long time. Not until they were on the dance floor jumping up and down and the strobe lights looked like crystals flashing all around her. As she turned, the lights wrapped around her like the fluorescent, lighted necklaces she and her brother used to get as children during festivals. Kaki and Brandon twirled them around under blackened summer skies, attempting to smack one another with them and laughing when one of them cracked the rubber tubing against the other one's arm or leg hard enough that it actually hurt and left little red welts.

Kaki wasn't sure if Damien was anywhere on the dance floor, but other men were dancing with her, putting their hot and sweaty hands on her hips, panting against her shoulders with their whiskey breath.

She didn't know how long she danced, or when Damien finally pulled her away.

She awoke. They were driving on I-66 West. Damien's music thumped away in the cloudy recesses of her head.

An exit. He pulled off. They were on a familiar road. Her vision cleared enough to see the sign that read *Welcome to Herndon.* They turned down one street, then another, then her street.

"Hey." He pushed at her shoulder to wake her. "You're home. Can you make it inside by yourself?"

"Yeah...yeah..." In a near catatonic state, she rolled out of the car. Somehow, she made it into her house and into her bed. She only slept a few hours, waking to dreams of demons chasing her, pawing at her, trying to get her to follow them into hell.

4

Tyler
Monday, October 10

Tyler locked the front door and stepped off the front stoop into the unseasonably cool fall morning. Swiping the newspaper covered in a damp, plastic bag from the driveway, he carried it to his car where a frost covered the windshield. He sat inside with the defrost on high and waited for his car to warm up. Removing the paper from the newspaper's plastic sleeve and unrolling it, he glanced over the headlines. One on the front page caught his attention. *Local High Schools Battle Sex Trafficking Within Their Own Walls.*

He backed out of the driveway. His morning routine consisted of a twenty-minute coffee stop, and sometimes a chocolate croissant, at Sam's Café—a corner mom-and-pop place where he could read his paper before heading into work. After ordering his dark roast coffee and doctoring it with three packets of sugar, Tyler settled into a table by the door—his usual booth was occupied. He smoothed the paper and began to read.

An investigation is underway to discover the whereabouts of two young females last seen entering their high school two weeks ago. On Friday, September 30th, Ariana Martinez and Marie Fuentes-Santiago were counted present in their first period classes, but disappeared shortly

39

thereafter—seemingly into thin air.

Principal Shep Miller declined to talk to reporters, but Security Resource Officer Brad Franklin reported the girls had been recorded on security camera leaving the building from a back exit at 9:38 AM. A classmate of the girls claimed to have seen them climb into the back of a silver car parked on the curb at the side of the building. It sped away soon after. No one has seen or heard from them since, despite repeated attempts to ping their cell phones and track them through GPS devices.

This incident has prompted an investigation unearthing a widespread sex-trafficking problem spanning over a large cluster of middle, secondary, and high schools in the Northern Virginia area in which a combination of gang-related sex crimes, underage prostitution, and wide-spread drug usage intersect.

"I was thirteen when my mother sold me the first time," says one sixteen-year-old girl now in safe housing and under custody of the state. "She said we needed the money, and so I did it."

This unimaginable trend is not an anomaly. At least half a dozen minors from three different schools claimed their parents sold them to fellow gang members or strange men for money, food, or housing arrangements. And these are only the ones who have come forward.

"You get good at hiding it. You wear clothes that cover the brands, the tattoos, the needle marks, the bruises. And what's going to happen anyway? So what if the school calls your parents? They're the ones who sold you."

Tyler took a bite of his chocolate croissant. Wow. It was almost too horrible to read. He was just glad this wasn't his kids' school.

"Hey there!"

Tyler looked up and into a familiar face. Mid-thirties, African American with the face of a model and the voice of a commanding officer. "Remember me? We've met a few times at the Wolfs' Christmas parties? I'm Josh's former colleague, Abbie Jackson."

Oh, yes. Now he remembered. She had been at their summer cookout. Detective Abbie Jackson. "Yes, of course. I'm sorry it didn't register at first."

"No problem. I just recognized you and thought I'd say hello."

"How are you doing? You still working with the Herndon Police Department?" Tyler remembered that she used to be Josh's partner when they were both on patrol.

"Yes. I'm wearing quite a few hats at the moment. I'm on a gang-related task force now. How are you doing? And your wife—what's her name again? Lara?"

"Lana. We're doing fine. Hey, you want to join me?"

"Well..." She glanced back up at the busy counter where the baristas called out orders and slammed down silver pitchers with clanging stirs. "Maybe just for a second. I'm waiting for my double, extra-hot, soy, skinny caramel latte. They got the order wrong the first time."

"I wonder why." Tyler laughed. "They're probably so relieved when I come in and order a black coffee."

Abbie slid into the chair opposite him. "How's Josh doing? I haven't talked to him in a while."

"I think he's doing fine. He and Molly had dinner with us a few weeks ago."

"Great guy, I think the world of him. I missed him so much when he left patrol to become SRO at Runnymede Secondary. But I still see him sometimes when he calls me in to check on a case up there."

Tyler smiled. "Yeah, he's a great guy. And a good friend. Let me ask you something, Detective Jackson. Have you heard about this case?" Tyler slid the newspaper around so that Abbie could read the headline.

She scanned the words, nodding her head grimly. "Recently I've worked on these types of cases. I sometimes join forces work with the county's human trafficking task force."

"Is this really going on?" Tyler asked. "Parents selling their children here in this area? That's some sick stuff."

"Afraid so. And more often than you'd think. Wherever you have drugs and gangs, you've got all kinds of stuff going on."

Tyler shook his head. "I didn't finish reading the whole article, but my understanding is that there's a much larger sphere than just this one incident of the two missing girls."

"It's so hot in here." Abbie stood and removed her coat, revealing the sidearm that hung on her hip. She draped her coat on the back of her chair before resuming her seat. "It's a highly complicated situation with lots of operators. As I said before, we're dealing with gangs here. We've got more than five thousand gang members in this area, and they've discovered sex trafficking in a big way. It makes sense, you know? People are a much more powerful commodity than drugs. Drugs—you use 'em once—they're gone. You gotta get more. People? Well, you can use them over and over again. There's a lot more mileage to be had in trafficking a person. Plus, these guys have such power over the women, you know? They get them so messed up in the head the girls don't know what's true and what's not. And they're completely committed to their pimps—or their *boyfriends*—as they call them." Abbie's tone of voice was both commanding and smart. She was very confident...and very attractive.

"As far as we know," Abbie continued, "these two girls were both children of gang members. I don't know anything for sure, yet—they're still questioning a lot of people—but my hunch is that they're probably in some other state right now. There're a few leads, but to be honest, once they're across state lines, it's really hard to track 'em down. We gotta get the feds involved."

"And it's not just this one school. It's happening all over the place, right?"

"Yeah. There's a long trail of interconnected underage prostitution—and it's not in an isolated area. There are cases here in Herndon and all over the DC metro area. All over the United States, for that matter. It's widespread. These guys are highly networked, and they're experienced at hiding the goods, which...in this case are under-aged girls."

"I've read about sex trafficking going on internationally and even in this country, but...I've never heard about it going on in high school. I mean, this just seems like something the parents in this area should know more about."

"They should. It'll be more and more commonplace. Mark my words." Abbie turned her head suddenly as the baristas called out something from the bar. "Oh, that's me." She stood, gathered her coat and stepped up to the bar.

Tyler remembered seeing Abbie at the cookout— with her well-toned figure and biceps in a short-sleeved shirt. She was in great shape—short in stature, but she still looked very capable. And she was a vibrant and enthusiastic woman. Smart, too. He had no doubt she had probably worked hard to rise through the ranks so quickly.

She made a pass by his table again. "It was nice talking to you, Tyler."

He smiled. "It was very nice talking to you, Detective Jackson. Be careful out there."

"Will do. You'll tell Josh I said hello, won't you?"

"I sure will."

On his way into work, Tyler passed by Runnymede Secondary School where Molly and Josh both worked. It was still early, and the school remained dormant and silent. In another hour, it would be teeming with kids. Parents and adults alike would drive by on their way to work, viewing it as a place of learning and knowledge and never knowing what went on beyond the walls. For that matter, he didn't really know what went on in there.

~*~

Tyler sat at the desk in his cubicle and stared listlessly at his computer screen. Crushing pain permeated his chest. It was only Monday. He'd somehow make it through today, and then he'd wait as late as possible before heading home to his depressed wife and noisy, needy children, along with a list of chores and expectations. Maybe this was what marriage looked like after ten years, but it hadn't always been this way.

"Happy Monday. Have a fun weekend?"

Tara Pickard stood in the entrance of his cubicle.

Tara had worked for CEF about six months. Fresh out of grad school, she'd assumed the graphic artist vacancy on the web services team left by a woman who went out on maternity leave and never returned. Tara was probably around twenty-four and cute as a button. She was gymnast-muscular and built like a cheerleader, with a personality to match.

Happy for the interruption, Tyler sat back in his chair, cracking his knuckles behind his head before resting them there, enjoying the full-length view of Tara's feminine floral skirt resting just above her knees. "I don't know." He smiled. "Let me think. It was all a blur. Watched some football. Went to the gym—first time in a while."

"Haven't seen you on the racquetball court lately."

"I've been pretty busy. Work and home and...you know. That kind of stuff."

"I get it," she said, smiling. "Hey, I finished that presentation you asked for—the one for the meeting tomorrow. The one with all the concentric, moving circles. I sent it to you."

"Oh, right. Great. Thanks. I'll take a look at it."

"OK." She moved as if she was heading back to her desk, but instead she clung to the side of his cubicle, her right leg raised behind her—one shiny pink pump frozen in mid-air. "And just so you know, I'm going by the gym today to play a little racquetball, if you want to join me. Blow off a little steam?"

Maybe after so many years of marriage Tyler was a little slow on the uptake. But that flash in her eyes and the model-like pose she held against the opening of his cubicle? Tara was flirting with him. He fidgeted with a pencil on his desk. "Maybe. Let me see how the day plays out."

A voice inside his head told him he was stoking a fire he had no business tending. He should go straight home, do not pass *Go*, do not play racquetball with Tara Pickard. On the other hand, maybe she was right about blowing off a little steam.

"OK. Think about it and let me know." Tara wiggled her fingers at him in a waving motion as she drifted slowly away from his cubicle, her eyes still locked with his.

The phone on his desk rang. His head still reeling from Tara's smile, Tyler lifted the receiver. "Hello?"

"Mr. Jones? This is Rebecca Hough. I'm an assistant principal at Runnymede Secondary."

Tyler's brain, which had been momentarily side-tracked with Tara's shapely legs, suddenly snapped to attention. "Yes? Is something wrong?"

"Well, there's an issue with your son, Brandon. I can't really talk about it on the phone. Would it be possible for you to come out to the school sometime today?"

"Have you tried to call my ex-wife?"

"Yes, we tried to call her first, but we couldn't reach her."

Tyler's irritation surged. What now? Where was Christina? And what was it with Brandon that he couldn't pull himself together and get with the program? Tyler sighed heavily into the phone. "I have a lot going on at my job today. Is this urgent?"

"Yes. I would say it is. It's pretty important."

"OK. Let me shuffle some things around, and I'll be out there as soon as I can." He hung up the desk phone and fished out his cell to speed-dial his ex-wife. It went straight to voicemail. With barely restrained anger, Tyler left a message. "Christina, where are you?

A principal at Runnymede just called me about Brandon. You know, I'm getting tired of this. I'm busy. I work for a living. Whatever this behavioral nonsense is that's going on with him, it needs to stop. Call me back so we can get this sorted out. In the meantime, I have to cancel a bunch of meetings so I can get all the way back to Herndon to find out what's going on."

~*~

The sight of Josh Wolf's uniform—the dark gray shirt covered by a flak jacket, a radio protruding from the shoulder—gave him a funny feeling in the pit of his stomach. Why was Josh here? What had Brandon done?

Josh nodded to Tyler as he sat on the opposite side of the conference room table. A teacher Tyler recognized from back-to-school night sat on Josh's other side. Ms. Richardson, or something like that. Young, twenty-something, blonde thing, first year of teaching.

Rebecca Hough, the assistant principal, pulled out a chair from the head of the table.

Tyler's hands were clammy as they intertwined in his lap, and he was careful not to allow them to rest on the table where they might leave visible, sweaty streaks on the surface.

The door to the conference room opened again.

"Sorry I'm late." A young woman breezed into the room and reached across the table to shake Tyler's hand. He noticed her nails were filed into claw-like shapes and painted pink. "I'm Melanie Hewick. One of the guidance counselors."

"We'll call Brandon in to join us in a few minutes,"

Rebecca Hough said. "We wanted to have an opportunity to chat with you first, let you know what's going on."

Tyler nodded, a knot forming in his throat. He met Josh's gaze. "I'm eager to know."

Rebecca motioned toward Ms. Richardson. "Kate, do you want to tell us what happened?"

Kate Richardson looked nervous. She leaned forward. "During first period this morning, two students came to see me and reported that someone they knew showed them a picture of some naked girls from this school. Apparently, the pictures are being uploaded and circulated around some social networking sites."

"OK. So…how does that involve Brandon?"

"We talked to the girls to get more information," Josh spoke up. "They said Brandon was one of the boys flashing the pictures around on his phone."

Tyler's face flamed.

Josh looked down at his hands.

The room was silent. Everyone staring at him.

Was he supposed to say or do something? Maybe express shock or horror? Instead, he sat back in his chair. "Isn't this pretty common? Boys looking at naked pictures on the Internet?"

"Yes," Josh said. "It's extremely common. In the past few years, sexting cases have been rampant."

"There are several factors here." Rebecca Hough said. "One, Brandon allegedly showed pictures to fellow students. Two, the pictures were of fellow students. We don't know who took them or how they were circulated."

"Did you talk to Brandon?" Tyler asked, a little defensive. He hoped they would bring Brandon in soon. He wanted to get to the bottom of this. "I mean, I have a feeling that he didn't intend for this to be a big deal. He's only thirteen, you know."

Rebecca glanced over at Josh with an expression that seemed to say, *you wanna tell him or do you want me to do it?* Something about her smug, middle-aged mouth suddenly bothered him. He didn't like her hair either—it was all wiry and disheveled. She reminded him a little of…Lana.

"Tyler," Josh began in a tone that suggested he was being as gentle as possible. "This is pretty serious. What these kids don't seem to understand is that once a picture like that is on their cell phone, they're in possession of child pornography, which is a felony. And if they send it around? Well, now they're guilty of distribution."

"Yeah, but…well, I mean, he's thirteen," Tyler repeated.

Josh shook his head. "Doesn't matter. We have to open a formal investigation."

"Investigation?" That seemed extreme. These were kids, for heaven's sakes!

"Especially because it involves other students within the school," Rebecca added.

"Mr. Jones?" Now the guidance counselor was leaning forward, using that same condescendingly gentle tone and a sickly sweet smile that made his stomach ache. "Have you known Brandon to look at any kind of inappropriate pictures? Online stuff? This is around the age when boys become interested in things like that. Sometimes even younger."

Tyler shook his head. "No. No, he doesn't look at anything." The words spilled from his mouth easily. He knew his son. Brandon didn't express interest in anything nowadays, except maybe video games. Definitely not girls.

A strained silence settled over the room.

"Well, let's bring Brandon in," Rebecca said.

"I'll go get him," the guidance counselor offered. "He's just outside."

The quiet of the room continued as she stepped outside to retrieve Brandon.

Tyler was all too aware of Josh's presence in the room. The awkward nature of the situation was nearly unbearable.

As Brandon entered, his gaze fell heavily on his father, and then Josh, before dropping to the floor. He slipped into the nearest chair as the voices all greeted him in unison.

The guidance counselor spoke in her irritatingly sweet tone. "Now, Brandon, we're here because we're concerned about you. We'd like to hear your side of the story."

"I already talked to him." With a quick flick of his eyes, Brandon motioned to Josh.

A sudden rush of anger coursed through Tyler, and he gritted his teeth. He'd had to leave work for this. And now they were going to waste his time with this ridiculous psycho-babble about hearing Brandon's side of the story? *Why not mete out his punishment and let's get this over with!*

"I realize you and Officer Wolf already spoke," Melanie Hewick said. "But I think your dad might like to know what happened."

"I don't know…it was just like…Jared and I were checking out our Trapster account—"

"What is Trapster?" Tyler growled.

Brandon looked down at his hands and shrugged.

"It's just a site where kids post stuff."

"Like naked pictures?"

Another shrug. "I guess. Sometimes."

"Well, you won't be using that account anymore." If they didn't move this little summit along, he would do it.

"So," Melanie Hewick jumped back in, once more steering the conversation, "so you and Jared were looking at your Trapster account…"

"Yeah, and he said, 'that looks like Caitlyn and Astrid.'"

"Two girls you know?" Melanie clarified.

"Yeah. And so then we started calling other people over to look at the pictures."

"Then you downloaded the pictures to your phone," Josh clarified.

"Yeah." Brandon looked down again.

"Did you repost them?" Josh asked. "Send them around to your friends?"

"I…don't…think…so." Brandon's eyes raised as though trying to remember. "I think maybe Jared did…" Which probably meant Brandon did, too.

Josh sat forward in his chair. "Like I told you earlier, Brandon, having those pictures on your phone is a class six felony possession. Reposting them or sending them out is a class six felony distribution…of child pornography."

"Really?" Brandon's blue eyes were wide.

Josh nodded, his lips pressed together, his eyebrows raised.

Tyler figured they were just trying to scare the kid with all of this class six felony stuff, and he was OK with that. Hopefully, he would learn his lesson from this little escapade.

Josh turned to Tyler. "You'll probably be contacted by investigators."

With another surge of anger filling him, Tyler turned to Brandon and held out his hand. "In the meantime, you can hand over your phone."

"They already took it," Brandon said.

Tyler looked at Josh.

Josh nodded. "Yeah. We had to confiscate the phones with the pictures on them."

Geez. Grimacing, Tyler rubbed his forehead. "OK. Well, is there anything else? I really need to get back to work."

"We'll handle it from here," Rebecca Hough assured him. "I'm sure Officer Wolf will keep you in the loop if we need to question Brandon again."

Melanie Hewick turned to Brandon, addressing him as if he were the only person in the room. "And sweetie, I want you to come see me every week, OK? I want to check in on you, see how you're doing. If you just need to talk…"

Tyler felt his upper lip curl involuntarily. *Give me a break.* He pushed his chair back and stood. He had to get out of there before he threw up. When he had been in school, someone looking at naked pictures of girls would have been taken to the principal's office, suspended, and that would have been the end of it. All of this drama—investigations, guidance counselors and their touchy-feely platitudes…

5

Kaki
October 12

Sneak-out mission #2. As Kaki crept down the stairs that night, she waited to hear, "Hey! Where do you think you're going, young lady?" But the house was silent. She guessed she was lucky her dad and stepmom were too wrapped up in their own problems to notice her. They hadn't really acknowledged her existence since she was twelve anyway.

Damien had told her he'd wait for her out front at eleven that night. "I'm not gonna wait long. If I don't see you out there right at eleven, I'm taking off."

Kaki didn't want to disappoint him, so she made sure to start her escape a half an hour earlier. It might take a while to get out without making a sound. It was easier than she thought it would be. She repeated her tactic from before, walking on the sides of the stairs, avoiding the middle section, trying to prevent each step from creaking.

One of the steps creaked anyway, so she just walked normally down the last few and right out the front door. It was that easy. As she looked back at the house, no lights popped on in the windows, and her cell phone didn't ring. No one knew she was gone. But it was a cold night, and she had to stand on the curb shivering for fifteen minutes until Damien finally showed up.

This was the third time seeing Damien, but her nerves still got the better of her when climbing into his car, almost as if those black leather seats that smelled of smoke, car cleaner, and pine-scented air freshener, held some sort of danger. And she couldn't make that feeling go away, no matter how crazy she was about the guy. She realized that was part of her attraction to Damien. The risk she took each time she was with him made him that much more appealing. Not everyone got to be with someone like him, and he had singled her out. In his eyes, she was special, and winning his attention made her somehow worthy of love.

"Anyone see you leave?" His dark eyes flashed in the glow of the dashboard.

"No. Everyone was asleep."

He nodded his approval and drove slowly out of the cul-de-sac, leaving her breathless with the anticipation of what would happen between them that night. Moments before, she'd been safe inside the warmth of her dad's house. With Damien, she was anything but safe. Even so, exhilaration filled her lungs and pumped blood through her heart, creating an electrically-charged friction inside her body.

"Where are we going?" she asked, as they turned onto Elden Street.

"You'll see." He looked over and raised his hand to touch her cheek. "It's a surprise."

Her heart hammered, and all the fluid in her mouth dried up as her teeth chattered together, partly from the cold and partly from his touch.

They drove down a road that took them through an industrial park and into a neighboring town—only a few miles from congested Herndon—where the lights and houses disappeared, and open, undeveloped land eclipsed the noise and neon. They passed a few tractor trailer stores, car shops, and warehouses and finally turned into a gravel parking lot marked by a motel sign, The Cove Motor Inn.

Damien parked the car and turned to her, his face shadowed from the overhead street lights. "Yeah, well, it's not the Hyatt, but I know the guy who owns this place. He won't give us any trouble." His meaning was obvious. By trouble, he meant the guy wouldn't care she was underage.

They kissed in the car for a long time before going inside, and when they finally did get out of the car, Damien wrapped his arm tightly around Kaki's neck and shoulders, almost as if he was worried she might take off running into the woods. And there were a lot of woods around them. Dark, silent. She shivered.

The lobby was small and smelly, with wood-paneling like in old houses. There were two couches positioned in an L-shape, both of them beat-up and tattered. On the brownish leather one, discolored and worn with decades of use, sat an old man and a much younger Asian girl. He was fat and greasy looking, and he puffed away on a cigar. Kaki nearly choked on the smoke that filled the room. The woman laughed and flirted, pushing at him with her small, thin hands. Her nails were painted green.

The second couch was orange fabric set into a wood frame. It also looked a million years old. The fabric was worn around the edges, pulling away from the frame, which allowed the stuffing to poke through.

Damien pointed at it. "Go sit over there while I check us in."

Kaki did as she was told, but she sat at the end

farthest away from the man and the woman pawing at each other.

Damien and the man at the counter mumbled something, and the man looked over Damien's shoulder at her. His dark eyes widened momentarily before constricting into a squinty smile. He dangled a key in front of Damien's nose. When Damien reached for it, the man snatched it away from him, laughing hysterically. Damien laughed too, but with a final "Give me that!" he managed to pull it out of the man's grasp.

"Come on," he said, wrapping his arm around her shoulders as she rose hesitantly from the couch.

The room was dark and covered in the same wood paneling as the lobby. It was also freezing. Kaki's breath materialized in the air like a puff of smoke as Damien flipped the wall switch and the fluorescent, overhead lights flickered and glowed.

She stood just to the side of the door, frozen, as Damien moved with expert ease around the room, turning on the television and the heat. He held a brown bag, and as he sat down on the creaky bed covered in an ugly, lime-green bedspread, he began pulling miniature bottles from it—a mixture of clear and brown ones—and lined them up on the dusty nightstand.

He looked at her briefly. "What are you doing just standing there?"

She shrugged, nearly paralyzed, and focused on a black-ink tattoo on his neck that said *Devil-Dog*. "I'm cold," she croaked.

Damien grabbed some kind of container from the long chest of drawers that held the television. "It'll warm up in here in a minute. Go ahead and take your coat off. I'm running down the hall for some ice."

As soon as the door closed behind him, Kaki looked around the room. This was her chance. She could just run. She could run right out that door. Or she could climb out the window. She knew what she was there for, and with the way things were going it seemed pretty certain what she thought was going to happen would happen. But Damien hadn't said he loved her, and she wasn't even sure if she loved him. She liked him a lot. The idea of being with him had filled her mind for the last few weeks, and she'd fantasized about him some. But now that it came right down to actually doing it? This wasn't how she'd pictured it happening at all. Not in an old, ugly, dusty motel room smelling of stale smoke and mildew.

Damien returned a few minutes later with the tan container full of ice, and remembering she was supposed to take off her coat, Kaki shrugged out of it, allowing it to fall onto a chair.

"What's your pleasure?" He motioned to the bottles on the nightstand.

Her stomach rolled at the idea of drinking. She felt as if she might throw up. "I don't know." Her voice trembled.

"Whiskey or vodka?"

She shrugged. "Whatever you're having."

"Well, I'm a whiskey man. My dad drank whiskey, his dad drank whiskey, and his dad's dad drank whiskey. I like tequila, too, but I didn't get any of that."

"I'll have whiskey, I guess."

The trembling moved into her legs as she watched him pour the brown liquid over the ice. He filled two glasses and handed her one of them. "Come on." He patted the bed beside him. "Sit down here. I won't bite."

Kaki wanted to talk. She wanted to talk more about his father and his father's father. "Did you grow up here?" She took a sip of the cold liquid that stung the back of her throat like the medicine she used to take for coughs.

"I've lived all over."

"Where'd you go to high school?" She stalled for time, even as his hand rested on her thigh, and then slid her knee-length black skirt upward.

Damien downed his drink in three quick gulps and turned to look at her. His breath was sweet from the whiskey as he leaned toward her. "Too much talking." He lifted the glass from her hands. She heard the ice clink against the sides of the glass as he shoved it onto the nightstand next to his.

He pushed her back onto the bed.

She didn't protest. She did everything he wanted. And afterward, she wanted to forget all about it.

6

Kaki
Friday, November 10

"I can't believe you dropped out of track." Kaki stood with Riley in the hallway as kids rushed by them in waves. The bell had rung signaling the end of the day, and there was a mad rush as freshman and sophomores moved toward the bus ramp, juniors and seniors toward the back parking lot. Riley was on her way to a big cross-country competition. The one Kaki had performed really well in the previous year. The one she would have been going to now if she had still been on the team.

Kaki shrugged. "I just got tired of it."

Riley's pale eyes were wide and she tugged at her wheat-colored hair, beginning to braid the ends of it as she so often did. "But you've been doing it forever."

"All the more reason for me to take a break," Kaki said casually. Out of the corner of her eye, she glimpsed Molly Jones closing her classroom door and rushing off in the midst of the kids. She threw Kaki a smile and a wave, and Kaki returned the gesture.

"But you're abandoning me," Riley mock-whimpered, her knees bending as she bobbed up and down.

"Oh, come on. You've got Sarah and Jordan and Emily with you. You don't even need me."

Riley shook her head. "I still don't get it. Is it because of that guy—Damien or whatever?"

"No," Kaki said quickly. "No, I just need more time for homework and stuff." That was a lie. She hardly did any homework these days. She didn't have time. She was too busy sneaking out and meeting Damien three and four times a week. She'd gotten good at silently navigating the steps at her mom's and her dad's house. She just wondered how long she could keep it up.

Riley sighed. "Well, I gotta go. Coach wants us all to be ready to travel at three fifteen."

"You'll be great."

"I still wish you were going to be there."

"Maybe next year."

Riley tossed her gym bag over her shoulder and disappeared into the throngs of other teenagers.

All of these kids were moving around her— dozens of them—walking to class, texting their friends, calling to one another down the hall. Some of them she'd gone to elementary school with, yet she didn't know them. They didn't know her, either. It was as if she watched someone else's life happening around her. She didn't belong here anymore.

~*~

"Lana?" The house seemed empty as she arrived at her dad's that afternoon.

"I'm in the bathroom!" Lana called out.

Kaki heard the toilet flush.

Lana was enjoying her afternoon cocktail.

Kaki threw her book bag on the chair in the living room and sauntered into the kitchen. She opened the fridge and spotted a bowl of grapes which she took out along with some packages of string cheese from one of the drawers. Then she sat at the island while unwrapping the plastic from the cheese and waited. *Bzzz.* A text appeared on the screen of her phone.

Hey baby. Pick u up tonite by 11:30. Dnt make me wait.

Why did he always say that? She had never made him wait. If anything, she'd been the one waiting most of the time. Slipping off the stool, she walked to the cabinet of glasses where Lana kept her hidden stash of vodka. Reaching to the back of the shelf, she pulled the bottle from behind all of the glasses, unscrewed the top, and swilled down a big swallow.

Blech. It was even worse than whiskey. It was nothing like the drinks doctored with juice or soda that Damien gave her. But after a few seconds, the not-unpleasant warmth filled her insides. That sensation was becoming familiar to her now. Holding her breath, she took another swig.

The front door burst open as Micah rushed in. Her younger half-brother's feet clopped across the living room floor to deposit his book bag and turn on the television.

Lana usually picked up Celia a few hours earlier, so she was probably napping now.

Kaki hoped Micah's arrival hadn't woken her. The longer she slept the better. That little girl had an awful temper and was so hard to deal with most of the time. And whenever Kaki was there, it was an unspoken expectation that she would help with Celia. Kaki quickly replaced the vodka bottle behind the glasses and returned to her phone and her bowl of grapes at the kitchen island.

"Mom!" Micah called out.

"I'm in the bathroom!"

Her stepmother just wasn't the right sort of person to have children—she didn't appear to even *like* children. When Lana was first pregnant with Micah she'd seemed excited. But her excitement had apparently faded as the pregnancy wore on.

Kaki had been nine years old when she put her hand on Lana's swollen stomach to feel the baby kick. That day Lana had been crying—her eyes were red-rimmed and her nose swollen.

"Aren't you excited for the baby to get here?" Kaki had asked.

Lana's reply had been delivered as though she were auditioning for a part in some dramatic play. "The excitement of having a baby has a shelf-life. And this one's past due. The joy never lasts. It's sort of like a bouquet of flowers presented for a celebration; the colors fade; the petals start out soft as velvet, but they become hard and brittle."

"Huh?" Fading colors? Petals?

Her father later explained that Lana had passed her due date and was very uncomfortable. OK, that made sense. But there seemed to be something more behind Lana's words.

Lana's cell phone jingled as it lay upon the island near Kaki's bowl of fruit. At the same time the doorbell sounded.

"Micah, can you get the door?" She lifted Lana's cell phone. She didn't recognize the number on the display—a 310 area code. She carried it to the door of the bathroom and knocked. "Lana, your phone is ringing."

The door opened a crack and a hand poked out

and grabbed the phone. Then the door shut again.

Micah appeared in the hallway and pointed behind him, "Miss Suzanne from across the street is here. And she brought a huge gift!"

"It's just me!" Suzanne trilled in her South Carolina accent. She held up a basket wrapped in red cellophane. "I hope it's OK I popped by. I just got home from the salon and thought I'd better do this while I was thinking about it." Suzanne's heavily styled hair looked even higher than usual, and the streaks of blonde through the light-brown strands appeared freshly highlighted.

Just then, a still sleepy Celia made her way down the stairs, her face smushed into a scowl as she rubbed her eyes.

"Hey, sweetie!" Suzanne said to the little girl. "You look like you just woke up."

Celia scowled and whined.

"Lana's in the bathroom," Kaki said to Suzanne.

"Oh, OK. Well, I'll just take this into the kitchen. I can't stay a minute anyway." Kaki followed in Suzanne's perfumed wake as she walked down the hall and into the kitchen and deposited the basket on the island. She turned to Kaki, her hand on her hip, her perfectly lined and shadowed eyes peering down at her. "So how are you doing, Miss Katherine?"

"Fine." It was always awkward when adults asked her questions. She never knew what to say back to them.

"Any boyfriends?"

Kaki's face flamed as she thought of Damien. Of course, no one could know about him. And why did adults always want to know if she had a boyfriend? "No."

Suzanne waved her hand. "Oh, well. Plenty of time for that. What grade are you in this year? Ninth?"

"Tenth."

"Oh my! Moving on up in the world. I remember when my daughter was that age. It seems like yesterday. Time goes so fast."

The bathroom door sprang open, and Lana emerged, nearly colliding with Micah in the hallway. She grasped her son by the shoulders.

"Miss Suzanne's here," he said softly.

"I know," Lana moved over to the island where Kaki and Suzanne stood together. "I heard her voice."

"Celia's awake," Micah added.

"Take her into the den and get her some cookies or something."

Micah was good at things like that. He entertained his sister regularly.

Celia followed her brother into the den, still rubbing her eyes and whining sleepily.

Lana's voice was unusually animated. "Hey, Suzanne. Great to see you. Would you like anything? Coffee? Or maybe something stronger?"

Suzanne shook her head. "No, I just wanted to drop off a little Thanksgiving gift. We're going out of town next week, and things have been so crazy with the holidays coming up and everything, so I wanted to make sure I brought it by."

"Oh, you didn't have to do that."

Suzanne smiled. One of her front teeth was smeared with butterfly-pink lipstick.

Lana picked at the cellophane wrapping that covered the basket of cheese, crackers, summer sausage, and a bottle of champagne. She plucked a small, red mesh bag tied with a white bow and filled with cosmetics—moisturizers, mascaras, lipstick. For the past three years, Suzanne had sold cosmetics through a company called Prism. "This is beautiful! Thank you so much!"

Suzanne motioned as though shooing away flies. "Oh, please. It was just a little something. Nothing much at all. I added a bag of goodies just for you. It's our winter line. I can get one together for you, too, Katherine. There's a really nice trial-size bottle of perfume in there. Lilac scent. Let me know if you want to order any more of it. And, Lana, like I said before, if you're interested in making a little extra money, I can set you up with your first in-home party."

Lana smiled. "Thanks, but my mind hasn't changed."

Even though Suzanne said it was due to Prism's microdermabrasion cream, Kaki knew through a girl at school whose mother worked at a cosmetologist's office that Suzanne had recently started using Botox. With her wide, neighborly smile, Suzanne's face should have crinkled with laugh lines, but due to the paralysis from the injections, her forehead was as smooth as Lake Placid.

Shrugging, Suzanne held up her perfectly manicured hands. "Can't blame me for trying. I think we'd have fun together. In a few years, Katherine, you might want to make a few extra dollars with Prism."

Kaki almost laughed out loud at the idea.

Lana pulled the bottle of champagne from the cellophane, shifting it in her hands. "Would you like some, Suzanne? I'd be happy to open it."

Suzanne shook her head emphatically as she pulled out a chair at the kitchen island and settled in. "Oh no, no, no. I've got to get back. Dale will be home soon, and I need to start thinking about dinner. You enjoy that with Tyler."

A look of disappointment crossed Lana's face as she put the bottle aside and sifted through the other contents of the basket.

"Did you hear the police cars the other night?" Suzanne asked. "I couldn't sleep anyway, and when all the cop cars started rolling down the street, the walls of our bedroom just lit up like a Christmas tree, and I just kept thinking, is this what we're in for now? Is this what we can expect in this neighborhood from here on out? And this is a good neighborhood!"

"No, I didn't hear a thing. I must have slept right through it."

"I think it was Sunday night. It was loud."

"Did you find out what it was?" Lana asked.

"Oh, you know. Some kind of domestic altercation or something."

Kaki sank down on one of the stools positioned in front of the kitchen island, just as the kids started to scream at each other in the den.

"You got to watch your show yesterday, Micah! *I* want to watch *Princess Pepper*!"

"You've only seen that stupid movie like forty-million times! You can watch it whenever you want! I want to watch *Ghost Aliens*."

"No! I was here first! Mommy!"

Kaki caught Lana's imploring glance. "Katherine, would you go check and see what's going on in there?"

Kaki hated it when she was asked to police the kids. "Why don't you let them fight it out?" It was so exhausting to referee their spats.

"Suzanne, I'm sorry. Excuse me a second," Lana said.

Kaki held up her hand and slid off of the stool. "No, I'll get it." Otherwise, Lana would be all annoyed with her.

"Thank you, Katherine."

She sauntered into the living room where Celia's shrill voice escalated into a scream and an all-out tantrum as she attempted to wrench the television control from Micah's hands.

Micah looked up as Kaki entered the room, his expression melting from resolve to resignation. He thrust the control at his sister, and she stumbled backward. "Fine! Take it! I don't care."

Kaki was thankful Micah had given in. It relieved her from having to break up a fight. She wasn't their mother.

The swigs of vodka from earlier warmed her, and she was tempted to go by the bathroom on her way back to the kitchen to take a few more swallows from Lana's other stash. But she didn't want to leave her phone unattended in the kitchen for too long. Damien might text.

"Celia's just become so obnoxious lately," Lana was saying to Suzanne as she came back into the room. "I thought the terrible twos and threes were all I needed to worry about—not the fearful fives. So anyway, what was your big news?"

Suzanne smiled and reached across the island, her bony fingers grasping Lana's, pinning them to the granite. "Well, you know how our daughter is living in Myrtle Beach now? Did I tell you that? She got a job as a dental hygienist there a few months back. She moved because a young man was sort of 'on the scene' at the time. Well, they're engaged now!"

Lana smiled. "That's wonderful! Congratulations.

I remember how excited my family was when Tyler and I got engaged."

Suzanne beamed, her eyes sparkling and her face flushing. "Yes. We're really excited, as you can imagine. And she's our only daughter, and Myrtle Beach is just so far away. So, we've decided to move to South Carolina to be near her."

"That's wonderful. You and Dale must be so excited," Lana said.

Lana was jealous. At least it sounded that way to Kaki.

"Oh, we are," Suzanne said. "We're putting the house on the market next week. But you know, we've lived there for fifteen years. It'll be weird to pack up everything and…start fresh, I guess. Anyway, I just wanted to let you know before you saw a For Sale sign in our yard. And of course, you, Tyler, and the kids have an open invitation to visit any time you like." Suzanne patted Lana's hand. "Well, I gotta dash, sweetie. I'll stop by later in the week, and maybe we can have coffee. Also, I have a great new hand cream I want you try."

Once Suzanne left, Lana began opening and shutting cupboards in the kitchen. She took down a canister of cocoa, sugar, and flour. "You wanna help me make some brownies?"

"Sure. I guess."

"I thought I'd make some for your father before he comes home. They're his favorite." Lana took mixing bowls from the pull-out drawers on the island and set them on the counter. "That was an interesting phone call I got. A friend from college. We studied theater together. She lives in California now."

Kaki nodded. "Cool." Lana passed eggs and a

mixing bowl across the island to her, and Kaki began to crack the shells against the side of the bowl.

"Yeah, she runs a talent agency in Santa Monica. It's been very successful, and she says they have an opening there for another agent. I think she was calling to see if I might be interested."

Kaki looked up. "In California?"

"Well, you know…your dad and I have talked about moving to California before. I know he'd like to be somewhere sunnier, and Micah and Celia are old enough now that I could go back to work."

A funny vibration burned in the pit of Kaki's stomach—a panicky, anxious sensation. Were they moving away? "What about me and Brandon?"

Lana measured out the cocoa and poured it into a separate mixing bowl. "You guys could come visit whenever you want."

"California's a long way away. It's like…the other side of the country."

"Who knows? Maybe you'd love it. Maybe you and Brandon would even want to move out there."

Kaki felt as if she was standing on a tilting platform. Leave her mom out here all alone? Her mom wasn't stable enough to take care of herself. She was bipolar and needed a lot of help. And what about Damien? If her dad and Lana were really moving away and leaving her and Brandon, then she needed Damien more than ever. Suddenly, he seemed like the most stable thing in her life.

7

Tyler
Friday, November 10

"Tyler, could I see you in my office when you have a chance?"

Tyler had been on his way to the elevator, but now he changed directions, moving instead into his supervisor's office. It was strange to hear John Cabrisi's voice, since he hardly ever saw or heard the guy. John was an office dweller and left most of his supervisory tasks to the underling micromanagers.

Tyler yanked the coat from over his shoulder, tossed it on the back of the chair, and dropped the plastic grocery bag containing his half-eaten lunch onto the floor.

"Go ahead and close the door," John said.

Tyler's thoughts fast-forwarded through the possibilities. Was he in trouble? Or maybe a raise was in the works? He closed the door and moved to sit in the chair across from John's desk. As far as he knew, John had occupied this office for years, but it didn't look like it. No pictures or books adorned the shelves. Nothing identified this as a personal space.

John was in his sixties and nearing retirement, and he appeared worn out—graying and balding, leathery pouches under his eyes.

Tyler winced at the thought that in a few years he

might look just as used up and exhausted.

John looked down at his desk as he talked, and Tyler stared at the bald spot on the top of the man's head. "Look, um, I don't want to scare you just yet, but there is the possibility we may not get funding for this task."

"What does that mean?" Tyler knew very well what it meant.

John took a deep breath. "It means if the funding doesn't come through—if the client goes in a different direction—then we'll be moved to a different task, or there'll be lay-offs."

"I see."

"We'll do what we can, of course. We'll try to shuffle things around. You never know. We might still get funding, so don't despair yet."

"I won't." He should feel shocked or angry or scared, but surprisingly, none of these applied to the numbness inside his heart. Nope. Nothing. No sadness, no regret. Staring down the barrel of a potential layoff, Tyler enjoyed a surreal sense of excitement and relief. If he lost his job, he'd be free from this laborious work. Of course, that would mean he was out of a job, which presented all sorts of other problems. Still, he couldn't help it. The idea of never having to set foot inside the CEF building again was appealing. He walked back to his office to grab his stuff.

Tara Pickard returned to the edge of his cubicle looking as fresh and adorable as she had earlier that morning. "I thought you were leaving."

"I was. I got waylaid."

"You know, I was thinking," She twirled around the post on the side of his cubicle. "I was thinking of playing racquetball this afternoon, but..."

Tyler sat back in his chair and watched her with amusement. "Yes?"

"I may forfeit my personal fitness regime today for an early drink at 1482. It's been a tough day. What about you?"

"Wow. Well, that's a departure from your original plan. Sounds like a better one."

"I think so."

"Are you asking me how my day was, or are you asking if I'm going to 1482?"

"Both, I guess."

He took a deep breath. He really needed to be on that three forty-five Metro. He usually worked six thirty to three thirty, and if he was lucky, he could make it home by four thirty. It was three now. If he went with Tara, he wouldn't be home until much later. He'd have to lie and say he was working late. "I don't know, Tara."

"Raj is willing to go along…if you need a chaperone." She smiled.

"Well, OK." His resolve caved. "If Raj is coming then maybe I'll join you." It seemed safe enough. He texted Lana that he had to work late and would be having dinner with Raj. It was partly true, but it was still a lie of sorts. Just as he pressed *Send*, his cell phone rang. His ex-wife's name appeared on the display. Christina. She was the last person he wanted to talk to right now. He clicked *Decline*.

~*~

The place was packed with after-work diners, and with over an hour's wait to get a table, the trio opted to sit at the bar. Raj Khan loved to talk to anyone. He talked to the hostess, the waitress, the guy sitting next to him, the guy sitting next to the guy sitting next to him. One question set Raj off on a conversational tear—his Indian accent more pronounced. "Yes, we all work together at CEF. Do you know CEF?"

"No," the server said as she rinsed out a pint glass. She looked a bit jaded—as though she'd been bartending a few too many years beyond her target career-switch date. "But let me guess. Government contracting?"

"That's right. How did you know?"

She sighed and rolled her eyes. "Because all that ever comes in here are you contractor types. You want another hot tea?"

"No. One hot tea and a cheeseburger is enough for me. I have to get home to my wife and three children. And she's pregnant again, so soon we'll have four."

"Congratulations," she deadpanned before moving to another customer on the other end of the bar.

"Wow! I didn't know, Raj! That's great!" Tara patted his arm, her smile warm and dimpled.

"I didn't know that either, Raj," Tyler said. "Wonderful news."

Raj beamed as he held his cup and moved it in a circle, sloshing the remaining tea around inside. "Yes, it is good news. I haven't told many people."

"Was it planned?" Tara asked.

The uninhibited tongue of youth. They said anything they wanted and everyone just chalked it up to their stage in life, along with a lack of understanding and life experience. He felt as if he lived in a world—at home, at church—where no one actually said what they thought or felt.

"Yes, it was planned. All of our children are planned—even if we didn't plan them. Because God did."

"Oh." Tara took a sip of her drink. She obviously didn't know how to respond to that.

Raj winked at Tyler. "God has told my wife that we will have six children."

"Six?" Tara gasped, nearly choking on her wine.

"Yes, six."

"How can you afford that?" Her voice reflected the horror in her expression.

"We don't worry." Raj smiled. "We know the Lord will provide. He has so far. Children are a gift from God. Don't you think, Tyler?"

Tyler looked up from toying with the edge of a napkin. "Hmm? I'm sorry. What?"

"I was just saying to Tara that children are always a blessing. Don't you agree?"

"Oh, yeah—yeah. A blessing. Yeah."

"You have four of them, don't you?" Raj asked.

Tyler shrank a little with the reminder. "Um…yeah."

"So you know it. The blessing of children. The more children, the more blessing," Raj proclaimed.

Tyler nodded, hoping for a change of subject. He didn't want to talk about the blessing of children. He'd been enjoying this time of separation from his family. He wanted to marinate in that feeling for a little while.

Tara grimaced. "I guess so. I mean, maybe one or two blessings—but six?"

"And if the Lord tells us there should be more, then there will be!" Raj's phone buzzed against the wood of the bar top, and he snapped it up. He placed it against his ear while he held his other ear closed. "Yes?

Snehali? What is it?"

Tara threw a shy glance in Tyler's direction. His stomach muscles clenched as he returned the smile.

"Oh yes. Yes, I'll be home right away. Should I stop and get anything on my way?" Even with the restaurant noise around them, Snehali's voice buzzed from the earpiece of the phone. "OK. Yes. Children's flu medicine. Right now. I'm leaving right now." Raj clicked off the phone and began to gather his things.

"What's wrong?" Tara asked.

"Manpreet, our youngest, is ill. She has a fever. I need to get home right away."

"I hope everything's all right," Tara said.

"Oh, yes, it will be. I just need to get the medicine to her. Good night. I'll see you both Monday."

"See you Monday, Raj." Tara smiled and waved.

A breeze of anxiety fanned over him at the prospect of being alone with Tara. Maybe he could just leave with Raj. "Do you need any help?"

Raj waved his hand. "No, no. It's fine. I've got my car. Thank you and God bless you both. See you Monday, God willing!"

Left in the hands of his captor.

Tara turned to him, her green eyes flashing. "So, here we are. All alone."

~*~

Tyler hadn't meant to spend two hours with Tara at 1482. Time had somehow slipped by and so had the number of drinks. He'd only meant to have one beer, but he'd ordered a second. The gold, bubbly beverage sat before him. Should he drink it? One was usually his limit. He really needed to catch the Metro. But on the other hand, he was really enjoying himself.

"I'm from Connecticut. Grew up in New Haven, attended University of Connecticut, and moved down to Northern Virginia because the job opportunities were good," Tara said. "My options were limited in New Haven. I could've married a friend of my father's, I could've gone to Europe for grad school, or there may have been an internship at the university. But I wanted to be where the action was, you know?"

He did know. He'd once wanted action and excitement and fulfillment. But then he'd met Lana.

She didn't wait for an answer. "So, how long have you and your wife been married?"

Wife. For a moment, he'd forgotten he had one. "Let's see. I think we've—"

"You think?" She laughed with a loud cackle, grabbing his forearm. "Don't you know?"

He laughed. "No, I know. I know. It's been over ten years."

"Wow!" Her eyes were wide. "That's a *really* long time."

The words spilled off his tongue: "It feels like it's been longer."

She jumped on it, snatching the opportunity and running with it. "Really? Why? Aren't you happy?"

Warnings from the pulpit chanted. *Don't discuss problems in your marriage with the opposite sex. Don't allow yourself to be alone with members of the opposite sex.*

But Tara was persuasive. "Come on. You can tell me. I won't tell anyone. I mean, who would I tell?"

Tyler signaled to the server. "My check, please."

Tara's stool squeaked against the hardwood as she sidled closer. She placed her well-toned arm on the bar top, and settled her pretty, pointed chin into the juncture between her knuckles. "Tell Tara," she purred.

Some of Tyler's discomfort was buffered by rationalization. He chuckled a little as he thought that maybe he could help her—sort of like telling her a cautionary tale. Maybe he could prevent her from making the same mistakes he'd made out of a false sense of obligation or expectation. "When I met Lana we were in our late twenties. I was coming out of a bad first marriage, and Lana was just gorgeous."

"How old was she?" Tara interrupted.

"I don't know. Maybe twenty-seven, something like that. Anyway, she was an actress, and she'd wanted to go to Hollywood and have a career out there. I talked her out of it, I guess."

"So what happened?" Tara seemed to be nearly salivating. "Why aren't you happy now?"

Tyler sighed, his shoulders dropping. "I don't know. Life happened. No relationship is happy all of the time."

"I think it can be. If you're with the right person."

Tyler recognized her seductive expression—the pouting lips, the strategically lowered eyes. He looked away. "Not even if you're with the right person. That's the problem with human relationships. At some point, they always sour."

"You wanna get out of here?" She ran the tip of her pointer finger over the top of his hand resting on the bar. "Get some more drinks at my place?"

A battle raged within him. One part of his heart and head were horrified, the other segments were attracted, intrigued, filled with longing… "No," he said quickly. He looked down at the remainder of his beer. "I need to catch the Metro and get home."

"Are you sure?"

Tyler's cell phone vibrated against the bar top. Turning it over, he spotted Lana's name on the screen. He smiled up at Tara, coming back to earth and his responsibilities. "Yes, I'm sure. I need to get home."

~*~

While riding the Metro home that evening, Tyler broke out in a cold, sweaty nausea. Shame flooded over him. Just like when he looked at websites he knew he shouldn't. *Very Nude Girls*, *Young and Fresh*, and *Hot Porn on Tap* were some of his favorite sites, and he was viewing them more and more frequently, despite the side effects of guilt and anger. The high was sometimes worth it. At least tonight he hadn't done anything really stupid. Looking at pictures was one thing, but it wasn't as bad as an actual affair.

As the Metro announced its entrance into Reston's Station, Tyler's mood nose-dived. Soon he would be home with his wife and kids. He retrieved his car and drove the ten minutes it took to get home. He still felt guilty as he pulled into the driveway and sat staring at the windows with dimmed lights glowing just beyond. It was late—just after seven thirty. The kids were probably in bed, and Lana was probably in the den, or maybe in their bedroom watching television.

He breathed into his cupped hands and to check how badly his breath reeked of alcohol. Popping a piece of gum into his mouth, he chawed it for several minutes before finally opening the door and making his way up the sidewalk.

Lana opened the door before he fumbled his keys out of his pocket. Usually clad in jeans or sweats and a stained T-shirt, her hair pulled severely into a ponytail or a bun, Lana looked different. She wore a long, black dress, accented with a red, form-fitting cardigan sweater that matched the lipstick she'd applied. Her blonde hair was loose, and it looked as though she might have spent some time styling it. But the most perplexing part of it all was her smile. He hardly ever saw her smile anymore.

"What's going on?"

She grabbed his hand and pulled him inside.

In the foyer, she pressed herself against him, kissing him as she hadn't done in ages. He was so shocked he didn't know what to say. He looked around, expecting to see the children running wild and Brandon glued to the television playing video games. But all of the lights in the house were off except for some dim lighting in the den, illuminated by candles and the smell of some kind of scented oil.

"What's going on?" A slight laugh broke his voice. "Where are the kids? Where're Brandon and Katherine?"

"The kids are in bed already." Lana led him into the fragrant, flickering room. "Brandon stayed at his mom's. Katherine's out with some friends."

"Oh." Where was all this going?

Lana sat down on the edge of the couch and pulled him down beside her, where two glasses of champagne sat on the coffee table. He couldn't possibly drink another thing.

"Tyler, I owe you an apology for the way I've been lately. I've been stressed out and completely absorbed with the kids, and I know I've treated you really badly. I'm sorry."

Tyler stared at her, unsure what to make of this moment of contrite humility from his wife. "OK. It's

OK. I know I've been a pain lately, too."

"I think it's this area, Tyler."

"This area?"

"Yeah. I mean, look at everyone around us. Everyone is just running around all of the time—rushing here and there—trying to keep up with everyone else. Trying to make enough, do enough to keep up with—"

"Don't say 'the Joneses'. That's us." Tyler laughed.

She laughed as if it was the funniest thing he'd ever said. "No, I was just going to say I think we need a change. We should get out of here while we can. I mean, is there anything really holding us here?"

Who is this woman? Lana spoke in fast and furious phrases—almost manic—the way his ex-wife used to chatter when she was riding the crest of the upward swing of her bipolar disorder.

Tyler shifted in his seat. "Let's see. We have a house. I have a job. We have four kids in school—"

"Yeah, but, the job could change, the house could change, and the kids could change schools. Nothing is written in stone, right?"

"I guess I don't get where all of this is coming from or why. What's suddenly making you want to move?"

"Do you remember my friend Erin? Erin Mullins? I used to go to school with her?"

Tyler shook his head. Lana had so few friends—just Molly, and Suzanne from across the street, and a handful of friends from college, all of whom lived elsewhere. He didn't remember ever hearing the name Erin Mullins.

Lana rushed on, telling him about Erin's talent agency and the possibility of working for them in Santa

Monica.

"Santa Monica?" Tyler drew back. "That's—that's California."

Lana stood up suddenly, pacing up and down the length of the living room as though making an opening statement to a jury. "Yeah—so? We've talked a hundred times about moving somewhere close to the beach—somewhere where it's sunny and more laid back."

"When we retire. Not right now."

"Why not right now? I mean, why wait until we're too old to enjoy it? Let's do it now. Why should we feel shackled to the Northern Virginia grind and all of the pretenses that come along with it?" Her voice was controlled, but a current of excitement rang out underneath the calm.

"I don't know, Lana—I guess a little something called money? I mean, what would I do in Santa Monica?"

She stopped pacing, spreading her hands out. "You'd find a job."

Tyler scoffed. "Come on. This is silly."

"Or you could finally start your own business—just like your father always wanted you to do. You could finally make him proud…and yourself happy."

Her words jabbed at that soft spot right in the middle of his heart that longed for his father's approval. "How long have you been thinking about this?"

"A long time. And I know it sounds crazy, but I really think we could do it. It would be a fresh start for us, and we could both feel as though we're doing something worthwhile for a change."

"Raising our kids isn't worthwhile to you?"

A storm cloud blew over her face, dulling the expression. "That's not what I meant."

"You know, Lana, if you want a job we could work something out."

"I don't want a job here. What could I do here? I could maybe be a substitute teacher or go work for a temp agency or something. Erin's offering me a real chance at a job I'd love to do. And there's something else."

"What?" Tyler braced himself.

"She wants me to come out at the end of the month for a formal interview."

"To Santa Monica?"

"Yes."

His head was spinning. Something about Lana's idea was enticing, despite the craziness of dropping everything and relocating to California. It was true they'd talked about moving to a sunnier spot over the years. On more than one occasion, Tyler had wanted to quit his job, jump in the car, and drive toward the sun, wherever it took him. Only his obligations and responsibilities held him here. And now his wife was giving him permission to shrug off all of that, throw caution to the wind, and break out of the model of expectations and societal pressures. "You know," he said. "John told me today the task may not get the funding to continue."

"So, you might get laid off?" Her eyebrow arched.

"Maybe. Or I might just get shifted into another role in another task or department."

"Which you'll hate. Why don't we just take this as a sign that we're supposed to move?"

Tyler stared down at his empty glass. "Maybe. I don't know."

"Let's just think about it. What if I go out to California and do the job interview? That way, I'll have a better idea about things, and then we can talk about it again."

Maybe it was the beers he'd had tonight, or maybe John's warning about layoffs had affected his judgment, but somehow, Lana's suggestion sounded reasonable. "OK. Go out there and do the job interview. If you get the job, then we'll see. We'll talk about it."

Lana lunged at him, kissing him with a passion and excitement he hadn't known since before they married. They clumsily kissed their way up the stairs and into the bedroom.

At midnight, Tyler watched the clock tick by as sleep continued to elude him. He might actually have a shot at a career he wanted and a chance to make his father proud all at the same time. It had taken his wife initiating the suggestion to light a fire underneath him, but now it seemed like the best idea in the world. From the bedside table, his cell phone buzzed with an incoming text.

He pushed himself onto his elbow and lifted the phone. Tara.

Had a great time chatting with you tonight. Maybe take me up on a game of racquetball next week?

He quickly deleted the message and glanced over his shoulder at Lana's sleeping form. Yes. Santa Monica was the best idea in the world.

8

Kaki
Saturday, November 19

There was no way she would do that. Absolutely no way.

"It's just dancing, baby."

"Yeah," she sneered. "Dancing while I take my clothes off. I mean, how can you even ask me to do that? Knowing that all of those guys would be looking at me? I thought I was your girlfriend? You said you loved me."

"I do love you. I just need this one favor from you. To help me out. Because you love me."

Parked in the lot just behind Damien's club, Kaki had never felt so sick in all her life. First of all, she was coming off of a bad trip. Whatever drug he'd given her that night was not having a good effect. She kept waiting for the high—the euphoric vibration that crept up from her calves and shot out along her arms and into her hands—that wonderful, tingly sensation she usually got. But he didn't give her the blue pill, like usual. Tonight it had been some white pill that made her sluggish and dizzy.

"It would just be this one time," Damien insisted. He slid his arm around her shoulders as he whispered and stroked her face. "It would be like you were proving to me how much you love me."

"What about Nishelle? Why isn't she dancing tonight?"

"Nishelle moved on."

"Really?" Nishelle didn't seem like someone who'd just quit. Nishelle seemed pretty desperate. "I thought she needed the money for her son and all."

"Yeah, well, she's not part of our game anymore. 'K?"

Kaki shook her head. Standing up and dancing in front of all of those people? No, just no. "OK, well, whatever, but I can't do it."

"You can. You can do it. You're beautiful and...well, look, baby. Look what Daddy brought you, right? This is your favorite, right?" He pulled some crackly paper out of his pocket.

"What did you give me earlier? It made me feel sick. Like, I could just throw up right now."

"That was just a little something to get you in the mood—you hear what I'm saying? A little something to make you feel good."

"Well, I don't, OK?" Her voice sounded foreign to her. "I don't feel good. I feel sick. And I'm not dancing. And I'm definitely not taking off my clothes."

The leather creaked as Damien sat back against the seat and stared out the window. "Yeah, OK. I see how it is."

Feeling confident she'd won the battle, Kaki shook her head. "I mean, I can't believe you would ask me to do something like that. I'm not like those girls. I think you know I'm better than that."

"Oh, I see." He glared at her like a demon. There was a strange blackness to his eyes—a flash of something evil. "Oh, I see how it is. Oh, see, see, you think you're better than all this? Is that it? You think you're better than all this?" His voice rose in volume, the tone sharp and angry.

"Yeah, I do. And I hope you think of me as better than all this too."

The slap came so suddenly and with such force that, for a minute, she wasn't sure what had happened. Had he just hit her? The radiating pain and heat across her cheek told her that he had. But no one had ever hit her. Ever.

Holding her hand to her face, she looked up at Damien. She no longer recognized the man in the car. He was yelling, screaming so hard his voice broke, calling her names—horrible names.

"I can't believe I ever thought you cared about me. All you care about is yourself. You can't even do me this one favor? Get out. Get out of the car. If you don't want to help me out, then you can find your own way home. Get out of my sight! You ain't even *as good* as those girls in there."

Bile rose in her throat and panic rendered her limbs useless, frozen. He was serious. He was pushing at her, shoving her out of the car as he reached across and opened the passenger side door. "Here I been buying you all kinds of stuff, making you out to be my queen, and this is how you repay me? Get out."

Kaki tumbled onto the ground, scraping her knees against the cold, icy pavement. Confused and disoriented, she pleaded with him. "Damien, please— please. Come on. You can't just leave me out here. How will I get home?"

He reached across the passenger seat, grabbed the door handle, and pulled the door shut. The car sped out of the parking lot, turned left, and with screaming tires, disappeared into the night.

Kaki looked around. Strange people stood in the parking lot and the alley. She recognized a few of their faces from the club, but without Damien there with her, protecting her, all of these people looked threatening and scary. She tried to think straight and figure out what to do. She couldn't call either of her parents. So far she'd gotten away with sneaking out every two or three nights to see Damien. If she called them, that would be the end of her relationship with him. They would probably press charges against him.

But do I really want to keep seeing this guy? He had hit her. She was from upper middle-class America where no one did anything like this. No one was desperate for cash. If she needed money she could ask her mom or dad and they would give it to her. So what was she doing hanging out with a guy who wanted her to dance naked in front of a bunch of strangers?

Standing in the middle of the freezing parking lot, Kaki tried to shake off the effects of the drugs. How had this happened to her? She'd never done drugs in her life before meeting Damien. She'd never done a lot of things. She shivered.

Maybe Damien was just messing with her. Maybe he'd come back in a few minutes, and they would make up. An involuntary sob erupted from her throat. What could she do? She began to move along the sidewalk. Maybe she could get a cab to take her back to her house, and then she could run inside and get some money from her dad's wallet or something. Great, now she was a thief on top of everything else.

A dark vehicle pulled up to the curb, and for a moment Kaki thought it was Damien coming back for her, but as the window lowered, the bald head of a middle-aged man looked out. "Hey, honey? You on the clock?"

Panic and fear tore at her heart. Now what? Would this guy assault her? He leered at her with a creepy smile and looked ready to jump out of his car to grab her. She'd worn a short black skirt and patterned leggings, her long legs ending in high-heeled ankle boots. She'd dressed for the club, not for running from strange, creepy men. She looked up the street to the corner where other women stood—actual prostitutes. She looked just like one of them.

Terrified, she ran. Darting in and out of parking lots, behind buildings, and through alleys, she ran until she reached an area that was well lit, just under the street signs on K Street. Holding to the pole, her fingers numb against its surface, she panted as tears streamed down her face.

As a kid she'd knelt by her bedside with her dad, saying night-time prayers. But that was before the divorce when she was still his little girl. "Now I lay me down to sleep. I pray the Lord my soul to keep..." Prayers of protection as she slept. Now she needed deliverance. "Help me, God! Please help me!" The desperate sound of her own voice spoken in a cloud of condensation scared her. If she hadn't met Sydney, none of this would've happened. Wait. Yes! She could call Sydney.

Grasping her cell phone, her numb fingers hit the speed-dial. As soon as Sydney's groggy voice answered, Kaki spoke loud and quick. "I need you to do me a huge favor. I need you to come right now. To the corner of K and 21st in the city and pick me up. OK?"

"Why? Where's Damien?"

"Just do it. Please?"

"OK. Give me half an hour."

It was an hour before Sydney arrived. Kaki was so cold she was sure her feet had frostbite. She walked up and down the street, trying to stay under street lights, trying to look busy on her phone in order to avoid the stares of men as they drove by. It was the longest hour of her life.

"You know I really shouldn't be doing this," Sydney told Kaki as she fell into the car, shivering and exhausted. "Damien'll be mad if he finds out, so do not tell him."

Kaki glared at her. "Yeah, I'm just fine. Thanks for asking. I didn't know what else to do, Sydney. I don't need you scolding me."

"Why did he leave you there? What did you do? Did you say something to make him mad?"

"He wanted me to strip at the club, OK?" Kaki blurted.

Sydney laughed. "Is that all? Seriously? You made him leave you here in the middle of DC because you wouldn't dance at his club? You are stupid."

Kaki leaned forward to get a good look at Sydney's face. "Are you kidding me? You think it's fine that he asked me to strip for a bunch of strangers? I'm not stupid, Sydney! I mean, I've watched enough movies to know how this goes."

Sydney laughed again — this time long and hard — as if that was the funniest thing she'd ever heard. "Well, this ain't no movie, honey. OK? I mean, first of all, Damien asking you to dance at his club is like, a huge compliment, OK? Not everyone gets to do that. That means he's like, super-crazy about you. Second of all, I've done it lots of times, and it's really no big deal."

"You've stripped before?"

"Lots of times."

"At Damien's club?"

"Yeah, and others, too. It's no big deal. I promise you. It's actually kind of fun."

Between this bombshell and the extreme cold and exhaustion, all Kaki wanted to do was go home, crawl into her own bed, and forget this night ever happened.

"Look, I'll talk to Damien for you if you want," Sydney continued. "I'm sure he feels really bad about what happened. I know he's crazy about you. He's told me he thinks you're like, the hottest girl he's ever had."

Despite the whirling confusion and brain fog, Sydney's words still settled her nerves just a little. Damien thought she was hot? No guy had ever called her hot before.

"I don't know." A smile threatened the corners of her mouth. But then she remembered. "You know, he hit me."

Sydney didn't even flinch. "He's just temperamental, you know? He's, like, a really talented guy. Guys like that have a temper sometimes. You got to take the good with the bad."

Her dad had a pretty bad temper, too, but he'd never hit her or her mom or stepmom during one of his episodes. She shuddered. How would he react if he knew she'd been sneaking out, sleeping with a twenty-five-year-old guy, and taking drugs? And now she would add stripping to that list of sins.

~*~

Sunday, November 20

All the next day, Damien sent her texts.

hey. U know I luv u bae.

sorry things got bad last nite. I got something for u.

can you meet me tonite?

She didn't respond to the first three or four, but by the eighth or ninth, she started worrying that he might get mad if she didn't. *OK. I'll meet u once everyone is in bed.*

She wasn't sure if God was real or not, but she could almost believe that He was for all of the *don'ts* resounding in her conscience. *Don't respond to his texts. Don't talk to him anymore. Don't agree to meet him.*

She was isolated from everyone and everything. Since she'd quit the track team, she had only seen Riley in class, and their conversations were forced. The girls she used to hang out with from the team were hanging out with other people now, and she was pretty sure they were talking some smack about her, too. She'd seen a few things online about how she was hanging out with a group of boys after school. She didn't even know the boys they were talking about. One of them was a football player. She didn't even know any football players. It was better to just avoid those girls.

Things were crazy at home, too. Her dad and stepmom were totally into their own lives and their own kids, and they might be moving to California anyway. Her mom was just crazy all by herself and always had been. She had some boyfriend now, too. So no one even noticed how bad Kaki's second quarter grades were, or if they did, they said nothing. She had gone from being an A/B student with the occasional C+, to a C- and D student.

Sydney and Damien were the only people in her life who actually talked to her and seemed as if they wanted to be around her.

When everyone went to bed that night, she enacted her usual exit strategy, narrowly missing her brother who was on his way back from the bathroom. Kaki froze in the hallway until his zombie-like form moved back into the bedroom. Once his door was closed, she worked her way down the stairs and out the front door. As always, Damien's car was there, heated with warmth and the spicy scent of his cologne.

They kissed for a while, and Damien assured her how much he loved her. "You're my only baby. You know that, right?"

She nodded and went in for another kiss, longing for the affirmation of his touch and the affection of his words. She wanted to forget about the slap and the parking lot argument—the fact that he'd left her there in the cold, alone and unprotected.

"I'll always take care of you." He pulled out a red bag with patterned hearts on the outside.

There were several sexy undies in the bag—red ones, black ones, white lacy ones. She giggled as she pulled them out of the bag one at a time.

"I want you to model those for me tonight," he said.

Next, she pulled out a new iPhone, the most recent model. "Now," he said explaining. "I've loaded this up for you. Every app you could ever want is on here, and if there's something else you want me to load on there, you just let me know."

Despite what had happened the night before, how could she not love this man who wanted to give her all of this stuff and really seemed to want to take care of her?

"And finally, there's this," he said, pulling out a

small, blue box and placing it in her hand.

Her heart pounded. It looked exactly like a ring box. Inside the felt holder a silver ring with a small diamond and sapphire sparkled. Later, she would find out that he'd bought it at a discount store for $20.

"Now, this is a promise ring. I know we got to spend a little more time getting money together, and I got to get us a house and all that, but one day, I'll get you a real engagement ring."

"I love you, Damien." She threw her arms around him. She did love him, after all. And didn't all of this mean that he loved her too?

"OK, then. Do you trust me now?" He grabbed her hands and rubbed her fingers under his thumbs.

"I trust you."

"OK. And we're all good now? We know who belongs to who and all that?"

She nodded, beaming. Warmth rushed all over her body. "Yes."

"OK, then. Now let's talk a little bit about that favor I need you to do for me."

9

Tyler
Saturday, November 19

Tyler had reclined on the couch all weekend, his feet propped on the arm at the opposite end, his head slightly tilted under the lumpy, brown, velveteen pillow as he flipped through travel shows. Monday, he'd have to go to work. Soon, if all things went according to plan, they would be living the good life in Santa Monica—sunning on the beach, watching the waves roll in and out. They'd both get rid of all of their bulky winter clothes, get fit, wear trendy clothes like they used to. Things were going to be so much better.

He hadn't even felt like surfing his usual sites online today. Life was looking up.

"You know what, honey?" He rolled his head to the side to look at Lana and reached his hand out toward her. She clasped his warm fingers in her own. The grasp was familiar, yet new to him all at the same time.

"What?" She perched on the edge of the coffee table and smiled down at him. For the first time in years, she resembled the woman he'd married. "I was just thinking how this idea of yours is sounding better and better."

"Is it?" She sat a little taller.

"Yeah." He propped on his elbow. "I mean, when

you first brought it up the other week, I thought it was crazy. But as I think more and more about it, I'm kind of like—why not? I mean, what if I do lose my job, and what if you do get this job in California? It makes sense somehow, you know?"

"I know." She leaned down and planted a kiss on his forehead.

Tyler's cell phone rang. He read the name from the screen. "It's Christina." Muscles tensed. Maybe he should just ignore it.

On the third ring, he answered it. "Hello?"

Christina's voice squawked away, but she must have been in a bad area for reception. She was breaking up, and Tyler could barely understand her. He caught Brandon's name and a tumble of words that clued him in that something had happened. So much for serenity.

"What? Where are you? You're breaking up, Christina. I can't understand what you're saying."

Finally, the line cleared just as she shouted into the phone. "Brandon got caught again for sexting!"

"What? Again? No, I can't believe it. How is that possible? The cops took his phone."

"Yeah, well, that was over a month ago. I got him another one."

"Christina!"

"He has to have a phone. What if I need to get in touch with him or something? It's dangerous for him not to have one."

"This is exactly why…" There was no use in trying to reason with her. "Never mind. OK, so now he was caught for the same stuff. So now do you see why he can't have a cell phone?"

Christina's voice was frantic. "I was out last night,

so I didn't get the school's message until this morning. Rebecca Hough, the assistant principal left a message for me to call her. I have her home number from the car wash fundraiser we did for the track team back in September. I just called her at home, and she told me. Brandon's going to be suspended for a couple of days, and there will probably be a detective coming out to talk to us. A bunch of kids are involved."

"Oh, that's just great. I knew I should have grounded him after it happened the first time."

Christina scoffed. "Yeah, it's kind of hard to ground your son for doing something that you're doing, too."

Tyler winced. He hated that after all of these years, Christina could still pull out that ammunition against him. "That's different."

"I don't think it's so different."

"I'm an adult, and I'm not posting photos of underage girls on social media."

"No, you're just looking at them."

Tyler fought the rage that threatened to derail the focus of the conversation. Clenching his teeth, he breathed in deeply. "So what did Brandon say when you confronted him about it?"

"Oh, he denied it. Just like you did all of those years ago when I confronted you about it."

"Christina, can we just keep this conversation focused on the problem with our son?" His voice shrilled. He was about to lose it.

She sighed. "So what do you want to do?"

"Well, obviously, he's grounded…for starters. No more cell phones. We need to make sure that's clear. The enabling has got to stop. At both of our houses. No computer use, no going out with friends. He does that too much anyway. He told me the other day that you let him and some other friend camp out in the woods by the school back in September. That's just crazy, Christina. He's only thirteen, and those woods aren't safe."

"He told me Jared's dad was going with them," she said.

"You need to stop believing everything he tells you. He lies."

"Our son does not lie!" her voice exploded into the phone.

"Yes, he does. He's lying all the time. We can't trust anything he says."

"We've got to find the right medication...the right psychiatrist for him. He needs help," her voice collapsed into sobs.

Tyler sighed, rubbing his forehead with his forefinger and thumb. Maybe Brandon had inherited some of Christina's mental illness. Finally, he said, "Well, maybe a psychiatrist can help and maybe they can't, but this whole thing is ridiculous." His skin prickled with stress...it was amazing how quickly all of his peace from earlier faded away. "I'll call a lawyer on Monday and find out what needs to happen...what sort of charges he could be facing." He was having to call a lawyer for his thirteen-year-old son. How had this happened? "I'm sure this whole thing has been blown out of proportion anyway. You know how these kids are. Probably some social media thing that's gotten out of hand. Don't worry."

As soon as Tyler disconnected the call, he looked up and locked eyes with Lana. "What's going on?"

"They think Brandon may have been involved in some sort of sexting thing at the high school."

"What?" Lana's mouth fell open.

"Someone is circulating photos of some nude girls around, and they think Brandon and a bunch of other kids are involved." Tyler reclined again, his feet resuming their position propped up on the opposite arm. "I didn't tell you about it, but last month I had to go up to the school to discuss it. Now, it's happened again. I'm sure this is all just blown out of proportion. It'll be fine."

Lana's forehead was lined with worry. "I hope so." She was probably thinking about California. She didn't want her plans messed up by Brandon's escapades.

For that matter, neither did he.

~*~

In the beginning of their marriage, Tyler had tried to hide his viewing of pornography from Lana. Whenever she'd walk into the room, he'd slam down the lid of his laptop or quickly minimize the images. Once while viewing, he had turned around and met Lana's eyes. He quickly made ready with apologies and excuses: the image just popped up, he'd been looking for something else, or another one of the excuses he'd used with Christina. But he hadn't had to say anything, because Lana simply turned and left the room as if she hadn't noticed the screen. So he'd decided to leave well-enough alone.

Tonight, Lana dressed up for dinner at the Wolfs'. She wore a red, form-fitting dress with a shorter hemline. "I haven't worn this since before I gave birth to Micah," she announced happily. "I've been starving myself all day. You know, in preparation for

California."

He sidled up behind her, nuzzled his face into her hair, and crossed his arms over her belly, which sagged slightly with that extra baby weight she'd never quite lost. She'd gained nearly eighty pounds with Celia. Tyler wasn't sure if that had been because of the stress of an unexpected pregnancy or a conscious decision to simply let herself go because it would be the last baby and she might as well enjoy the eat-a-thon.

After Celia's birth, Lana had suffered from post-partum depression—at least that's what the doctors told them. So she drank a little now and then to make herself feel better...to take the edge off. But he didn't think it was really a problem.

By the time Tyler and Lana arrived at the Wolfs', Tyler had put the whole Brandon thing out of his mind and a sense of peace returned. But as soon as they walked in the door, Josh approached him, his face lined with concern. Of course, he knew all about Brandon's second sexting offense at the school. He was probably the one who interrogated him. Tyler cringed. He did not want to talk about that tonight.

"Hey man, how you doing?" Josh shook Tyler's hand and patted him on the shoulder.

"Doing fine. Doing great. How 'bout you guys?"

"Yeah. Fine, we're fine. I guess Christina got in touch with you? About yesterday?"

"Yeah." Tyler nodded tersely. "Yeah, we've got it all under control."

There was a strained pause before Josh answered. "OK. Great. Well, listen. I was as shocked as you, and I just want to let you know that Brandon was not alone in this. I mean, I can't really get into the case right now—"

"Yeah, and I wouldn't worry about it. You know? I think it's all just being blown out of proportion."

Josh's brow furrowed.

Tyler waved his hand as though shooing a fly. "As I said, Christina and I have it under control, and Lana and I just want to have a good time with you guys tonight. OK?"

Josh's expression clouded. "Yeah, OK. Sure."

Molly jumped in, steering the conversation toward the kitchen as she grabbed Lana's arm and led them from the foyer. "Well, come on in, you guys. I've got all kinds of stuff to eat in here. I made way more food than I meant to, so you can take some home with you. Where are the kids? I thought you might bring them. Katherine keeping them?"

"Oh, no, no. Katherine's out running around somewhere tonight. They're across the street at Suzanne's."

"OK," Molly said, offering a tray of appetizers to Lana and then Tyler. "But please don't feel like...I mean, you guys can bring the kids over anytime you want. You know we love them."

"Thanks," Tyler said. "But if we get the opportunity to have a night sans kids, we're taking it."

"That's right," Lana agreed. "And they're having fun over there. No doubt Suzanne has Celia knee-deep in Prism products. She'll come home smelling like a lilac farm."

Lana and Tyler perched on the bar stools at the island in the kitchen and grazed on sausage balls and spinach artichoke dip while Josh dumped boiling pasta into a colander and Molly poured water into mason jar glasses.

"Anytime I have the opportunity to eat carbs I'll

take it." Molly beamed. "I'm breaking bad tonight with the spaghetti."

"Any news?" Lana asked.

Molly shook her head, her eyes downcast. "No. No news. Same as usual."

Dinner was a little strained, and Tyler assumed it had something to do with the whole Brandon-elephant in the room. Josh talked to him as though they'd just met one another, sticking to safe topics such as sports, church, and television shows.

Lana and Molly barely talked at all, and when they did, it was about something funny Celia and Micah had done, or some story about Molly's grandparents and their winter home in Florida.

Lana was drinking quite a bit tonight. She'd polished off most of the bottle of wine they'd brought all by herself. Her words were a little slurred when she spoke. "So, Tyler. Should we tell them our plans?"

"Yes." The corners of his mouth curled. This was the moment he'd been waiting for all night. "Yes, Lana and I are about to embark upon an adventure. Well, maybe we're about to embark. It really depends on Lana." The slightest sensation of pressure squeezed at his chest. The idea of them moving to California with Lana as the only one employed made him a little nervous.

"Really?" Molly asked, twirling a forkful of spaghetti against the bottom of her plate. "What kind of adventure?"

Lana sat back in her chair. "I have a job interview."

"That's great!" Molly and Josh said in unison.

"Yes," Tyler joined in. "And tell them, honey, where it is and what you might be doing."

"Well," Lana began, her face stretched with an

uncontrollable smirk. "I would be working as a talent agent."

"Really? Wow. When's the interview?" Molly asked.

"Next week. And it's in California. In Santa Monica."

Josh's mouth fell open, and Molly's stretched into a sort of incredulous smile. An uncomfortably long silence accompanied the announcement.

"Wow," Josh said finally. "Wow. So, you'd be living and working there? In Santa Monica?"

"Yep," Tyler said proudly. "You knew Lana had a degree in theater, didn't you?"

Josh and Molly nodded.

"I have a friend there," Lana jumped in. "I went to college with her, and we both majored in theater together. She has an agency."

"What exactly does a talent agent do?" Molly asked.

"They work for the actors—they book auditions and jobs, negotiate contracts, and basically act in the best interests of their clients. Kind of like a real estate agent, but instead of finding properties they find entertainment gigs."

"So...so what about you, Tyler?" Josh asked.

Tyler swiped his hand at the air. "Aw, you know. I'll find something. I'm pretty employable."

Josh reached over to grasp Molly's hand. "That sounds amazing. I know you guys must be so excited. I mean—we're excited for you, too."

Molly nodded enthusiastically. "And if it all works out, we'll definitely want to come out for a visit. It's Santa Monica, for heaven's sakes."

"Of course," Tyler said. But he doubted the four of

them would actually continue their friendship once they settled in California. Their lifestyles would be too different.

"And the kids?" Molly asked with a little shrug. "The kids—Brandon and Katherine—they're OK with this? You wouldn't be able to have them living with you part of the week anymore."

"We haven't said anything to them yet," Tyler said. He wasn't worried about that. It would all work out somehow. The kids could visit…whenever. "Once Lana is officially offered the job we'll deal with all of that."

"How do you think they'll take the news?"

Tyler was a little irritated. They couldn't base their entire lives on how their kids would react. Molly and Josh didn't have kids. They didn't get it. "I'm sure they'll get used to it. They might not want to at first, but eventually, I'm sure they'll love coming out to spend vacations with us. Don't you think so, honey?"

Lana nodded, smiling. "Yeah. I'm sure that's right."

"Don't you have a custody agreement with your ex-wife?" Josh asked. "How does that work?"

Tyler's jaw clenched and unclenched, a separate spasm from his prior chewing motion. "Christina and I will work that out. I've got it all under control."

10

Kaki
Thursday, December 1

"You look awful," Riley said to Kaki as they settled into their seats in history class.

"Thanks." Leaning across her desk, Kaki rested her head on her arms. She could go to sleep right there and then. She was so tired. "I feel awful," she mumbled to the surface of the desk.

"You're never here anymore," Riley said. "How come you're always absent?"

Can't she see I don't want to talk? "I've been sick a lot." Kaki looked around the bustling class where kids were settling their book bags, playing games on their phones, or yelling across the room to each other, and dropped her head again.

"Did you get your flu shot?" Riley asked.

"No."

"You should get it. It's supposed to be a bad strain this year. My mom says that some people have died from it already."

"Hmm." Kaki wondered what it would be like to die. Would that just mean she got to sleep forever? That sounded really good to her right now.

"Do you think you have the flu?"

"No, I don't have the flu," Kaki growled. "I'm just really tired."

"What do you think is wrong with you? You're never around anymore. I feel like we never get to talk. Are you going to join track for the spring?"

"Would you stop talking?" Kaki snapped. "Your voice is like, really grating on my ears right now. I just want to sleep."

Riley's face crumbled, her eyes flew wide open. "Sorry. I was just trying to talk to you. We used to be friends."

A surge of guilt flooded Kaki's chest. "I'm sorry, Riley. I don't know what's wrong with me. I'm not sleeping much, and…things are just really weird."

Riley looked unconvinced. "OK. Whatever."

The bell rang, and the students began making their way to their desks. The teacher was talking—which teacher was it? Miss Moss? No, that was math. Sydney was in that class with her. This was…oh yeah, history. Her head flopped back onto her arms. She just couldn't do it today.

The "one night" Damien had insisted Kaki would have to dance turned into one week, and three weeks later…it hadn't stopped yet. She was arriving home later and later. After her second week of working at the club, Kaki started skipping classes. It was too difficult to stay awake. When she skipped an entire day of school, an automated phone call went home to her mom that Kaki had an unverified absence for that day. Kaki heard it on the voice mail when she got home and quickly deleted it. As long as she could get home before her mom did, she could make sure her mom never got those messages. She was just glad they weren't sending any to her dad's house. Not yet anyway.

Kaki still tried to attend school as much as she

could, but she missed at least two days every week and started falling so far behind in her classes that she couldn't catch up. There were a few mornings when she barely made it back inside her mom's or her dad's house before they woke up. Some days she went to school after having had no sleep at all.

This was one of those mornings.

There was a tap on her shoulder. "Kaki? Kaki, wake up." It was Ms. Shephard. "Come on. Sit up. You need to know this stuff for the test."

She tried to sit up, but her eyes kept closing. Finally, in the middle of the lesson on the War of 1812, Kaki held up her hand. "Can I get a pass to the clinic?"

~*~

"You got any more of those blue pills?" Kaki asked Miranda, one of the other dancers.

"Take this. It works quicker." Miranda poured some liquid into Kaki's drink.

Kaki didn't even ask what she was taking anymore. It didn't matter. Anything that kept her from feeling the fear of walking out in front of a crowd of cheering, slobbery men—their eyes like night-time weasels glowing from within a forest. More like a jungle. A jungle of hungry, drooling jackals ready to pounce on her.

Miranda danced at Damien's club the same nights Kaki did, and she always had a supply of all kinds of pills to take or powders to snort or smoke. She was just about the tallest woman Kaki had ever seen. Miranda said she was only six feet, but when she wore her six-inch heels and the rabbit ears, it was like looking into the face of a giant, angry Easter Bunny.

"These are my signature, see?" She adjusted her pink ears in the mirror. Her curly, light-brown hair spilling over her shoulders matched the color of her skin. "They know Miranda's in the house when they see these. Plus, they make me feel like I'm a little more upmarket, you know? Like I'm a Playboy Bunny in Hugh Hef's mansion, you know what I'm saying?"

Unlike Miranda, Kaki didn't want to feel like anything. She just wanted to disappear. She sipped at her drink and waited for that to happen. Taking something was the only way she could do this. "How long have you been doing this, Miranda?"

Miranda rested her backside against the dressing table and rolled her dark eyes to the ceiling. "Oh, let's see. I guess I been dancin' a coupla years now." She waved her hand in the air, her pink-painted nails with their intricate designs were shaped like claws. "You know. Time all runs together after a while. But I done a little bit of everything. I'm just doing this right now until I save a little. Then I'm movin' down to Atlanta. Openin' up my own little place. Then *I* be runnin' the show."

Even with the stuff Miranda had poured into it, the drink wasn't hitting Kaki fast enough. Her stomach was all fluttery and rolling with that sick feeling she always got before she went out on the floor. She gulped several more swallows and watched the clock on the wall. Fifteen more minutes before she had to be out there.

In the three weeks she'd been dancing at Damien's club, she'd only tried to refuse once. That time, Damien whipped her with his belt. It was the most humiliating experience of her life. She fought him until he had her on the ground.

One of the other girls stood by and watched. "Just stop fighting him, honey," the girl had called out to Kaki. "If you just take it, it won't be so bad. It'll only be worse if you fight him."

The beating left some welts on her backside, but Damien still made her go out on the floor. "No one'll care once you're out there swinging around a pole."

Kaki learned not to cry. If she cried, she was sure to have her head shoved into the toilet while it was flushed. Finally, she'd learned never to be a minute late onto the dance floor. The punishment for that was to repay the customers for the time they'd lost, which meant private dances. And there was nothing more degrading and horrible than having to do that. One night, Kaki had to do twenty private dances while disgusting, drunk men breathed beer breath into her face.

According to Damien, the biggest problem they faced was with her dancing itself. "You 'bout the worst dancer I've ever seen. You act like you don't know what to do."

"I don't," Kaki protested. "I'm not a dancer. I don't know what I'm supposed to be doing up there."

Damien had grabbed her where her chin and neck met and pushed her against the wall. "You do the same kind of moves you do when you're with me. It shouldn't be that hard."

She had done everything he'd wanted, so she didn't know why he was suddenly so rough with her. Before he'd talked so sweetly, told her she was beautiful and wonderful and how much he loved her. She just wanted to hear that stuff from him again. He still bought her gifts—clothes, jewelry, gift cards—but she never saw any money from the stripping.

After her first week of dancing at the club, she'd asked him about it. "Are you going to pay me for doing this? I know the other girls get paid."

He'd snort-laughed. "Yeah, we'll see about that when you get better at dancing. Right now, you stink."

She hated standing out there on the stage holding onto the pole—her only anchor of security—while the lights swirled around and the music pounded in her ears.

"Start moving!" The men sometimes called out.

Between sets, she usually took another pill or drank another rum and Coke—anything to drown out the voices.

"Hey girl, don't fall asleep on me now," Miranda's voice was like a sharp knife cutting through her drift. Whatever she'd put in the drink had finally taken effect. Instead of feeling euphoric, Kaki wanted to curl up in a corner and sleep.

Miranda's hand slapped at Kaki's cheeks gently. "Come on now. You'd better get up and get moving. You got like three minutes before Damien be gettin' all over you." Miranda helped Kaki to her feet. She staggered to the door, steadying herself against the wall.

"Maybe I gave you a little too much," Miranda said. But her voice sounded as if she was speaking from the other end of a tunnel. "You smaller than me."

Using the wall as a brace, Kaki stumbled along the hallway leading to the stage.

Damien stood by the stage door, his arms crossed over his chest. "You're almost late. Thirty more seconds and you'd owe some private dances."

She didn't look at him. It was best to keep her head down. That way he couldn't accuse her of giving him attitude.

He smacked her on the backside as she staggered through the stage door, and she almost fell. Her legs felt as if they were buried in sand. Calls and hoots from the men erupted all around her—their voices warped as though special effects had been added. Kaki grasped the metal of the pole, slippery under her fingers from other dancers' baby oil and lotions. Was she moving? She couldn't be sure. She saw different sides of the room, so she must have been swinging on the pole. Men's voices hooted.

Kaki didn't remember taking off any clothes, but she walked off the stage naked. She didn't even bother to redress before returning to the dressing room and collapsing in a chair. It was some time later when she woke up. Miranda had covered her with a blanket.

Miranda's eyeliner-exaggerated eyes came into focus. "You really can't dance, can you?" she said, shaking her head. "Baby, I don't think this is the right work for you. You got moves like a chicken, and Damien never gonna pay you for doing this."

The door to the dressing room opened, and Damien walked in.

Miranda got up. "I gotta get out there," she whispered.

Damien pulled a stool up in front of Kaki. Holding her hands, he smoothed the hair back from her face, a slight smile on his lips. Kaki's mood lifted a little, seeing him look at her the way he used to. As if he really loved her.

"You wanna quit dancing? Huh?"

His tone was gentle, but Kaki was still afraid to answer. What if she said yes, and it was the wrong thing?

She shrugged.

"I got an idea. I got something better for you to do, baby. Something where you can make us a lot more money."

11

Tyler
Friday, December 2

"Did anyone ever tell you that you look like Buddy Holly?" Tyler greeted Raj with their usual exchange as he entered his cubicle on Friday morning.

Raj, as always, was glued to the computer screen, the light from the screen reflecting off of his retro, black, horn-rimmed glasses. "Yes, you. Every day. But I don't have his money, and I don't want to die like him."

Tyler smiled, plopping down in the chair by Raj's desk and stirred the coffee in his cup. "Were any of your guys in your department told about possible layoffs?"

Raj raised his eyebrows. "Where did you hear about layoffs?"

Tyler looked into his cup and watched the powdery fake cream form a filmy veneer on the top of his coffee. "John Cabrisi. Mentioned it to me a couple of weeks ago. He said the task may not get the funding."

Raj was a lead programmer working in a different department and task, but his office was on the same floor as Tyler's. "I haven't heard anything about layoffs."

Tyler shrugged. "It's probably not affecting your

department."

"I hope it doesn't affect yours either."

"Doesn't matter," Tyler said cheerfully. "'Cause Lana and I are moving to California."

"You're moving to California because of a possible layoff?" Raj removed his glasses.

"No, it's not just that. You know, we've been thinking about it before now. This news just kind of sped it all along."

Raj squinted as though trying to understand Tyler's words. "So, I still don't get it. You don't have a job out there, right?"

"I'll get something, of course," Tyler said quickly. "Or maybe I'll finally start up that business I've wanted to get going. Santa Monica has a thriving business community."

"There's a thriving business community right here. Why not get it off the ground here before pulling up all your roots and moving thousands of miles away? What are your kids saying about this?"

Why did everyone keep asking what his kids thought? Micah and Celia were too young to have any opinions, and Katherine and Brandon were teenagers. They would both adjust. "They'll be fine."

Raj crossed his arms and sat back in his chair. "Teenagers really need their fathers around."

Tyler drained the rest of his coffee. He didn't want to talk to nay-sayers about their plans. He felt good today, and he didn't want anyone squelching his mood. "Yep. Well, I guess I'd better go do some work, Raj."

"OK. Don't book any plane tickets just yet. See you at lunch today?"

"Maybe." Tyler moved toward his own cubicle.

He didn't want to commit to anything. Leave everything open—who knew what might happen? That was his new attitude and mantra.

His good mood continued throughout the day as he surfed the Internet for images of Santa Monica and the southern California coastline. He imagined once they got settled, he and Lana would take daytrips to Northern California—Sacramento, San Francisco, Sonoma County and the wine country. It felt good to "step out in faith" and act as though this was definitely going to happen, even before he had confirmation. Wasn't that what the Bible said the faithful should do? Act as though you've already received what you've asked for? He remembered reading something like that in Scripture.

Tyler floated through his day, accomplishing his usual tasks without the usual amount of stress. Because really, what did it matter how well he wrote this report or spreadsheet? He was on his way out of here. He didn't even bother to micromanage his underlings. After all, if they didn't know what they were doing by now, then they shouldn't be working here. By next week, it might be that none of them, including Tyler himself, would be working there.

He was on his fourth cup of coffee by noon, and he'd knocked out several reports, made three or four important phone calls—something he would normally dread and put off until deadlines were approaching— and he'd even started plotting a list of topics for the task members' meeting by the end of the next week. He was ahead of the game.

Tara appeared at the edge of his cubicle. "Hey there."

Oh, no. A terrible distraction and temptation. If he

wasn't careful in his dealings with her, he'd veer off in a wrong direction. He had to stay on the course of the current plan. Things were going too well to allow a cute little blonde to mess with his head—even if she was only eye candy. "Hi," he said, trying not to look away from his computer.

"Headed to the gym today?"

"No, not today. Too much to do."

Out of the corner of his eye, he glimpsed her short red skirt and high-heeled ankle boots.

"You still don't want to compete against me in racquetball, do you?"

"I don't know, Tara. I only like to play when I have a chance of winning." He laughed a little and tried to look busy while staring at the blank screen. Moments before, he'd been geared up to compose a flow chart as part of the proposed project for which they were awaiting funding. "It's not that I don't want to play racquetball with you. I just need to get home tonight. Lana's out of town, and I should be there for the kids." Mentioning his wife's name might act as a deterrent. Sort of a *Remember? I'm married* maneuver. But then telling Tara that his wife was out of town probably wasn't the smartest thing...and he'd confused the issue a couple of weeks before when he'd joined Tara for after-work drinks.

The flashing light on his office phone was an opportunity for diversion. "Oh, you know what? I've been waiting for a call, and this might be it." He pointed at the phone on his desk. A ripple of disappointment crossed her face.

"Yeah, OK. Well, maybe one of these days you'll have the courage to take me on."

Tyler nodded and smiled, trying to make light of

her double entendre as he picked up the phone. "Tyler Jones."

"Hey, Tyler. It's Josh."

"Hey, Josh. What's going on?" A sinking feeling assailed him. "I need you to come out to Runnymede. I got Brandon here with me. He got into an altercation with another student."

"A fight?" Brandon had never been in a fight before.

"That's my understanding."

Brandon had just come off of three days of suspension for the sexting. This kid was just not learning his lesson. "All right. I'll be there."

~*~

Tyler was becoming far too familiar with Runnymede Secondary's conference room. When he arrived, the room was already crowded. Brandon sat at one end of the table, his head down. Oliver, another one of the school's security guards was there as well— a big, African American man, larger and more muscular than Josh, and in some ways, more intimidating.

Rebecca Hough, once more in attendance, threw Tyler a half-smile and a wave as he entered. "Hello, Mr. Jones. Here we are again."

Tyler pulled out the empty seat next to Brandon and sat. "Yes. Here we are again."

Brandon didn't move his gaze from his lap. His right hand held an ice pack to the other side of his face.

"What's going on now, Brandon?" Tyler tried to control his voice. "You haven't had enough trouble yet?"

"Brandon had a little tussle with someone in the front parking lot," Oliver began. "Isn't that right, Brandon?"

The boy nodded, his mouth fixed in a sullen pout.

Oliver turned to Josh. "Happened just before lunch. Couple of girls saw it and came and got us."

"Who was it? Who'd you get in the fight with?" Tyler asked.

Brandon sat tight-lipped as he stared at the adjacent wall.

"Who was it, Brandon? You will tell me."

"No, I won't," he said in a low tone.

"Yes. You will—"

"One of the girls recognized the boy," Josh said quickly. "She said he doesn't go to this school."

Josh and Oliver exchanged glances. Oliver spoke. "Judging from the footage we saw on the security cameras, Officer Wolf and I don't think he goes here either. We've opened an investigation into this incident, but we think there were two males, neither of them actually attending Runnymede, who rode to the school on buses and disembarked with the kids."

A ripple of alarm flowed through Tyler. That seemed like a breach of security.

"How did that happen?"

"We don't know yet," Josh said. "But we're looking into it."

"You guys sure have a lot of investigations going on." Tyler was starting to think the school—and possibly even his friend's own lax security—was to blame for Brandon's troubles.

Josh nodded. "We're not denying that there are some issues going on here."

"Did this girl say anything else about who the guy

was or anything?"

"No. The girl just said the guy was not in school anymore," Oliver said.

"Not in school anymore?" Tyler was trying to make sense of it, but nothing was coming together. "Brandon, who do you know that doesn't go to this school?"

"Nobody."

"Obviously, that's not true. You didn't just fight the guy for no reason."

Rebecca spoke, reaching toward Brandon as though trying to get his attention. "Brandon, Gianna George said—"

"Gianna George?" Tyler looked at Brandon. They knew Gianna. Her father was Vincent George—a city councilman. Her brother was Gio George—a star football player—the reason the team had gone to state that year. Gianna and Katherine used to play together.

Brandon shrugged.

"Here's the thing," Rebecca said, lowering her voice. "Gianna said she thought she recognized the guy, and she thinks he's in a gang. Do you know anything about that, Brandon?"

"No," Brandon said.

"A gang? You have gang members showing up at the school now?" Tyler leveled his words at Josh.

"There's gang activity all over this area. And yeah, there is definitely activity in the school. It's hard to avoid in a place of this size...and very difficult to battle."

The school's role aside, how did Brandon know someone in a gang? Did he not know his son at all?

"Brandon, are you in a gang?" Rebecca asked.

"Of course not," Tyler answered for him.

"Brandon's not in a gang. He has nothing to do with any of that." But he didn't know for sure.

Oliver stared hard at Brandon. "Well, I can tell you that Brandon here had a pretty strong reaction when Gianna came in to the room to talk to us earlier. Brandon, I overheard you tell her not to say anything because the guy's a member of Masters of Sin. Didn't you say that, Brandon?"

"I don't know," Brandon said, looking up at Oliver suddenly, his eyes blazing with venom—reminding Tyler all too much of himself. "You're so smart—you seem to know everything. Why do you even ask me? Why don't you all just go to—"

Tyler shoved the chair out from under him and grabbed Brandon by the back of the neck. If he'd ever spoken like that to another adult, someone in authority, his father would have decked him. "You do not speak to anyone in this room like that. Do you understand?" He let go of Brandon's neck and made eye contact with Rebecca.

Her mouth gaped.

"Calm down, Mr. Jones. It's all right."

Disbelief at his son's insolence and his own angry reaction washed over him, and he sank back down into the chair, the anger replaced by embarrassment.

Oliver leaned across the table to address Brandon in his gruff, commanding voice. "Young man, let me tell you something. I used to be a bounty hunter. Do you know what that is?" When Brandon didn't answer, he continued, "That means I chased down criminals who were wanted for unspeakable crimes. I've chased men down to Tijuana. Do you really think you're any kind of challenge for me? 'Cause I'm telling you right now—you don't want to tango with me. You won't even come close to the dance-off!"

"OK, that's enough," Rebecca cautioned. "Everyone needs to calm down. This is not at all productive. Brandon, I'll send you back to class, and we'll have a talk with your dad. I'm assigning you one day of in-school suspension next week for the class skip and the fight."

Brandon kept his head down as he left the room. Once the door slammed behind him, Tyler exhaled a shaky stream of air. "I don't know what's going on with him."

"He's very angry," Rebecca observed. "Any idea why?"

Tyler shook his head. "No idea. The kid has everything. What else does he want?"

Rebecca looked tired, too. Her chin-length, mousy-brown hair seemed a little messy this morning, and there were puffy pouches under each of her steel-blue eyes. She was about his age. Did she have teenagers keeping her awake at night? "I'm referring him to the school psychologist—"

"Oh, good grief. My ex-wife has been sending him to every psychologist on the east coast for the past six months. As we see, it's not doing him any good."

"OK," Rebecca said calmly. "Well, Mr. Jones, this is part of the process here. Brandon may need to be screened for special education services, and a psychological evaluation would be part of that—"

"Special ed services?" Tyler balked. "Are you kidding me? This is ridiculous."

"The greater concern right now," Josh jumped in, "is the possibility of Brandon being involved in a gang. Now, we have no proof of anything, but Gianna mentioned Masters of Sin…and those guys are bad news."

"We've had some trouble with them recently," Oliver added. "We've had the county gang task force up here about that group."

Tyler's head was reeling. "Well, Brandon's not involved with them. I mean, I've seen some stuff about them on the news, but I just can't believe that any thirteen-year-old kid…"

"I've seen nine-year-olds involved—not as members, but they run favors for them. Sometimes they get caught up in their older brothers' stuff, you know…it happens," Oliver said. "These guys prey on kids who are vulnerable. Socio-economic level is often a factor, but in this area, it doesn't have to be. A kid who's looking to belong—looking for somewhere to fit in—they're all over that."

Josh nodded. "And these guys are not small time. They don't play around. Super-violent, drug traffickers, sex traffickers."

Tyler couldn't remember the last time he'd cried, but he had that weird, unstable feeling that accompanied an onslaught of emotion. He needed to get out of there. "Why would Brandon have been fighting with a guy from a gang?"

"That's what we need to find out," said Josh. "It seems like Brandon is protecting someone, or he's just not ready to talk."

"Could be a lot of reasons," Oliver added. "Could have something to do with a girl or money or something."

"You want to look for gang symbols," said Josh. "Tattoos are a big identifying factor. These guys use a dragon-type symbol."

Tyler had had enough. He stood. "I've got to go."

"We'll be in touch with you as soon as we know something more," Rebecca said.

Tyler left the school and drove straight home. Originally, he'd planned to go back to work, but now he needed to lie down. Micah and Celia had been staying with his parents since Lana had left, and he was more thankful than ever for that. There were some days he wished he'd never had kids. And this was one of them.

12

Kaki
Monday, December 5

"It's really no big deal," Sydney said. "Seriously. It's really easy once you've done it a few times."

Kaki stood with Sydney in the hall in front of their math classroom, staring over Sydney's shoulder as she flipped through pictures on her phone of the party she'd attended the night before. "But I don't want to do it ever again, Sydney. Doing it one time made me want to throw up."

Sydney tossed her a glance meant to warn her. "You wanna be with Damien, don't you?"

Kaki wasn't sure what she wanted anymore. She was riding a tidal wave, looking down at the world below, and if she tried to get back to them by stepping off the crest, she'd drown. "I guess."

"Well, you'd better make up your mind. There are a ton of other girls who'd love to take your place and be with Damien. You're really lucky, you know."

Lucky was hardly how she would describe herself. Stupid? Yes. Weak? Yep. Trapped? Absolutely.

It was rare for Sydney and Kaki to be in school on the same day. Sydney attended once or twice every two weeks—just so they didn't take her name out of the system or send out a truancy officer. Sydney only came to school to recruit other girls. She did it in the halls, standing by some mousy-looking girl's locker, talking up how they could make a lot of money and be part of something really important. Sydney had tricked her, too, and she'd fallen for the whole lie. And now she was in neck deep.

"Come on," she said, motioning for Kaki to follow her down the hall where people looked at her as if they knew what she was—what she'd become.

Sydney palmed something into her hand. "Take two of those right before you get with a guy. Then you won't even care what's going on."

"What is it?"

"It's heavy-duty anxiety medication. It's the best stuff ever. If you can snort it, it works even better. I get it from a guy whose mom is like a doctor or something. She's got this kind of stuff all over the place."

"How do you know the guy?"

"You know. He's one of the guys Damien set me up with. I give him what he wants, and he gives me good drugs. And a lot of money."

The way Sydney talked, Kaki almost believed she didn't mind what she was doing. Being high was the only way she could get through another experience like the first one.

~*~

The temperature gauge outside read thirty degrees, but with the wind chill factored in it felt more like fifteen. Kaki sat on the curb, shivering with dread, waiting for the sight of Damien's blue car to turn the corner. Instead, a silver car pulled into the cul-de-sac and circled around as though it was going to head back out onto the main road. Suddenly, it stopped. A dark-headed man wearing a black coat got out of the driver's seat and opened the back door of the car.

"Come on," he said in a rough voice. "Come on. Get out." At his gruff command, a dog jumped out of the backseat. It sniffed the ground at first, but as the man climbed back in his car and drove off, the dog turned, appearing confused, momentarily trying to follow the car. As the car pulled up to the stop sign and turned left onto the main road, the dog turned its sad, brown eyes toward her.

"Come 'ere." She used a high-pitched voice and patted the cold ground next to her.

The dog, a mutt—maybe a little dachshund, a dash of beagle, a smattering of terrier—appeared pregnant. Her belly hung heavy with puppies, the teats swollen and prominent. She approached hesitantly, stopping at the curb just before she reached Kaki.

She moved toward the dog slowly, her hand outstretched, her voice soft and high. "C'mere girl. It's OK." Had that guy really just abandoned the dog? And in freezing temperatures. Kaki wasn't sure what to do. She finally reached the mutt and rubbed her fingers across the top of her head, staring into soulful eyes. The dog looked up at her even as its whole body shook violently.

"Hey there!" Molly Wolf stood at her mailbox pulling out the day's deliveries. "Who you got with you?"

"I was just sitting here, and somebody just dropped her off. Right there." She pointed at the spot where the car had been moments before. "They just drove up, opened their door, and let her out. And then they left."

"What on earth?" Molly squatted to pet the

shaking dog, whose tail was tucked between her legs.

Kaki shivered so hard her teeth chattered together. Her bulky leather jacket did not help her bare legs fend off the cold.

"How could someone do that? I mean, look at her. She's pregnant and it's freezing out here." Molly's face was wreathed with lines of concern.

"Yeah, people are mean." Damien would be there any second. Kaki didn't want to leave the dog outside, but she couldn't very well dump it inside her dad's house and leave. *Hey, Dad. Here's our new dog.* He'd never go for that.

"We had a dog when Josh and I first got married," Molly said, a puff of smoke-like, condensation circling her face. "It was Josh's dog, an old Labrador named Winnie. She died three years into our marriage. It practically destroyed Josh, and after that he said he didn't want any more dogs. It's so hard to lose them." Molly scooped the dog into her arms. "Even pregnant with puppies you probably don't weigh twenty pounds."

"I don't know what to do. I'm waiting for someone, and I can't dump her off in the house with nobody home."

Molly looked down at the dog. "Hm. I guess if nothing else we could always take her to the animal shelter. It would be cruel to leave her out in the cold."

"Will you take her?" Kaki was hopeful.

Molly shrugged as the dog licked under her chin. "I don't know. I'll take her inside. This isn't weather for human or animal. Which makes me wonder what on earth you're doing out here. You're not dressed for this weather."

Kaki shrugged. "I'm OK. That's nice of you to take

her in. I love dogs. I'd take her, but...I'm waiting for my boyfriend to pick me up."

Molly stroked the dog's head. She was shivering too. "You can't wait for him inside your house where it's warm?"

No. She really couldn't. She might miss the car when it pulled up. And she was privileged that Damien was even picking her up on this day. It was rare he did that anymore. He usually expected her to find her own way to parties and "dates." Kaki hugged herself and looked off toward the road. Her teeth chattered again.

Molly moved toward her house. "Well, come in my house if you need to. But I've got to get back inside and see to this little girl. It's freezing out here. You should call your boyfriend and tell him to hurry up."

Relieved that Molly had taken pity on the dog, Kaki smiled. But the smile soon melted as a blue car swerved into the cul-de-sac, forcing Molly to take several steps back to avoid being run over. Kaki quickly stood and clambered into the car.

As soon as she was inside, Damien sped off, the car tires whooshing against the icy pavement. Kaki looked out the passenger window. Molly carried the dog inside her warm house. She only wished she were going with them.

~*~

Kaki never knew where they were going. If she asked, the response was always, "You'll see." Tonight, she didn't even bother to ask. They were headed down I-66 East, so they were probably going to Damien's club.

Damien pulled the car around to the back of the club and stopped by the door. "Once you're inside, go like you're heading to the dressing rooms. One of the other girls will meet you there and show you where you need to go."

"You're not coming in with me?" A sudden rush of panic coursed through her.

"No, I got some other business to take care of."

Kaki thrust her hand into the pocket of the leather coat. Relief. The pills Sydney had given her were there. She'd even crushed them up before she left the house so she could snort them and not have the long wait for them to take effect.

Hand shaking, Kaki grabbed the latch and stepped into the freezing air. She stopped just in front of the door and turned to look at Damien. His black gaze warned her. *Don't try anything. Don't even think about running.* He was staying to make sure she went inside.

She placed her hand on the cold, sticky doorknob. Inhaling sharply, she turned it and went inside. Might as well get this over with. Inside, another girl was waiting for her. Kaki didn't know her, and the girl didn't introduce herself.

"You Kaki?" she asked, her pale face unchanging in its drone-like stare.

"Yes."

"Come on. They're waiting."

Kaki followed her to a room at the backend of the club. Yeah, they were waiting. Four of them.

"You don't go with any guy ever until Spider or Jak collects the money. Understand?"

Kaki nodded.

The girl pointed to one of the men—a nameless, faceless, dark entity that stood like a shadow in the corner. "There's your first one. He's all paid-up."

They moved into a private room behind a door and down a dark, smelly hallway.

Kaki never saw one dollar of the money. She didn't want any of it anyway.

13

Tyler
Friday, December 9

Tyler couldn't wait for Lana to come home from California. Between dealing with Brandon's situation, running the younger kids back and forth between his parents' house, and trying to keep things running at work, he was exhausted. He was just thankful it was Friday, and Lana would be home on Sunday.

Their phone conversations had been a little strained. She didn't call the first night, and when she finally called the next day she was hungover.

"I was calling the airlines to make sure your plane landed safely and you weren't swept away in some sort of disappearing flight or something," he said.

"No, I'm fine. I'm fine. I went to dinner with Erin to talk business, and I think I had too many Apple-tinis."

"Oh. So you got drunk, and that's why you didn't call me?"

"I had a little too much to drink, yes."

"OK." Was she in California to party? To live out some fantasy or recapture her youth or something? "Well, it just would've been nice if you'd called and let me know that you were safe. You know, Lana...I'm dealing with a lot of stuff here. There's stuff going on with Brandon, and the kids are asking all sorts of questions about where you are and why, and I don't know what to say to them." He endeavored to reel in the familiar, angry tone. "Lana, I want you to call me tonight. Without fail, OK?"

"OK." Her tone was clipped, terse. She was just pacifying him.

And then, just the night before, she'd called to tell him that she'd gotten the job. Should he be happy? Maybe he should feel relieved. Maybe, like Lana, he could just walk away from all of this—jobs, house, responsibilities involving his delinquent, teenage son—get away from the trouble and the pain and soak up the sun in Cali. The whole idea seemed ridiculous.

He staggered into the corner coffee shop, herded into the line behind the other customers, and moved cattle-like through the ordering queue.

A tap on his left shoulder turned his head. "Hello, again."

Abbie Jackson stood in the line.

"Hey, good morning. Happy Friday, Detective Jackson." He tried to force energy into his voice.

"How's it going?" She gave him that great smile.

"It's...uh...it's going. My wife is out of town on some business—so I'm taking care of kids and all that." The words tumbled out of his mouth in nervous chatter. "You got kids?"

"No. Not married."

She was really cute. If he were still single, he'd— Tyler had to force his mind away from Abbie's single state. His mind was drifting into that place it always went when he needed some mental medication.

"Saw Josh yesterday," she said. "I was up at the school for some gang-related stuff, and I got to catch up with him a little."

Gang-related stuff. Did she know about Brandon's parking lot incident from last week? "What do you know about the gang called…I think it's Masters of Sin?" he asked.

"What do you want to know?"

"Well, my son got into trouble at the school last week…" he gave a nervous laugh. "Actually, it seems like every week now he's getting in trouble. Anyway, when I was up there, Josh mentioned that Runnymede has some Masters of Sin gang activity going on."

"Yes, there are Masters of Sin gang members at Runnymede. I was just there dealing with it this week."

The line moved up. Tyler ordered his large, black coffee and handed the barista his debit card. He turned back to Abbie. "So what does that look like? I mean, what does their gang activity entail?"

"Well, they deal in drugs…and a lot of gang-controlled prostitution. That's their game. It's much more lucrative for them than drugs or robbery. And it's much more difficult to prove. They're really well networked with a lot of cash flow."

"Where do they get the girls?"

"They're pretty good at recruiting them—from the schools, the malls, the neighborhoods. They know which girls are vulnerable, which ones they can pull in. Then their MO is to brand them."

"Brand them?"

"Yep. It's a tattoo—usually the boyfriend's name or initials, or sometimes it's a dragon or a devil."

"So it's like they're livestock or something." It was appalling. "Where do they brand them? On the neck or arms or…?"

"In various places. Necks and arms are common,

but I've seen girls with their pimp's initials tattooed on their eyelids before. I mean, make no mistake, these are bad guys."

An acidic taste burned at the back of Tyler's mouth. Brandon would never be involved in that kind of stuff.

"When I talked to Josh yesterday, it sounded like things are heating up over there with the gangs, so we'll be keeping a close eye on things."

"That's good to hear, because I have two kids going to school there. I'm starting to worry a little about their safety." Tyler picked up his coffee and waited for Abbie to retrieve hers.

They walked out to the parking lot together.

"If you're worried about your kids' safety, the main thing is to talk to them. Make sure you know what they're doing, who they're hanging out with—that kind of stuff. Kids with really involved parents—you know what I'm talking about, right? Like parents who are all up in their kids' business and stuff? Those kids are much less likely to get involved with gangs."

Well then, he didn't need to worry too much. Tyler climbed into his car and drove toward the Metro station. He was involved in his kids' lives. He had always known who they hung out with. At least, he used to know…

~*~

Tyler upturned his CEF mug, dumping the dregs of the day's coffee into the waste basket. Time to head home. He was just about to stuff his cell phone into his pocket when he glanced at the screen. Voicemail from…oh, no. Christina and her drama. He pressed the message replay button. "Tyler, you need to call me right now. I know you don't like it when I call you at work, but it's about Brandon, and it's really, really important. As a matter of fact, I really think we need to talk in person about this. I'll drive out there and meet you after work."

Her elevated tone and the words all tumbling together indicated she would be primed for histrionics. He dialed her number, hoping to catch her before she drove all the way out to Arlington in late afternoon traffic.

She picked up immediately.

"Christina, do not drive out here. I've got to get home, and whatever we need to discuss we can do it over—"

"Some really rough kids came by the house today looking for Brandon, and—"

"What?"

"Tyler, I'm in the parking lot. Would you please come out here and talk to me? Now? Please?" Her voice broke. She was crying.

When they were married, Christina cried all the time. Her hysterics drove him crazy. Ultimately, her bipolar mood swings were too much to take. She wouldn't stay on medication, and even when she was on it, she had a propensity for violent outbursts—usually directed toward him.

From the door of the building he could already see her short and spiky blonde hair behind the wheel of her blue sedan. He tapped on the window of the car, and she pressed the automatic lock to let him in. Tyler swung into the passenger seat, assaulted by the stale, artificial fragrance of a pine-scented air freshener.

Christina's ocean-blue eyes were red-rimmed and

watery, the whites shot through with spidery, red trails of emotion. "I've been calling you all day," she croaked, glaring at him with the hatred she'd displayed when they'd been married.

"So you told me. What's this all about?"

"I don't know. There's just a lot of crazy stuff going on. These guys showed up at the house today looking for Brandon. Really scary-looking guys with tattoos and piercings. They said they were friends of his. But I know they're not." Christina drew a shredded tissue from her pocket and held it against her crimson-tipped nose. "I was scared to death. I was getting groceries out of my car when they just walked up to me."

"What did they want?"

"I don't know. I told them Brandon wasn't around. I'd dropped him off at school after the appointment with the psychiatrist, and it seemed like they were acting kind of shifty anyway, and...I'm just really, really scared."

"Did you call the police to report it?"

"No, because that's the other thing. Last night some detective came by to ask Brandon about some party. I couldn't follow everything she said. Something about the party being where those sexting photos were taken—the ones circulated all around the school. Some of the photos were on Brandon's phone. So, apparently, he's been going to all of these parties? I don't know. He won't tell me."

"I told you not to have Brandon talk to anyone unless I was present."

"Well, she was at my door. What was I supposed to do?" She sniffed and wiped at her nose. "So was he at the party or not?"

"I'm not following you. What party?"

"I don't know which party they're talking about. She said Brandon's been seen at a lot of parties lately. I would never have let him go to a party like that. That must have been your night with him. You never called me to ask if Brandon could go to a party! You know how fragile he's been this year! How depressed he's been. How could you do that?" The annoying, shrill tone, as though she couldn't control the anger rising up, made her eyes bulge. Her face mottled with malice.

"What night was it? When was the party?"

"I don't know. Sometime around Homecoming."

Brandon had never asked about going to a party. But Brandon's visits had been sporadic lately. He hadn't been keeping to the regular visitation schedule. Tyler scratched his head. "Look, Christina, I'm sorry. There's been a lot going on. Lana's been in California, and—"

"I don't care about her and what she's doing," Christina spat. "I'm talking about our son. Don't you understand how serious this is?"

"Oh, come on. I can't even keep track of all the nights Brandon's supposed to stay over but doesn't because you have some doctor's appointment scheduled the next day. I didn't know that he even wanted to go to a party! He never told me or asked about it. When he's at our house he just stays in his room all the time."

"He's thirteen, Tyler!" she shrieked.

"I know that!"

She paused, taking deep, slow breaths. When she spoke again, her voice was calmer. "I went to see a lawyer yesterday about Virginia sexting laws. Did you know what Brandon did is considered distribution of pornography? That's a class six felony. It carries jail time. He could be required to register as a sex offender."

"They're not going to prosecute a thirteen-year-old as a sex offender."

"That's not what the lawyer told me," Christina said. "He told me it would probably be prosecuted in juvenile court, and there's a wide range of possibilities for punishment."

Tyler couldn't believe this. These were kids, and they looked at dirty pictures and yeah, they probably passed them around to their other friends. In this age of the Internet, there were new apps and sites the kids used that Tyler didn't understand or even know about. "This is such a mess."

"It's clear that our son has been running around doing whatever he pleases when he stays with you and Lana. Because you two are too wrapped up in your own lives to parent our kids."

Her words stung. "You're the one dragging him to this psychiatrist and that psychiatrist."

"And, obviously, he needs to go! Something is wrong!"

Tyler looked out the windshield, pressing the back of his head against the headrest until his neck ached. The car had grown very cold, and he could see his breath. "Fighting about this isn't helping. I'll talk to Brandon when he comes over next."

"Yeah. I'm sure that'll do a lot of good." Christina scoffed. "What're you gonna talk to him about? How it's OK to look at porn but not actually send pictures of naked girls to your friends?"

That arrow stung, but he held his tongue.

Christina's upper lip raised in a sneer. "No doubt

he learned about all of this stuff from you anyway."

~*~

Saturday, December 10

Saturday afternoon, Tyler answered a knock on the front door. Through the beveled glass, he could make out the forms of three boys. In this neighborhood, weekend solicitations were common, and Tyler figured these were probably neighborhood kids selling something for the school band. But these boys were not in the school band.

Three faces stared back at him—one of them partially covered in tattoos. All of them had tattoos of varying sorts—some on their hands and necks—but the one who spoke sported a black dragon climbing up the side of his cheek toward his temple. "Hey. Yeah, we're looking for Brandon."

"Brandon's not here." Tyler's mind reeled. What could these guys possibly want with his son?

"You know when he will be?"

The boys stood in a triangular formation and reminded Tyler of birds or a school of fish, especially since all of their dark hair was gelled and molded into fins on the top of their heads. The one who spoke stood in the front, his hands in the pockets of his jeans, his dark eyes darting all around. The other two looked past Tyler and into the entryway of his house. His blood chilled even as goose flesh rose on his arms from the cold air outside.

"What do you want with Brandon?" His fingers curled stiffly around the doorjamb.

"We're friends of his. You know, we just wanted

to come by and say hi," the guy said, and a small laugh punctuated his speech. His eyes shifted from the ground to Tyler to inside the house.

"You look a little old to be friends of my son's. You go to his school?" An electrical current of fear and anger ran through him. These were the gang members who had been harassing his son.

"Yeah...yeah." The boy with the black dragon tattoo threw a glance over his shoulder at the guys behind him. They all smiled. "Yeah. We go to school with him."

"Uh-huh." There was no way Brandon was hanging out with these guys—ever. These were probably the same rough-looking guys who'd showed up at Christina's home. A frisson of unease spiraled in his brain. Micah and Celia were inside. He could hear their voices upstairs. "Well, Brandon's not here."

"You know where he is?"

"No." Tyler jutted out his lower jaw and crossed his arms. "What are your names?"

The three males all exchanged glances and snickered. None of them made eye contact with Tyler.

"Yeah...uh, I'm Fred," the ring leader said. "And this is Bert and this is Ernie."

The trio burst into fits of chuckles, obviously amused by their clever leader.

Rage rushed through him as he growled, "Yeah, OK, Fred Flintstone. You and your cronies need to hightail it off of my property before I call the cops. And I'd better never see you around here—and I'd better never see you around my son!"

Coughing and chortling with hilarity, the three made their way down the steps and out to a black truck parked at the corner of the street. As they drove off, they held their hands out of windows with their middle fingers raised high. "We'll be back!" one of them called out, followed by a string of expletives.

Tyler closed the door and called Josh.

~*~

The sun was sinking as a police cruiser arrived to take Tyler's statement. Josh and Tyler met them in the driveway. The patrol car's lights flashed, blending with the Christmas decorations at several of the houses along the street. Various neighbors, including Suzanne, stood out in the freezing cold, hugging themselves and trying to garner some gossip-worthy information.

"What's going on, Tyler? Josh?" Suzanne called across the street. "Is everything OK?"

"Everything's fine, Suzanne. Nothing for you to worry about. Get back inside. These are frost-bite-worthy temps out here."

Tyler gave his statement, mentioning that his ex-wife had also received a visit from the thugs. The young officer said they would be in touch as soon as they knew something. He nodded to Josh before he left. "See you at the gym? Monday morning?"

"Bright and early," Josh responded.

Josh laid his hand on Tyler's shoulder. "If these guys show up again, give me a call. If I'm home, I'll come over in uniform. If not, I'll make sure another officer gets out here pronto. These guys will not bully you and Brandon, or anyone else in this neighborhood."

Tyler had never felt so helpless. "Thanks."

Somehow those guys had known Brandon was supposed to stay at his house that night. He meant to have a long conversation with his son. Laying down the law was the only course of action Tyler knew to help rectify Brandon's thoughtless—and reckless—behavior.

He went into his son's room, which smelt faintly of the pungent body spray so many teenage boys wore, mixed with the unmistakable odor of reeky socks. He shifted a box sitting on his chest of drawers and lifted the top to reveal a jumbled mess of video controls, headphones, and a rubber snake. The corners of Tyler's mouth lifted at the simple boyhood trinket.

Tyler opened Brandon's closet and shifted his clothes—at least those actually hanging—from side to side. What was he looking for? He wasn't even sure. Drugs? Some kind of gang propaganda or paraphernalia?

Stepping over the pile of laundry on the floor, he moved to Brandon's nightstand, opening the drawers and sifting through several cell phone chargers, some loose change, and a few metal badges Brandon had received when he'd been part of the Scouts. Funny. Brandon had once been so proud of those medals, and now they were relegated to the back of a dusty nightstand drawer. One day, they would probably end up in a box full of items to be given or thrown away, just like his own Scout medals.

Kneeling, Tyler lifted the edge of the comforter and peered underneath the bed, surprised to find it void of anything except the tennis racquet and can of tennis balls he'd bought Brandon last year. He'd hoped they could take some lessons together. But Tyler had gotten busy with work, and Brandon had gone to summer camp, and just like so many ideas to spend time with his son, that one had gone by the wayside.

Brandon's computer loomed like a sleeping giant. It was Tyler's old computer, one he'd retired for his current, more practical laptop. The old, fold-out metal chair creaked as he sat. Tyler's chest tightened as the desktop illuminated, and a sea-blue wallpaper with photographs of dolphins swimming appeared. Several old games Tyler used to play in his spare time remained on the desktop, ancient, mindless time fillers he no longer used.

Tyler pulled up the Internet browser. It was set to open on Brandon's e-mail account. Brandon didn't use his e-mail account very often, except for school. As Tyler scanned down through the contents of his son's inbox, a hot, tingling sensation disseminated through his chest, up his neck, and into his face. Almost every subject line read something like: *Hot Hot Hot, Katya and her friends want to meet you, Asian women looking for husbands, hi I'm looking for someone like you.* Many of the subject lines were familiar to him, ones he received in his own inbox. Some spam was unavoidable no matter what sites were visited, but nearly every e-mail in his son's inbox was pornographic.

Moving the cursor to the address bar, Tyler clicked on the browsing history. His heart sank. The only URL addresses present were XXX pornographic sites. He propelled his weight backward with such force that he nearly upended the chair. Leaning forward once more, his hand swept over his face, resting on his open mouth as he stared at the screen. "What?" he breathed.

When he clicked on one of the sites, intensely graphic, violent, and kinky images materialized on the screen. This went well beyond the sites he frequented. He flipped through a few of the pages. An image so disturbing, vile, and abhorrent caused him to look away. This was what his son was viewing? He grasped the computer cord and yanked it violently from the socket.

~*~

When Brandon arrived home from school, Tyler was waiting in the living room. He'd set up Micah and Celia in the den, watching one of their favorite movies. He didn't want them to hear the serious conversation he would be having with their older brother. It was past time to have this talk, and he berated himself for letting things get so far out of control.

He'd allowed Christina to take the reins, carting Brandon from one doctor to another, when he should have been manning up as Brandon's father. Through the living room window, Tyler observed his son as he exited his mother's car. With clenched jaw and compressed forehead, Brandon pulled his bag from the backseat. Christina said something to him through the open window, and Brandon nodded absently before moving up the front steps.

As Brandon came through the front door he locked eyes with his father.

"Come on in. Sit down. Let's have a chat," Tyler said.

Frowning, Brandon threw down his bag and slunk to a chair. His head went down and his fingers knitted at one another.

Tyler stood with his back against the wall. "So...you wanna tell me what's going on?"

Brandon shrugged.

"Look, Bran. This is all getting very serious. Fights at school. Sexting, pornography. Come on, I saw the pictures on your computer. That's some messed up stuff. Why are you doing all this?"

Another shrug. More silence.

"What you're looking at...I mean...that's some sick, sick stuff."

"All the kids look at it," Brandon spoke to his hands.

"Do all the kids have to hire defense lawyers?"

Brandon's face reddened.

"Do all the kids have gang members showing up at their house looking for them?"

Brandon's head popped up then, and his eyes widened. "What?"

"Three guys showed up here this afternoon looking for you. I had to call the police. Yeah, Brandon. It's that bad—it's that serious. Who are these guys? Do you know these guys?"

The boy shook his head.

Tyler brought his arm back and hammered his fist into the wall. "Brandon! Look at me. There are other people in this house besides you. Micah and Celia. I do not want them exposed to this kind of filth or violence, do you understand?"

"I don't know those guys."

"Your mother told me they showed up at her house, too. They said they know you."

"I don't know them."

"Then what do they want with you? Why are they looking for you?"

"I don't know." Brandon's voice shook.

"Tell me about this party then. Your mother said you went to a party one night when you were supposed to be staying with us."

"I stayed with Jared that night."

"You stayed with Jared, and you didn't tell

anyone. Your mother thought you were with me, and I thought you were with her. You took advantage of both of us." Anger burned in Tyler's chest. "Brandon, let me tell you right now. At the rate you're going, you're headed straight to juvie!"

Another shrug. "I guess."

"Is that where you met these guys. At this party?" Tyler willed his speeding heart to slow.

"I might have seen them there. I mean, they might have been there. I don't know their names or anything. Look, they asked me if I wanted to be part of their group. That's all."

Brandon's nonchalance stoked Tyler's irritation—every shrug was a poker pushing against the fiery coals burning in his stomach. "Do you realize how serious this is? Because I don't think you do."

"I said I didn't want to."

"You're facing potential criminal charges! And you've put us all in danger with these roughnecks you hang out with. And why are they looking for you? What do they want with you if you told them you didn't want to be part of their gang?"

"I don't know, Dad. You keep asking, and I don't know. I don't know why they keep coming by. I don't even know how they know where I live!"

"We can't have these kinds of people coming into our neighborhood." Tyler pushed himself away from the wall. He'd made his point clear. "And I'm moving your computer out of your room. You're grounded. You're not to use the computer at all. Do you understand?"

Brandon nodded, wiping at his nose with the back of his hand.

~*~

"I don't want to go to Grandma's! I want to stay with you! Where's Mommy?" Celia wailed directly into Tyler's ear.

It seemed safer for Micah and Celia to stay with his parents for a few days. "It's only for a couple of nights, sweetheart," Tyler soothed. "Mommy will be home and Grandma and Grandpa will bring you back. Anyway, you love going to Grandma and Grandpa's house. You'll have a great time there."

"No!" she screamed. "Why can't you come, too?"

"Because I can't, honey. I've got to take care of some things here."

Lyman, Tyler's father, pried the screaming child from Tyler's arms. "No need trying to reason with a five-year-old. Just give her to us. She'll calm down once we get her home."

"She's just upset by everything going on—her mother gone this whole past week..." his mother, Nancy, said softly. She placed her hand on her son's arm.

He wanted to howl with pain. Looking at his daughter's distraught face, streaked red with hysteria and glistening wet with tears, proved almost more than he could bear.

Micah, always calm in every circumstance, put his hand on his father's other arm. His forehead was lined with an all-too-mature concern. "It's OK, Daddy. I'll make sure she calms down. You know she gets like this sometimes."

Tyler pulled Micah close. "Thanks, Micah. I'd really appreciate it if you looked after your sister, OK?"

"Yeah, I know, Daddy. Don't worry."

He didn't know how he'd managed to father four such different children. Micah, the little adult, quiet and responsible even at eight-years-old. Celia, the firecracker—exploding at the most unpredictable moments. Brandon, sullen and withdrawn, barely communicative, impossible to read. And then there was Katherine. It was as if she wasn't in the world these days. She kept to herself. She didn't say much, and it was hard to know what she was thinking. In the midst of all of the chaos, Katherine flittered in and out, and he wasn't keeping track of whether she was supposed to stay with her mother or with him.

Nancy shook her head as she threw a few of Celia's toys into a bag. "I still don't understand why you two are thinking about moving across the country. It seems crazy to me when you have such a good life here. And it'll just be hard on the kids."

"Mom, I really don't want to get into all of that. I'm not even thinking about the move right now," Tyler said. "Right now, I just need to deal with Brandon."

He helped his parents bundle Micah and Celia into the car. "Give me a kiss before you go." He leaned inside the car but Celia, her mouth hanging open in a silent, shaking scream, tried to push him away.

"We'll call you a little later, once we get them in bed." His father's face was drawn and sad.

"And you'll call us if you need anything, won't you?" his mom asked as she climbed into the car.

"Of course, Mom. And thank you for this. I really appreciate it." The weight of the situation settled upon him. He could almost sense his father's disappointment and the thoughts rolling through his head: his son's dead-end job, failed marriage, troubled son, and now some harebrained plan to move across the country. Would he ever make his dad proud?

14

Kaki
Saturday, December 10

"Damien told me to make sure you buy some higher heels," Sydney said as they drifted from mall lingerie shop to shoe shop. Sydney flashed Damien's credit card. "I think you'd look cute in those." She pointed at a pair of shiny, blood-red pumps with a black heel that looked like a spike long enough to kill a vampire.

"I don't think I can walk in those."

"You don't have to *walk* in them."

Kaki hated clothes shopping with Sydney. She used to go out with her mom and buy sports-tees, shorts, and track shoes—gear good for running. Now, all the clothes were about tight, short, high—shackles to prevent her from running.

"Come on." Sydney grabbed the box containing the shoes and thrust it under her arm. "Let's get these in your size and go. We got an earlier start tonight. House parties in the 'burbs start earlier than city gigs."

Through the window of the shoe shop, a scene just outside the store caught her eye. Two girls sitting on a mall bench—Kaki knew them from school; one of them had run track with her—were looking up into the face of a guy Kaki had seen around. He was a gang member. As he turned his head and flashed a wide smile at the girls, the head of a dragon tattoo peered out from the top of his white collar. The girls giggled at something he said, their faces alight with intrigue, probably flattered at his advances.

Kaki's stomach rolled. She wanted to run over and warn the girls to stay away from him. Run! He was danger. He was the death of their lives as they knew them. He was—

"You ready?" Sydney's vice-like grip on her upper arm propelled her from the store and away from the girls and the gang member. Even so, his head turned as he saw them, his black stare darting back and forth between hers and Sydney's. His eyes seemed to say, "I'm watching you."

~*~

Sydney didn't drive all the way into the cul-de-sac. "I gotta run get ready for the party," she said as she pulled up to the corner. "We're all meeting out at The Diggs tonight."

Kaki said nothing as she climbed out of the car. Before she closed the door, Sydney called out to her, "Hey, what's wrong with you? You seem all drippy and emo. You need something?" She started to dig in her purse. "I got some anti-depressants with me."

Yeah, she *did* need to take something. All the time now. She never had a normal feeling anymore. In fact, she never knew what she was feeling from one moment to the next. "No, thanks. I got some in the house."

Sydney nodded and put her hands back on the steering wheel. "OK. See you later, then." She gunned the car and sped off.

Kaki turned and made her way into the subdivision. She glanced at her cell phone. It was five o'clock. She had about five hours until Damien or Sydney—or someone—picked her up. She'd head back to the house and take something to sleep until then. What else was there to do? Otherwise she'd just sit around dreading the passing hours.

Molly was at her mailbox, and Kaki gave a half-hearted wave. Molly waved back.

"How's the dog?" Kaki crossed the street.

"She's doing fine. I think she's going to have those puppies pretty soon."

"You keeping her?"

Molly nodded and smiled. "I think so. She's a little cuddle-bug. She's pretty much been on my lap all afternoon."

That would be wonderful—relaxing all afternoon on a couch with a dog curled up in her lap—no worries, no men waiting for her, no Damien. Kaki lingered for a few seconds just in front of the driveway. Her legs were tightly pressed together as she tried to keep out the cold.

"Anyway, I won't hold you up. You must be freezing," Molly said, waving her on. Kaki was happy to talk to someone normal. It took her mind off of the things she would have to do that night. "It's OK. I'm used to it. Hey, could I come by and see the dog sometime?"

"Do you want to come in now?"

"Just for a second."

Clasping their arms around themselves and against the biting wind, they made their way inside. Stepping into the dry, warm air, Kaki shivered against the contrast.

Megan Whitson Lee

The little dog was curled on the couch, the fleece throw bunched up underneath her. She looked up as though she'd always lived there, her tail thumping.

"You've just made yourself right at home, haven't you?" Kaki said, a reflexive smile spreading across her face. It was impossible not to smile when looking into this little dog's doe-eyes. Kaki had always loved animals, and especially dogs, although her family had never had one. Her mother claimed she had enough to take care of with two kids, and although Micah and Celia had begged for a dog repeatedly, her dad kept putting them off. Still hugging herself, Kaki sat down next to the little dog and stroked the top of her head. "Aw. She's so cute!"

Molly smiled down on the mutt as though she were a proud parent of a newborn baby. "Yeah, she is pretty cute. We're calling her Trixie."

"Trixie. She looks like a Trixie."

"I used to read a lot of Trixie Belden books when I was a kid. Did you ever read those?"

Kaki shook her head. She wasn't much of a reader before, now she couldn't remember the last time she'd picked up a book.

"Oh, well, Trixie was this young girl who went around solving mysteries... the stories would probably seem pretty dated if you read them nowadays."

Kaki ran her hand over the dog's soft fur. "That's so cool that you took her in. You rescued her. She probably would've died out there."

"Well, I couldn't leave her out there in the freezing cold. But I don't want to let myself become too attached. The owner may come looking for her."

Kaki shook her head, remembering the heartbreaking scene of the car speeding away from the cul-de-sac and leaving the cold and confused dog behind. She wiped at a tear in the corner of her eye. She figured it was just her eyes watering in the dry heat. Her finger came back with smeared eye makeup. She'd put on a lot before going out with Sydney. "I don't think so. If they were throwing her away, they won't want her back."

Hugging the mail close to her chest, Molly shuddered, still shaking off the chill. "Can I get you anything warm to drink? You want some hot tea or hot chocolate or something?"

Kaki shook her head, unable to take her eyes off the dog. "No, I'm fine."

Molly set the mail on the coffee table and sank down onto the couch on the other side of Trixie. "You going out tonight with your boyfriend?"

Kaki nodded. Her stomach dipped with dread at the thought of what she would be doing that night. "Umm…yeah, sure."

"How long have you been seeing each other?"

"A few months."

"Where'd you meet him?"

Molly asked so many questions. It was probably the teacher-thing rearing its nosy head, prying, reporting any strange behavior. These days all of the teachers were on high alert to make sure the kids weren't depressed or planning to kill themselves. Just last week her school had set up "safe zones" where kids could go during the day if they were feeling overly stressed and needed a break. Anytime she passed by them, they were filled. She only wished they really were safe zones. She'd live there. "I met him at school."

"Oh." Molly eyebrows raised. "Does he go to

Runnymede?"

"No. He came to one of my track meets in the fall."

Molly nodded. Her lips set in a line. Kaki longed to change the subject.

"What's his name?"

Kaki didn't know if she should tell Molly his real name, but she didn't want to make something up. "Damien."

Molly laughed a little, her eyebrows raising again. "Damien? Wow, that's quite the name. That makes me think of that movie I saw when I was little. Actually, I wasn't supposed to see it, but I had a babysitter keeping me, and my grandparents didn't know we were watching cable TV. Anyway, this movie came on about this kid named Damien who was evil— possessed by the devil or something."

That description wasn't too far off of her Damien. Kaki gave a terse smile.

Molly waved her hand, dismissing the conversation. "I'm sure you feel like you're getting a lesson in seventies pop culture today. I'll shut up now."

Kaki was relieved they were moving away from the boyfriend topic. "No, it's fine. My mom talks a lot about movies she used to watch and stuff. I've seen some of them from the eighties. I think there was one called *Sixteen Candles*?"

Molly's eyes lit up. "Yes! I loved that movie! That was my favorite movie when I was growing up. I must have watched it twenty-five times when it came out on video. I knew practically every line. And the lead actress shared my name, so I thought that was pretty cool, too."

Kaki laughed. "Yeah, it was a good movie."

Molly pulled her long, dark braid over her shoulder. "You know, high school was tough in the eighties, too—lots of cliques and bullying and all that—but I think you guys have it a lot harder. You just have so many things competing for your attention now. Technology pressure, social pressures, pressure to get into a good school. I had the situation with my mom to deal with, but school was OK."

"What was the deal with your mom?" Kaki was curious.

Molly's dark eyes met hers. "Oh, my mom was a drug addict. I was raised by my grandparents."

"Wow. I didn't know that." Molly seemed so normal and well-adjusted. But she was almost forty. Maybe people got over stuff by then. Maybe she would too…if she made it to that age.

"Yeah, my mom kept disappearing for days at a time. She'd leave me with this friend and that friend, and finally my grandparents stepped in. They got legal custody of me when I was around six."

"What about your dad?"

"I never knew him. Don't have a clue who he is." Molly's eyes shifted and her mouth tightened. "That probably gives you some insight into my mother and her dealings with men."

What would Molly think of Kaki and her dealings with men? "Where's your mom now?" Kaki asked.

"Haven't heard from her in years. We think she might be living out in Arizona somewhere but can't say for sure."

A silence settled. Kaki looked down at Trixie. She hadn't stopped petting her. Now the dog was sleeping—her eyes closed, her paws twitching with dog dreams.

"It's starting to snow," Molly said, pointing out the window.

White flakes rained down, coating the tips of the grass with a white gloss.

"Later in the week, I think they're calling for a heavy one. Maybe enough to get us out of school."

Kaki hoped so. She'd love to have a couple of days of being snowed in where she couldn't get out of the house and no one could get to her.

"Hey, you hang out some with Sydney Diaz, don't you?"

Kaki's muscles tensed. "Sometimes. Why?"

"Well, she's rarely in school. I'm concerned about her."

"She told me she's failing your class."

"Yeah, but it's more than that. Her attendance has never been good. She hardly turns in any work, but when she takes a test, she does well. She's smart, you know? I can just tell she's got other stuff going on that's more important to her."

"Yeah, I don't think school's at the top of her list."

Molly's gaze rested upon Kaki. "Tell her...if she needs to talk or she wants—or needs—anything...she should come talk to me. I'll do what I can to help her. I try to keep a professional distance from my students most of the time, but I have a special burden for girls like Sydney. Maybe because I lost my mom to drugs and bad men...I know the signs, you know? All too well. I've lived them."

Kaki's chest tightened. Molly's heart was in the right place, but Sydney was too hardened. She didn't think she needed any help. Kaki wondered if the same thing was happening to her.

15

Tyler
Sunday, December 11

Tyler had stopped going to church. It had been an integral part of his life when he was growing up. No matter what was going on, if the church doors were open, his parents had taken them to church. When he was a teenager and had gotten his first car, his father told him and his brother in a stern voice, "You can ride with us or you can drive yourself, but once your mother and I are sitting in the pew, I'd better look over and see your faces somewhere in there."

Lyman Jones was not a man to be questioned. When Tyler and his brother Brett were kids, they lived with the fear of their father's leather belt—the administrator of justice. He snapped it before he used it on them—that always made Tyler mad. "Just use it already!" he'd wanted to scream at his father. But he wouldn't have dared. To do so would be to show disrespect—the one thing Lyman Jones never tolerated.

Before Tyler and Brett were born, his father had fought in Vietnam, and when he returned, he'd set up a successful real estate business. Lyman often told his boys that he was proud he had forged his own way in the world. Unlike many of his fellow soldiers, he had not returned with PTSD—or if he had he did not know it—and he wasn't bound to anyone or anything. He was his own man with his own success. He encouraged both of his boys to do the same thing. "Don't work to make someone else money. Be innovative, boys. Find what you're good at and do it. Put your own money in your own pocket. That's what this country is all about."

But Tyler figured that when his father said those words, he had not imagined that Brett would find that he was good at playing guitar. Once he was old enough, he moved to Los Angeles to play in a rock band. They rarely saw him but once every three or four years. Lyman had probably not figured that Tyler would end up being good at running government projects—a job that required him to be tied to an employer—and the government. Both things his father hated. So both sons were probably great disappointments to him.

Tyler sighed and looked at the clock. Twelve thirty-eight. Too late to go to church now. An unsettled and restless feeling swept over him as he glanced at his laptop resting neatly on the dining room table. Lana wouldn't be home until this evening. Micah and Celia were at his parents' house. Katherine and Brandon were still sleeping. Maybe he should wake them up. Then there would be accountability...

With a surge of anticipation tinged with an underlying sense of guilt, Tyler made his way over to the laptop. With all the stress he'd been under, he deserved a few minutes on his favorite sites. He'd been pretty good this week and had only looked once or twice. Now was the perfect time. This evening, Lana would be home, the kids would be home, and he probably wouldn't have opportunity.

His fingers twitched and his heart pounded as he moved the mouse, and clicked on the address bar. He didn't know how much time he had until Katherine and Brandon were up, so today he would go straight to his favorite. His body relaxed. It was like taking medicine, soothing every part of his brain, his heart, his mind. He was lost in the images of women in various poses and state of undress. Time and place shrank away as his longings were filled in the webpages of *Girls, Girls, Girls*. Oh, how he'd missed these pages this week. It was like coming home again. All that mattered was this moment—these images— and the pleasure he got from it.

When his cell phone buzzed against the table, he thought it was his stomach growling. The sound pulled him from the comfortable trance, out of the warm waters, and back into the cold, stark reality.

Christina. *Could you wake up Brandon? Been trying his phone and he is not answering.*

He could ignore it, but then she'd just keep texting…and then she'd start calling. With a sigh, he closed the site and shaking off the brain sedation, headed upstairs. It wasn't entirely unusual for his teenagers to stay up late and sleep until afternoon, although it was after one o'clock, which was pretty late for them. He rapped his knuckles against Brandon's door. "Brandon? You awake in there?"

No response.

"Brandon?" Tyler grasped the doorknob and turned. Locked. Anger gushed through his veins. The kids knew they were never to lock a door in this house. Ever. "Brandon, unlock this door now!" Tyler pounded on the door with his fist, rattling it in its frame. "I'm telling you right now—if you don't open it, I will break it down. Don't test me."

Another possibility occurred to him—one that

eclipsed the anger and replaced it with fear. Images of Brandon dead in his bed stampeded into his mind's movie screen, along with a picture of the thugs at his door the day before, and news headlines of teenage suicide or gang-related murders. "Brandon!" Tyler called out frantically, rattling the doorknob and throwing his shoulder into the door.

"Dad? What's going on?"

Katherine floated from the doorway of her room, her voice soft and gravelly from having just woken up.

"Your brother's not answering and the door is locked," he said between thrusts to the door. The door gave way with a crunch, jarring against the frame at an awkward angle, the force of which propelled Tyler forward, staggering into the room.

The bed was empty, blankets and sheets strewn across it as though Brandon had been in it during the night. Impulsively, Tyler rushed to the closet and peered in. Nothing but a heap of clothing on the floor and some soccer balls.

Katherine, pale and ghost-like, stood in the broken entryway. Her gaze was fixed on the partially open window and the snow flittering inside, accumulating on the sill.

Tyler shot forward, grasping the sill and thrusting his head outside to the ground below. Nothing. He felt the cold, wet snow melting underneath his fingers. His breath made puffs of smoke-like panic into the air. Where was Brandon? How had this happened? He wrenched his head back inside and turned to his daughter, still standing like a zombie in the doorway. "Katherine, call 9-1-1."

She stood without moving, her eyes wide and staring as though trying to focus and understand the situation.

Tyler jolted toward her, grabbed her shoulders, and spun her around to face the hallway. He gave her a little push. "Go! Call 9-1-1. I'm going next door to get Josh."

Katherine skittered down the hall like a frightened doe, and Tyler rushed the stairs, taking two and three at a time. He flung open the front door and dashed out into the snow, nearly falling as he scaled the slippery embankment between the two houses. Arriving at the Wolfs' front door, he pounded upon it, praying they were home.

The sound of a dog's alarm-like bark sounded from within. It seemed to take minutes, not the thirty or so seconds that actually passed before the door opened.

Josh stood before him, still dressed for church in a wool sweater and khaki pants.

"It's Tyler," Josh called to Molly over his shoulder. "Hey. What's up, my man?"

Tyler's voice sounded shaky and unnatural to himself. "Hey, sorry to bother you, but Brandon's gone. I don't know where he went."

"He's not with Christina?"

"No. He was staying with me last night. Christina texted me because she was trying to reach him on his phone and he wasn't responding."

"Did you call 9-1-1?"

"Katherine's doing it right now."

"Be over in a sec. Let me just get my coat." Josh ducked back inside the house and closed the door.

Tyler stepped backward off the front stoop, feeling as if he might be sick. He trekked around the side of the house to the place below Brandon's window. A fine mist of white powder sifted from the sky, and with the cold temperatures, it was quickly accumulating. In the distance, he heard the whine of sirens. He couldn't tell for sure, but it looked as though there were some drag marks around the side of the house. *Oh, dear Lord, please no.* If he walked around the side and found…

The crunching sound of snow under foot accompanied Josh's arrival. "There you are." He moved to stand beside Tyler.

Tyler stared at the ground and the faint marks that trailed around the side of the house. Wordlessly, Josh followed the trail. With dread and fear rising in his throat, Tyler followed him. Around the corner, the metal structure of a ladder rested against the siding.

Josh pointed. "Yours?"

Tyler exhaled. No bodies. Just a ladder. "Yeah. That's mine."

"Looks like that's how he got out of the house."

They made their way around to the front yard just in time to meet the police pulling into Tyler's driveway. Josh waved to the first officer who emerged from the first car, and out of the second, unmarked car stepped Detective Abbie Jackson.

Her face was solemn. "Hi Josh, Mr. Jones." She pointed to the two male officers who stood on either side of the patrol car, the radios attached to their shoulders buzzing with communications. "This is Officer Phillips and Officer Mendoza."

Tyler held the front door open as they all entered. Snow blew inside and across the threshold. "Thanks for coming," Tyler said softly, shutting the door just as a gust of wind tried to force its way in. He ushered them into the living room.

Officer Mendoza took out a notepad.

Tyler motioned for them to sit, but they all continued to stand.

"What time did you last see him?" Abbie asked.

"Last night." The inside of his mouth was bone dry. The phone in his pocket buzzed. He needed to contact Christina.

Officer Mendoza scribbled something on his notepad.

"When did you notice he was gone?"

"Not until twenty minutes ago. I just thought he was sleeping in. His mother texted me that she couldn't get in touch with him. I went up to his room. The door was locked."

"Is that unusual—for his door to be locked?" she asked.

"Yes. We don't allow locked doors in this house. I had to break the door down."

"You broke down the door."

Tyler nodded.

Officer Mendoza continued to scribble.

The sound of pen against paper irritated Tyler. "Katherine," he called out.

His daughter sat silently in the corner. Her face was pale and drawn—eyes swollen and puffy. One even looked a little bruised.

"Call your mom. Let her know what's going on."

She lifted her phone from the table.

"Can we see his room?" Abbie asked.

"Yeah. Come on upstairs." Tyler motioned for them to follow. Tyler flipped on the hall light leading up the stairs.

"Lana still not back?" Josh asked.

"Tonight."

"Where are Micah and Celia?"

"At my parents. I felt safer with them there—you know, after what happened yesterday."

"What happened yesterday?" Abbie asked.

Tyler quickly filled her in on the visit from the thugs. "I called you guys in yesterday for that, too." They were quickly becoming that house on the street—the one that was always plagued with trouble.

"I was one of the officers who answered that call," said Officer Phillips.

"I'll want to get some more information on that, too," Abbie said. "But right now, let's take a look at Brandon's bedroom."

Tyler led them into Brandon's room—a room that had *teenage boy* stamped all over it—the mess, the wall posters, the clothes strewn everywhere. It was freezing cold from the open window. On the floor, a pile of clothing and other articles lay in a mound, and Tyler stood over it, as though observing a dead animal at the side of the road. When he spoke, he spoke to the mound, not to Josh. "I found porn on Brandon's computer. Sick stuff. Violent, disgusting stuff." Tyler's eyes watered. "Anyway. I took the computer out of his room. I grounded him, too. I guess I might have said some pretty harsh things to him."

"Did you call any of his friends?" Josh asked. "He's probably with one of them."

Tyler shook his head. "Haven't had a chance yet. I only know a couple of his friends."

"We'll want to make those calls," said Abbie. "See if they know anything. You never know—he could be hiding out with them. Open window." Abbie pointed at its partially open position. "Escape route there, I guess."

"Yeah," Tyler said. "That window sticks when the

weather's cold."

Abbie and the officers trolled around Brandon's room, taking notes and talking amongst themselves.

Tyler's heartbeat pounded in his throat.

"Mom's on the way," Kaki announced from the doorway.

"Great," said Tyler. That should add some hysteria to the mix.

When they had finished inspecting the room, Tyler and Abbie Jackson moved outside the door which hung lopsided from one hinge.

"I'd like to talk to your daughter...and your ex-wife when she gets here, see if they know anything. You should call the friends. After that...well, Brandon's a minor. There's no twenty-four-hour waiting period to report a minor missing. We'll file the report. Could be a runaway situation, but with what you reported yesterday...could be something else, too."

Tyler rubbed at his eyes and nose as if that would scrub away the horror of the situation.

Josh moved to stand beside him, placing his hand on Tyler's shoulder. "Hey, look. I'm sure he hasn't gotten too far. With it being as cold as it is outside, you can bet he'll call or come home soon."

"Or freeze to death," Tyler said. He swallowed bile.

~*~

Lana's plane landed late that afternoon as the newscasters all around the region began broadcasting numbers associated with accumulating inches of snow. "A lot of flights were canceled," she told Tyler as they retrieved her suitcase from baggage claim. "Too bad mine wasn't one of them." The words were mumbled under her breath, but Tyler heard them. They stabbed at his already aching heart.

"The kids are waiting for you at home with my parents."

It was only a seven-minute drive from Dulles Airport to their house, but it was already dark, and with the roads icing and the snow whipping, Tyler had to concentrate on his driving. He decided to wait and tell Lana about the situation with Brandon until they were on their way back, but she was talking full-force.

"It was eighty-degree temperatures the whole time I was there. And you should see the house where Erin lives. It overlooks this beautiful manmade lake in a gated community...and Dan, her business partner, he lives nearby, too. I got some information about that subdivision in case we want to look at houses there. Or we may want to look at the luxury condo units. They aren't too far away from the office, and they're within walking distance of the ocean."

Tyler wanted to get home as soon as possible to stop her incessant talking about this California fantasy. He didn't want to hear about gated communities and ocean-side views. Brandon, his son...was missing.

Lana was still talking as they turned into their driveway.

"Go on inside," he told her. "The kids are waiting for you. I'll get the bags." Tyler grabbed the bags out of the trunk and carried them inside, anxious to hear whether there had been any word from Brandon.

Micah held yellow flowers for Lana, telling her proudly he'd purchased them at the grocery store when Tyler's parents had run out for bread, milk, and toilet paper earlier in the day.

Celia had drawn a sign in simplistic green crayon that said *Welcome Home Mommy!* The W-E-L took up the top half of the page, and the rest of the letters were pushed together on the bottom half. The exclamation point hovered in the bottom corner. On the back, Celia had drawn a princess in gold and silver crayons with bubble-feet peeking out from under a triangle skirt. "I made this for you, Mommy!" Celia held out her sign.

"And it's beautiful, baby!" Lana squatted down and let her purse and carry-on bag fall from her shoulders as she embraced first Celia, then Micah.

Tyler's mother moved forward and politely hugged Lana, and a cordial nod was exchanged between Lana and his father. As they all made their way to the kitchen, Lana chatted animatedly about the new job, the opportunities in Santa Monica, the great weather, and the wonderful, laid-back place it would be for the kids to grow up.

Tyler's parents listened politely and silently.

"I know a move to California would mean you wouldn't see us all as often, but we could arrange holiday visits—or you could fly out and see us."

Tyler gritted his teeth, waiting for Lana's stream-of-consciousness retelling about her trip to end.

"Mommy, where is California?" Celia interrupted.

"It's on the west coast of the United States, sweetie. And it's beautiful. We'll be by the ocean, and it's always sunny there."

"Is it far away from Grandma and Grandpa?"

"Sort of. It's about a five-hour flight."

Celia appeared to be considering this. "Would we still be able to see them every week?"

Everybody in the room shook their heads at this

question, and Lana answered, "No. Not every week. But we'd still see them."

"How often?"

Lana, still smiling, sighed with exasperation. "I don't know, baby. We'll work all that out when the time comes. Definitely we'd see them at Christmas and during the summer."

"I don't want to go. I don't want to leave Grandma and Grandpa."

A few more seconds of this line of questioning, and there would be a scene. "Let's not worry about that right now, Celia. Grandma and Grandpa are going to stay with us for a few days. You'll like that, won't you?" Tyler asked.

Celia clutched her grandmother's leg, and smiled. "Yes! And we can play all the games we played at Grandma and Grandpa's house. It was so much fun! We got to sleep over two nights this week."

"They were very good," Lyman confirmed. "I taught Micah how to play chess."

"And I beat Grandpa a bunch of times!" Micah beamed.

"Yes, you did." Lyman pointed to his head. "This old brain's not quite as sharp as it used to be."

"And we get to play games again tonight, don't we Grandpa?" Celia asked.

"Yes," he answered quietly.

"Really? You're staying the night?" Lana's smile drooped and her eyes widened. She looked from Tyler's parents back to Tyler. "Why's that?"

"We need to talk about some stuff," Tyler said. A sense of dread settled. He needed her to tone down all the talk about California. He couldn't even imagine going now.

"And what did you do all week?" Lana asked Tyler as she sank down on a stool at the kitchen island.

Celia pulled at her mother's arm, forcing Lana to lean severely to her right. The little girl whispered in her ear, but it was loud enough for the rest of the room to hear. "Mommy, Brandon ran away."

In the sudden silence of the room, the thud of little pellets of ice pelting the roof became loud.

Lana's expression wrinkled with confusion. "What's going on?"

"I'll fill you in on it upstairs. We can take your bags up to the room."

"I don't really think you can go out in this weather to look for him tonight," Tyler's mother said.

"I gotta try, Mom."

"But the roads—"

"You want me to come along, son?" Lyman asked Tyler. "Help you look for him?"

"No, thanks, Dad. I think Josh may help me. It would be better if you and Mom stayed here and helped with the kids, waited to hear any word, or if he comes back…"

Lyman looked at Micah. "You up for a game of chess?"

"Yeah!" Micah's serious mouth spread wide in a grin.

"Can I watch?" Celia asked.

"Of course," Lyman said in a tone of enthusiasm.

Tyler never heard words like that from his father while growing up. He couldn't ever recall playing chess or any other game with his dad.

Lana hugged Celia and Micah again. "I'll be back down in a little while, OK? I've got to unpack a bunch of gifts for you."

The children seemed happy to follow their grandparents into the den.

Tyler and Lana carried her bags upstairs.

"What's going on? Where's Brandon?"

Tyler sat on the bed, staring straight ahead, his chest constricted with anxiety. "We think Brandon sneaked out of the house last night or this morning early. No one's heard from him. Christina and I had to file a police report."

"Have you called all of his friends? Could he be staying with Jared or—

"We've called everyone we can think to call. No one has seen him."

Lana's face paled. But Tyler knew her too well. The horror on her face wasn't for Brandon. He could practically see the wheels in her brain whirring, fueled by fear that this would mess up everything and unsettle the delicate balance of her hard-won plan.

"And there's more. These rough, gang-type kids came by yesterday looking for him. Brandon said he met them at some party or something."

"Gang-type kids? They came here? What did they want with Brandon?"

"I don't know. He claims not to know. The police are looking into it. I didn't want Celia and Micah in the house last night in case they came back. And then today, I needed Mom and Dad here to help in case Brandon comes back. And I sent Katherine home with her mother. It's been a case of musical houses. Just— everything's a big mess, Lana. Before I picked you up, Christina and I spent two hours out in the snow hanging up posters with Brandon's picture."

Lana's face was blazoned with anger. "I blame Christina for the way that kid is. With her crazy life, and the way she's shuffled them back and forth between two houses, it's no wonder."

"Let's not waste time placing blame," Tyler said. "I've got to see if Josh still wants to take me out in this weather to look for Brandon."

Lana grabbed his hand. "This is all going to be so much better once we're in California."

Was she nuts? Had she not heard a word he'd said? He tried to keep his voice calm. "I'm sorry, Lana. But I really can't talk about California right now."

Her face drooped and she let go of his hand. The room fell silent as he walked to the closet, pulled out the heaviest wool sweater he could find, and slipped it over his head. Maybe the roads were pre-treated early enough that they wouldn't be so bad. And Josh had a four-wheel-drive truck...

"Maybe I can go out there early with Micah and Celia and get settled. Then you can join us after all of this is resolved."

Tyler turned to look at her, shocked. He shook his head, a sardonic laugh punctuating his words. "You have got to be the most self-centered woman."

Lana's eyebrows shot up. "Excuse me?"

"Have you heard a word of what I've just been telling you?"

"Yes, I have. But our plans are set. And I'm sure Brandon will show up again."

The lines of his face melded into firm, angry edges of stone. He whipped a hand through his hair, grabbed a handful and pulled until his scalp hurt. A growling, guttural sound of frustration exploded from his throat. "You're living in La-La Land, Lana! I don't know what planet you're on. My son is missing. Don't you understand that?"

Lana's mouth compressed into a hard line and the look in her eyes seemed to defy him as she walked into the en suite bathroom. The door slammed behind her.

16

Kaki
Wednesday, December 14

The roads were finally clear enough by Wednesday for school to resume. Three full nights of being snowed in with her grandparents and her little brother and sister had afforded her a little glimpse of normalcy. Three full nights of not seeing Damien and only stealing a little vodka from Lana's stash or popping a pill or two just to get a little lift, and she could actually think pretty clearly. Even so, Damien's text messages never stopped.

Keep ur mouth shut.
Don't forget how much I love u.
Remember u belong to me.
I bought u a new phone.
I bought u a new mp3 player for ur car.
U better b quiet.
Brandon was gone.

That reality played over and over in her head like a song that got stuck in her brain. *Brandon is gone. Brandon is gone. Brandon is gone.* Something had happened on Saturday night. Something that had caused him to run. But she couldn't remember enough of the night to piece it all together. And of course, she hadn't been able to tell the police she knew anything at all. If Damien found out she'd told anyone…

"If you ever tell anyone—your mom, your dad,

anyone at school…we'll kill your whole family." When he'd said the words, he'd spoken them in the same tone he'd used when he first told her he loved her.

Kaki hated what she was doing, and she hated herself for doing it, but she didn't have any choice. Some of the guys in the MOS gang were killers, and she knew they didn't make idle threats. But that wasn't the only thing that kept her shackled to this life. No matter how much he scared her, she was just as addicted to Damien and the ebb and flow of his love as she was to the drugs he gave her. Even so, Damien made it no secret that Kaki was one of about five other girls in his "stable."

Sydney was Damien's bottom girl. She'd been around the longest, and she did a lot of work for him and some of the other guys in the gang. She recruited new girls, prepared them to work, and set up the parties they attended.

The night before the party, Kaki had tried to talk to Sydney about how horrible she felt doing this, how much she wanted to stop…had Sydney ever known anyone who had stopped?

Sydney just brushed her off. "Why would you want to stop? Damien takes care of you, doesn't he? We're like a family."

Kaki was tired of hearing these empty assurances from Sydney. "Does your family make you do this kind of stuff?"

Sydney had laughed in response. Her face hardened and her eyes took on this cold, dead look. "How do you think I got started with all of this? Honey, I've been doing this since I was fourteen…when my mother pimped me out to her boyfriend's friend."

Looking at her then, Sydney was a totally different person. Sydney wasn't the cool girl who recruited her friends into the trap of prostitution. Sydney was a girl in trouble. Sydney was in even worse shape than her.

She'd tried to contact Sydney since Saturday, but her texts were never answered and her phone went straight to voicemail. And Kaki had a sneaking suspicion that something bad had happened that night that involved Sydney as well, but she couldn't remember. Her memory was all flashes and fuzzy images. Usually that was a good thing following a party where she'd been one of the items for sale, but this one…she wanted to remember. She needed to remember.

~*~

Saturday, December 10, the party date. Kaki remembered because it was her mother's birthday. She got dressed and ready to meet Damien, silently talking to herself. *Don't look at them. Don't think about them. Numb. Numb. You feel nothing. You are nothing. You're not even here.*

Her mom's name appearing on her cellphone interrupted her attempts to convince herself that she didn't exist.

"Hey. It's supposed to snow. Eric's got a whole birthday thing going on for me, so I'm just going to stay at Eric's this weekend. So if you need me, I'll be over there. Are you out tonight?"

"Yeah."

"Is your dad at home tonight?"

"Lana's out of town. I don't know about Dad. I guess he's going to be at home."

"Well, remember that your brother's going through a tough time right now. He really needs someone with him at all times. I don't trust your dad to really watch him, so promise me you'll come home at a decent hour."

How could she promise that? She didn't know what time she'd actually be home—or *if* she'd be home. Brandon might be alone all night if it were up to her. Kaki rolled her eyes. "Mom, Brandon's all right."

"No, Katherine, I do not want him left alone. Do you understand? And he is not to leave the house."

"Yeah, OK, Mom. I gotta go." When she hung up the phone, she called out to Brandon through the open door of the upstairs bathroom. "She thinks you're going to kill yourself or something, you know."

"Are you crazy? I'm not going to kill myself," he said as he came out of his room.

Kaki believed him. Brandon was a weird kid, moody and sneaky, but she didn't see him as suicidal. She hadn't been at all surprised about the sexting. She knew exactly what he was doing when he came home and got on his computer—when he pretended he was looking up stuff for his history class. There was nothing even remotely historical about those sites.

She also wasn't surprised about the fight at school. This year in the eighth grade he was in some classes with kids who were much rougher than he was used to. In fact, she knew a lot of them—and they weren't the sort of people she wanted her little brother hanging out with. Her life was a lost cause, but his didn't have to be.

Kaki hurried to gather her stuff and put on the rest of her makeup. Standing in the upstairs bathroom, cringing at her own reflection in the mirror, she heard

Brandon's voice from the open door of his bedroom.

"By the way, I know what you're doing." His voice was low and it sent a chill through her.

"What are you talking about?"

"I know what you're doing with those guys."

Kaki's fingers shook, and her eyeliner fell into the sink. Brandon moved to stand in the hall, his arms crossed as he watched her. Kaki turned sharply and stared at him. "Who told you that?"

"Some guys at school."

Slowly, she picked up the eyeliner, turned back to the mirror, and tried to finish the cat-eye line across her eyelid. "Yeah. Like your friends would know."

"I heard it from a guy who knows your friend."

Her heart pounded. No one knew anything about this other side of her life except Sydney and Damien. "What friend?" she growled, trying to pretend she didn't believe what he was saying.

"Your friend Sydney. They know her."

"How?"

"You know how."

She swung around and glared sharply at him. "You're telling me that your thirteen-year-old friends—"

"They're not thirteen. They're older. One of them's like, nineteen. He's failed a bunch of times, but he's special ed so he can stay in school until he's like twenty-one or something."

"Why are you hanging out with those kind of guys?" Her chest felt tight. She knew those guys from Runnymede who were already adults and still attending classes. They were gang members.

"Why are you?"

A knot formed in the pit of her stomach, but she

had to be tough. She couldn't show any shame or fear. She was a Masters of Sin girl now. Moving toward him, she grabbed the neck of his shirt, and twisted it so hard he pushed at her.

"Ow!"

"Brandon, no one—no one can know about this. Do you understand?"

"I won't tell anyone."

"Good." She let go of his shirt and pushed him away as she returned to the mirror. "And stay away from those guys."

Numb, numb. *Feel nothing. You are nothing. You're not even here.*

~*~

Originally the party was supposed to take place at The Diggs, a cinderblock shack out in the middle of a field. This was where they usually brought "the new girls"—the gang's term for very young girls who had recently arrived from Honduras or El Salvador. Girls who didn't speak much English and had no idea what was happening to them until it was too late.

Kaki and Sydney had ridden together, and when they arrived, Damien and two other guys were standing in front of the cinderblock shack waiting for them. Damien tapped on the hood of her car and walked around to her window. "There's been a change of plans. We're moving the party to Gio George's house."

"Why?"

"Better venue," he said, rapping the ledge of the driver's side window with his knuckles. "Leave your car here. You two can ride with me."

"No," the words burst from her mouth in a rush of panic, and his eyes darkened. She would much rather leave directly from the party. Then she could go straight home and not have to risk any secondary stops. "I mean, I'd rather drive. I need to make sure my car makes it home."

"You probably won't be able to drive from the party anyway." Damien pulled a plastic bag containing blue pills from his pocket. "I've got your favorites." He turned and walked toward his own car, and Kaki knew there was nothing else she could say. She had to ride with him.

"Just pull over there and park." Sydney pointed to a space behind some large bushes. "No one'll bother it."

Sydney was well schooled in the operations of the gang. She knew how they worked, and how far and how hard to push. Sometimes she fell under Damien's wrath, but not very often these days. She'd learned to stay on the sunny side of his street.

"I think we're under Hubby's watch tonight anyway. Damien has new girls to break in, so I wouldn't mess with his head too much."

With what they were doing, there was never really a good night, but at least with Damien, they knew his expectations. When they got passed along to other guys in the gang tasked with minding the stable, they never knew what they were in for. It was hard to know when they were doing something wrong, when someone might go off on them. Kaki didn't know much about Hubby, except that he was the big, tall guy who hung out with the football players.

"He used to play on varsity for Runnymede," Sydney said. "He graduated last year, but he still hangs with Gio and those guys."

Gio was star varsity football player, homecoming king, and an honorary member of the Masters of Sin. He was Italian and very good looking, but an egomaniac, and one of the most popular boys at Runnymede Secondary School. He was also a fledgling pimp with a stable of four girls and looking to add more. Damien was down to five girls after Vera's family moved to New Mexico. Lucky her. She'd escaped through default. The rest of them had no out.

Gio was one of those guys who got a kick out of power and wielding it over women. He liked being in control and he liked the danger of being a pimp on the down low. He didn't need the money, that was for sure. Gio's father was a successful businessman and sat on the town council; Gio's mother came from big money. His family lived in a gargantuan mansion off of Route 7 that looked out of place sitting just off the main road. A turret and archway connected the four-car garage with the ten-bedroom, eight-bathroom house.

Kaki knew their daughter, Gianna, from track. The only relief Kaki experienced on this night was Gianna's absence from the party. At least she would not see her former track mate while dressed up like the prostitute she was, practically led on a leash with other girls into the basement.

These parties were money-making ventures for the gang. They charged a $30 cover fee, and the guys were let in with access to all the booze and girls. No questions asked. Sometimes other girls from school came, ones who didn't realize they were part of the money-making equation. Realization struck them, often after it was too late, usually the next morning after they awoke and understood that someone had slipped something into their drink.

No girls ever reported anything. The embarrassment was too great, and they didn't want to be grouped in with the likes of girls like that.

Mattie, another girl Kaki had gotten to know through parties and the club, was already there when she arrived. Mattie was one of Rocket's girls. Although they never dared talk about how much they hated this life and themselves, they could read it in each other's eyes, and it drew them together. Mattie attended Harper Park, an alternative school.

"Only a few more months," she whispered to Kaki as they waited together in the corner chugging cheap vodka and downing the pills the guys gave them. They waited for the euphoria to kick in—or the numbness, which sometimes was nearly as good.

"Only a few more months until what?" Kaki cleared her glass and poured another.

"Until I graduate," Mattie said, following suit.

"Yeah. Then what?"

She looked up, her dark eyes sweeping over the room with a determined hatred of the men within it. "And then I'm so out of here."

"Where you gonna go?"

"I don't know. Anywhere but here. I have an aunt who lives in Lake Tahoe. Maybe I'll go there and live with her for a while. I want to go really far away...to make sure they don't find me."

Kaki shuddered. Was there anywhere far away enough for that? "You gonna go to college?"

"Yeah. Maybe."

Both silent for a few moments, the girls emptied a second glass of vodka and poured a third.

"How long does it usually take for your stuff to kick in?" Mattie asked.

Kaki shrugged. "I don't know. It's never fast enough."

"Yeah, I know, right?" But Mattie's eyes dilated, and her slow smile said she was already starting to feel it. "I think I'm getting a dog when I move away."

"I love dogs. One day I'm going to have a dog and name her Hope."

"That's nice." Mattie's eyes were swimming. "I'll bet she'll be really cute. Just don't ever let Damien know you got one. He kills dogs."

Kaki's gut twisted at the image. She'd never seen it happen, but she had heard Damien talk about it. She'd tried to pretend he was kidding. "No, I'm getting one. Sometime this year. I'm going to name her Hope."

"Yeah, you said that."

Everything was moving with floating colors and woozy, gauzy textures all around her. "Thank you," she heard herself say, as her head lolled toward Mattie and her form blurred. "I'm finally taking off."

Suddenly, Hubby grabbed her arm. "Time to get this party started." His voice sounded as if he were at the other end of a tunnel. One more glance around the room. Flashing lights and loud, pounding music. And her brother was talking to Sydney. *Wait, what?*

As Kaki was pushed through the door of one of the bedrooms by some guy she didn't know, she heard herself say, "Hey, hey—that's my little brother."

Maybe she'd hallucinated his face onto someone else's? Why would her little brother be here? There was no reason for him to be here.

It was hard to remember anything else.

One other blurry scene remained in her mind:

staggering out of the bedroom to the sound of shouting and the scene of Hubby and Gio pushing each other. Her brother was nowhere around. She was sure she'd dreamed that she'd seen him.

~*~

Back at school on Wednesday, Kaki's stomach clenched and nervous tremors ran up and down her arms and legs. Damien's spies were everywhere. Most likely they would let her know they were watching her, too. While sitting in her math classroom, Sebastian Riviera poked his head into the room and stared at her. He gave her a two-finger salute and puckered his lips. Chills ran down her back and she dropped her gaze. When she looked up again, he was gone.

Breathing a sigh of relief, she looked at Sydney's empty seat. Tightness gripped Kaki's chest as she wondered why Sydney had not replied to any of her texts or phone calls. What had occurred during the rest of Saturday night's party? Had something happened to Sydney that she just couldn't remember?

At the end of the day, Kaki stopped by Molly's classroom to find out if Trixie had her puppies yet. Molly was sitting at her desk, her laptop open in front of her and a stack of papers beside her. She looked up when Kaki entered the room.

"Hey, Katherine."

Kaki felt a little awkward just stopping by like this, but she moved closer to Molly's desk. "Hi. How's Trixie?"

Molly smiled. "Oh, she's settling right in."

"Any puppies yet?"

"Any day. The vet said she's ready. Maybe within

the week. We've taken her to the vet twice now, and the vet says she seems healthy. He's given us all kinds of material on what to do during a dog birth, how to help, when to get professional help..." Molly shrugged. "I guess we're going to have a crash course in dealing with puppies."

Kaki slid into a desk. "I'm glad you're going to keep her."

"Well, I don't think Josh really wanted a dog—especially not a pregnant dog—but I think she wore him down with those sad, sagging eyes. She cuddles up close against his leg when we sit on the couch and watch television."

"That's so cute."

"It's almost as good as having a baby of our own." Molly's smile slipped from her face. She looked down at her hands, silent for a moment. Then she drew a sharp breath and looked up again. "So any word about Brandon?"

Kaki shook her head. "No."

"I really hoped he would just come back. I know your parents are beside themselves."

"Yeah, pretty much. Mom's been calling all day every day, and Dad hasn't gone to work."

"I know Josh regretted that the weather was too bad on Sunday to go out looking for him."

"It was really bad out."

Her dad had trudged around in the snow, walking through all of the neighborhoods around them.

Kaki cleared her throat. "Sydney wasn't in your class today, was she?" Sydney hadn't been in math class, but sometimes she went to one class and not another.

Molly shook her head. "I haven't seen Sydney in

weeks. She's pretty much stopped coming to my class. Have you seen her recently?"

Kaki needed to be careful. "I saw her on Saturday at a party. I haven't been able to get in touch with her this week, though."

Molly's brow furrowed. "Hm. You worried about her?"

Kaki nodded. "Yeah, a little. She hasn't answered any of my texts or anything."

"Do you know her mother at all?"

"No. Never met her."

Molly turned to her computer and began to type. "Let's call home right now, and see if we can find out what's going on. I should have done that before now anyway."

Kaki didn't want to make any waves. But maybe Sydney's mother would have some information. "I don't think her family speaks English."

"That's OK. I'm pretty fluent. My grandmother was Argentinian. I can get by." Molly picked up the phone. "Let's call." She punched in the numbers and held the phone to her ear.

"Ola?" she said after a few seconds. *"Ola. Mi nombre es Molly Wolf. Soy profesor de Inglés de Sydney."*

There was a long pause.

"Si?" Molly continued in Spanish.

Three years of French meant Kaki didn't understand much of what was said.

Molly's face took on an expression of concern. Finally, she hung up the phone. "That was Sydney's aunt. She said Sydney and her mother haven't lived with her for some time. She said Sydney's mom moved to New York. Sydney was supposed to stay with her and finish school, but she left and moved in with her boyfriend a couple weeks ago. Do you know her boyfriend?"

Kaki cringed. "Um, not really." Molly would never understand the truth. It would be dangerous to try and explain it.

She really had known very little about Sydney. She'd never been to Sydney's house or met any members of her family. The only places she'd ever gone with Damien, Sydney, or any members of the gang were the club, some motels, the cinderblock shack they called The Diggs, and a few house parties. She'd never been to Damien's house. She didn't even know where he lived. It was kind of weird how little she knew about the people in her life. But what part of this nightmare was normal?

17

Tyler
Saturday, December 17

On Saturday afternoon, Tyler drove up and down the streets of Herndon looking for Brandon. Snow banks lined the roads, and salt crews were still out trying to keep the roads from refreezing. He tried to take deep breaths and maintain some patience as he slowed to a crawl behind one of them.

From the passenger seat, his cell phone rang. He glanced down at it. Abbie Jackson's name appeared on the screen.

"Hello?"

"We've got a lead on Brandon."

Tyler's heart leapt. "Where?"

"Winchester."

"Winchester? That's fifty miles away. What's he doing there?"

"We got a call from police in Winchester who thought they might have him in their custody," Abbie explained. "Some woman in Winchester called the police after she chased a kid off of her back porch. Anyway, the Winchester police got him as he was running through backyards in the neighborhood."

"I can't believe it," Tyler breathed. He had been so sure Brandon was still in Herndon, staying at some friend's house he didn't know about. Tyler had driven up and down every road he could think of every day. And he'd spent a lot of hours driving through rough neighborhoods where gang members were known to live. "Are they sure it's Brandon?"

"He gave them another name," Abbie said. "But one of the cops recognized his face from the news and the missing poster sent out to all Virginia police. They're pretty sure it's him. I'm on my way there now."

Tyler hung up and called Josh.

Daylight was almost completely extinguished when they backed out of Josh's driveway. As they drove down Route 28 toward Interstate 66, the sunset off to their right was at its end—only a small ball of fire burned in the distance as it sank below the line of businesses and strip malls.

"I'm glad you called me," Josh said.

"Thanks for driving me out there. I…I didn't want to call Christina until I'm out there and know for sure it's him."

They drove in silence for a few moments.

"You know," Josh said. "I always pegged you for one of those guys who never shows a crack. You know…you always have your brave face on and look like you've got it all together. I figured it was either that, or you really did have it all together."

Tyler exhaled a short, terse laugh. If Josh only knew… "Josh, I don't have anything together. I think I can readily admit that my life is a mess."

"Well, you need help, and you're willing to admit it," Josh said. "That's a move in the right direction."

They turned onto Interstate 66 going west toward Winchester and were immediately forced into the far left lane to crawl behind a line of other cars as rubberneckers all gawped at an accident on the shoulder.

"There's still a lot of ice out here," Josh remarked. The grass was still piled high with the white walls of snow, now turning black with road debris.

"It'll take months to melt," Tyler said. "I can't believe Brandon's been out in this for a week."

"And Winchester?" Josh scratched his head. "How did he get to Winchester? Fifty-five miles away."

"I don't know. I just can't believe any of this is happening. All of this craziness started with that sexting thing. And now running away? I just can't believe he keeps doing these stupid things."

"Just so you know," Josh said. "It's not like this is the only sexting case we've ever had—or even the first case we've had this year. Unfortunately, we see this all the time. We used to prosecute every case. Now, there are just too many of them. I'm confiscating phones from kids every week because of the sexting epidemic."

A heavy, rattling sigh escaped Tyler's throat, and he covered his eyes with his hand. "I guess I should have known Brandon was hooked on pornography."

"How would you have known?"

"I should have been paying more attention." And he should have been looking to his own behavior as a compass to that of his son's. The apple didn't fall far from the tree...the sins of the father...

"It's hard, you know? These kids are sneaky. You can be the best parent in the world and still miss this stuff," Josh said.

Despair settled over Tyler. He suddenly felt much older than his forty years. How had he ended up here? How had he let this happen to his son?

"You OK, man?"

"No. There are so many things going through my mind right now." Tyler focused on the windshield wipers squawking against the glass, sweeping the delicate, mist-like snowflakes to the sides of the windshield where they turned to slush. There was no reason to keep his secret anymore. "I should have known...because I think I may have a problem with it myself."

"With what?"

"Pornography."

"Oh."

An uncomfortable silence followed. Should he have told him? Would Josh judge him? If anyone seemed like they were straight-laced and had it all together, it was Josh. He probably wouldn't understand. He might just think Tyler was a sicko.

After a few seconds, Josh spoke. "You know—all of us guys struggle with that. Whether it's pornography or lust. All of us. Anyone who tells you different is lying—or too old to care."

Tyler was relieved at his candor. "You look at porn?"

"Well, no. But I used to—when I was in college. I mean, I even went to a few strip clubs, I'm ashamed to say. But look, I don't have to use pornography to know what it's like to be tempted, man. All I have to do is open my Internet browser, watch a movie, or even an ad on television. Some days it's bad enough just walking around the school building. You know how some of those teenage girls dress."

Tyler was quick to follow up his first confession with his second. "I've met a girl at work, too." He might as well let it all fly tonight.

"Have you done anything with her?"

Tyler shook his head. "I've had drinks with her, we've played racquetball. Mostly I've thought a lot about what it would be like to...you know...*be with* her."

Josh paused a minute before he answered. "Hmm … I guess this is how the devil operates. He keeps us in a state of dissatisfaction."

"What do you mean?"

"I was just thinking about how the devil keeps us all chasing our tails. No matter how much we have, we'll always want more. Partly it's our own human nature, but the devil takes advantage of that—shows us what we're missing out on. 'Look at all the thrills you're missing!'" Josh removed one hand from the steering wheel and waved it in the air for emphasis.

"I guess that's true," Tyler said absently.

"We hate being told what to do by our parents, so we rebel and do all kinds of stupid stuff we later regret. Then we grow up a little, go off to college so we can party and get all that out of our systems, but then we can't wait to get out, get our degree and find a great paying job, which, by the way, we're sure will just fall into our laps. Then, we get the job, it's not what we hoped, so we get married to the person we're sure will never disappoint or betray us. When they do disappoint us, we figure there's something else we're missing. A big house, maybe? So we buy that. What comes next? Oh, yeah, kids. OK, so now what? And it never, never ends."

Tyler was quiet for a minute. Out of nowhere, a verse that he was pretty sure was from the Bible shifted into his mind. "'The eyes of man are never satisfied.' Isn't that in the Bible somewhere?"

"Yep. Ecclesiastes," Josh confirmed.

Wow. Where had that come from? It wasn't as if he'd tried to remember an applicable saying. It was as though God had plopped it into his mind.

Only the sound of wet tires and wiper blades filled the car. "And then your wife tells you she's disappointed with her life and the kids, and she wants to pack up everything and move across the country to California so she can fulfill her fantasy. Then you find out you're not enough for her either."

"I thought you wanted to go, too," Josh said.

Tyler rested his head against the window pane. "I guess I did. I wanted a change, you know? But now, it just doesn't seem important anymore."

"I'm so sorry, bro. Have you talked to Pastor Simmons about this at all?"

"No. I haven't been to church in ages. I think I've moved away from God. And let's be honest, Lana was never a believer. My parents warned me before we ever got married that this was the way it would be. I went from a mentally ill wife with no faith, to one who faked her belief to get me to marry her. Then all she wanted was kids. So we had the kids. I thought that might change her—that she might have more interest in church after that. Instead, the kids just made her want a different life. Something more glamorous. Her parents were rich, and they traveled all over...our life just isn't enough for her."

"I urge you to call Pastor Simmons. You need someone to talk to, man. And Brandon probably needs to get some counseling, too. Once you get him home, you need to sit him down, have a talk with him. Don't use this as an opportunity to alienate and punish him. Use this as an opportunity to connect and come clean to him. Tell him you understand."

Tyler's head swiveled as he looked in Josh's direction, a slight smile tugging at the corner of his mouth. "What do I need pastoral counseling for? You seem to have all the answers right here and now."

Josh chuckled. "No. I assure you. I don't."

The exit leading to Winchester was just ahead of them. Josh turned onto the exit ramp, and the snow pelted the windshield harder. As they pulled into the parking lot of the Winchester Police Station, Tyler's heart was in his throat. What if it wasn't Brandon? Then he'd have to keep searching, worrying, wondering…

Tyler and Josh climbed out of the car. As they walked across the icy parking lot, their feet made crunching noises. Tyler held his breath as he pulled open the glass door and stepped inside the police station.

Then he exhaled.

Brandon sat on a bench near the front door. An officer in charge sat nearby.

Tyler's heart soared at the sight of him, covered in bruises, cuts, and lacerations, his expression as sullen as ever. He didn't look up as Tyler and Josh entered.

Abbie Jackson was there, talking to the officer on duty. She waved as they came in.

Tyler approached his son cautiously. His hand shook as he placed it on Brandon's head. "Come on, son. I'm here to take you home."

Brandon's head didn't raise, and he didn't move.

"They're getting him another hot cocoa," Abbie called over.

A female officer brought a steaming cup to Brandon. Brandon reached for it with hands riddled with black spots.

Frostbite? They needed to get him to a hospital right away. Tyler walked up to the front desk where an officer on duty sat. "Did he say anything about what happened to him?"

"Nope. Only that he was on that lady's porch to get out of the weather. But I think he needs some medical attention. He's got some cuts and bruises, and I'd be surprised if he didn't have some other injuries, too."

Abbie moved to stand beside Tyler. "Take him straight to the Winchester Medical Center. We'll worry about all the details next week." Her dark eyes were soft, compassionate. She patted his arm. "It's going to take some time. And you'll need to keep a close eye on him. He's at risk for running again."

Brandon's brows were furrowed, his mouth pushed out in an angry expression reminiscent of when he was a little boy. Fear was there as well. What was going on in that boy's head? Would Brandon ever let him in?

The doctor in the emergency room spoke of Brandon's numerous superficial scratches and bruises, at least two lacerations that required stitches, and frostbite to Brandon's hands and feet.

"Several of the toes are bad," the doctor told them. "But I think all of them are salvageable. Everything else should heal pretty quickly."

But Tyler knew the majority of Brandon's injuries were internal—those of the heart, soul, and mind. Those would take the longest to heal.

~*~

Sunday, December 18

It was a relatively quiet homecoming other than Christina, who descended on the house early the next morning. They all sat in the living room, Tyler and Lana on one sofa, Christina and Brandon on the other. Katherine stood in the doorway looking on. Brandon remained taciturn throughout the hugging, the questions, the insistence that he immediately go and see one of the many doctors at Christina's disposal.

"Christina, let's just get through the weekend before we worry about that," Tyler said calmly. He was already making his own plans to take Brandon to see someone at the church.

"What were you doing? Why did you run away like that?" Her voice was hoarse as though she'd spent the night screaming or crying or both.

Brandon shrugged.

"And how did you get to Winchester?" She grabbed his cheeks with the vise-like fingers of her right hand and turned his head to examine his bruises.

"I got a ride with a truck driver."

"What?" Christina shrieked.

It was the first Tyler had heard of it as well.

"What if he'd killed you? Or—or something worse?" Her eyes bulged.

"Christina, I think all of these questions can wait for now."

She ignored Tyler and spoke directly to Brandon. "Well, it'll be better when you're back at home in your own bed."

Tyler tensed. He didn't want Brandon in the middle of a fight, but he definitely wanted him staying put. "I think it best, if Brandon stays where he is at the moment. Let him adjust to one house before he flies off to another one."

A muscle in Christina's jaw clenched as she glared at Tyler. She rose. Tyler stood to meet her advance. She moved her face close to his, spitting her sharply whispered, vitriolic words in his face. "Haven't you done enough? You're the cause of all of this. He needs to be with his mother."

"He needs to be here. Leave him be," Tyler said.

Katherine stood nearby, watching with a ghost-like silence. Since Brandon had come home, she'd stared at him as though she didn't know who he was—not once coming near him.

Christina whirled back to her son. Her eyes flashed with anger as her voice trilled with false exuberance. "Brandon, honey? Would you rather come home or stay here with your father?"

Brandon looked up at her, the expression in his eyes making him look too old. "I'm fine here."

Tyler's heart soared with relief. In the morning, he would call the church, schedule a counseling session. Get Brandon on the path to recovery—and maybe himself as well.

Christina turned toward Tyler again, her hands on her hips, jaw set, head nodding with bitter derision.

Tyler bit his tongue, resisting the temptation of telling her to get back on her broomstick and fly away. She was in pain, too.

Christina's face hardened as she turned to Katherine. "Are you coming, Katherine? Or are you staying here, too?"

Katherine shrugged. "I guess I'll stay."

Tyler almost felt sorry for his ex-wife. "I'll call you tomorrow." He quickly moved toward the front door and held it open for her.

Her head nodding as though to say, *I should have*

expected as much, and her mouth pressed into a thin line, Christina exited the house, climbed back into her car, and peeled out of the cul-de-sac, nearly colliding with the local news van as it rounded the corner.

~*~

Monday, December 19

Tyler returned to work, grateful for some normalcy. If they lost this contract, maybe he could apply for another position within the company. Sitting at his desk, he unpacked his things—his notepad, his lunch, a clean coffee cup.

"Hey." The voice was like an unexpected touch that startled him. He glanced up at Tara, standing at the edge of the cubicle as she usually did, kicking the toe of her red, high-heeled pump into the edge of the dividing wall. She looked perfect as always—her shoulder-length, strawberry-blonde hair flipped up at the ends, her bangs resting in a perfectly straight curtain, barely touching the top of the bridge of her nose.

"Hi, Tara," he said a little brusquely, more irritated with himself that he felt a tingle and surge of adrenaline at her appearance than he was at her openly flirty mannerisms.

Her manicured fingernails, the same red as her dress and shoes, tapped the side of the cubicle, and she cocked her head to the side as she smiled at him. "Missed you last week. I've been thinking a lot about you. You know…wondering how your son is doing. I heard you found him in Winchester?"

What was it about twenty-somethings these days that they seemed to have no filter? They didn't know how to ask a sensitive question. They just blurted it out as if they were inquiring whether a lost fact sheet had been found or if a deliverable had reached the government point-of-contact in the correct format.

"That's right," he said.

"Is he OK?" Her tone melted into a whispery puddle of sympathy and concern. "How long was he missing?"

"About a week."

"Do you know—I mean, did he run away or was he kidnapped or…"

There were far too many intricacies, and Tyler didn't expect a twenty-five-year-old who'd never had a bad day in her life to understand. He was being a bit harsh, but looking into her gorgeous green eyes right then simply reminded him of his weakness. It wouldn't take much to push him over the edge, and he was trying really hard. "We think he ran away, but it's just…there are a lot of outside details to work through."

"Sounds complicated," she observed, her eyes resting on his with a devastating amount of responsiveness.

Why couldn't his wife look at him like that? "It is."

Slowly, Tara ceased her pole dance with the anchor of the wall and stood with both high-heeled feet on the ground. "You'll let me know if there's anything I can do, right?"

Tyler forced a smile. "Right. Sure. Thanks."

"Well, there's been a lot going on here." Her eyes widened as she emphasized the *lot*.

"I'm sure there has."

Tara looked over her right shoulder, and tilting her chin upward, she shot off in that direction, as though she'd seen someone with whom she needed to speak. Her form was almost immediately replaced by John Cabrisi's.

"When you get settled, stop by my office for a sec, would you?"

"Sure."

John made a thumbs-up sign before heading off in the same direction as Tara.

Weeks had passed since he'd heard anything regarding the contract renewal. This was probably the moment when John would issue him a pink slip and the last date of his employment. Hopefully, there would be a respectable severance package of some sort. Tyler had been with the company for quite a few years—plus, he had employee stockholder options. That should count for something. As he walked toward John's office, he passed Raj's cubicle.

"Anyone ever tell you that you look like Buddy Holly?"

"Yes, but I don't have his money, and I don't want to die like him."

Tyler offered Raj a fist bump.

Raj returned it.

"How are you my friend? How is your son?"

"He's doing OK. He's at home. Lana's keeping an eye on him. And I'm doing OK, I think. I'm actually glad to be back at work. Keeps my mind off of things."

"I get that. I've been praying for you and your family."

"Thanks. Hey, John wants to see me in his office. You think the axe is going to fall today?"

Raj took a deep breath, his eyes searching the

rafters overhead as he considered the possibility. "I really don't know. I haven't heard anything about anything. No word of whether CEF got the funding or didn't. It's been silent."

"Well, who knows? Maybe no news is good news."

"Let's hope. I know you're off to greener pastures, but I really need to keep my job. Especially with the newest chicken coming along in a few months. Dave's wife is having another baby too."

"Wow," Tyler observed. "Lots of new births on the horizon."

"You're next!"

"Ha," Tyler laughed at the irony. "I think Lana would rather go work in the coal mines than have another kid. She's already fast-forwarding thirteen years to when Micah and Celia are out of the house, and she's on a beach in Santa Monica reading her book under an umbrella with a pina colada."

Tyler tried to picture himself as a man of leisure— supine on those beaches, drinking something smooth and reading a political thriller novel. But every time he tried to envision it, the image was foggy, as if he had something under his contact and the view wouldn't come into focus. He couldn't smell the ocean air, the suntan oil, or the coconut.

"Hey, Tyler! It's good to see you. Glad you're back. Come on in. Shut the door behind you if you would."

Tyler couldn't help but dread the lowering of the axe.

"So," John began, smacking his hands on the top of the desk, "how's Brandon doing? Saw you on the news the other night."

"Yeah. He's doing OK. He's home. That's what matters."

"I'm sorry you're going through all this." A moment of silence passed.

Tyler waited with his hands underneath his twitching legs for the fateful words.

"I really am sorry...and I'm glad he's home," John assured. "But in a complete and total switch of subjects, I have some good news for you. At least, I hope you'll think it's good news."

Maybe the contract had been extended?

"You know Roger Pearson?"

"I know of him, yes." Pearson was a substantial step above Tyler's rung and had been with the company for over twenty-years.

"He's retiring."

"Oh."

"And Colonel Snowden nominated you to replace him."

"What?" Tyler exclaimed. "Was our task not renewed?"

"Yes, it was renewed. But, obviously, this is a much better opportunity for you. There's a lot more money involved. It would be a promotion."

A tire iron striking him on the head couldn't have surprised him more. "Yes, I know it is. It's just...wow."

John's bushy eyebrows elevated at Tyler's reaction. "I know you've got a lot coming at you right now."

"Yeah." Tyler's head was spinning. Did he accept it outright? He could always change his mind.

"This is a major opportunity, obviously. You're not thinking of turning it down or anything, are you?" John asked with a short laugh.

Tyler rubbed his hand over his mouth. "Well, it's just that Lana and I were toying with the idea of moving to California, but with everything going on..."

"What? When?"

"Well, it depends on a lot of things."

"Did you get a job out there?"

"No, not—no. Lana has a job offer out there."

"Oh." John's tone changed suddenly, and Tyler detected a note of disappointment. "Well, you have to do what you have to do."

"It depends on what happens with Brandon, of course. I can't really go right now."

This must have sounded convoluted and personal to John, who probably wanted to stick to business and not get involved in the sticky, crusty elements of domestic issues and problematic children. Tyler didn't dare tell him that his son might also be facing felony charges for pornography distribution.

"Just so you know, I don't think they want to wait too long." A note of warning tinged John's voice. "But maybe you can talk this over with Lana and see what she says. We're also talking a significant raise. I don't know what's in California, but she might find that life can be just as good, if not better, on this coast."

~*~

Tyler's temples pounded and his stomach rolled with acid indigestion at dinner that night. Pressure constricted his head and chest as Lana talked about what this or that realtor said and how they should update the kitchen before listing it. Now that Brandon was home, Lana just assumed the move to California was back on.

"The one realtor I talked with thinks folks might not want the stainless steel anymore. They're looking at built-ins and butcher-block countertops and clean lines, instead of the flashy coldness of granite and steel."

Tyler stared at her. "We spent a lot of money for those granite countertops and stainless steel appliances. That's what you wanted—had to have—couldn't live without."

"Trends change."

"Well, I'm not spending another cent on this house for the latest design trend," he said, gulping his water. He could feel the anger rising, constricting his ribcage with painful resentment. "Since you came back from California, all you talk about is how unhappy you are with every aspect of our life. You don't like our house, you don't like my job, and you don't like being a stay-at-home wife. Do you even like our kids? 'Cause I'm beginning to wonder."

"Where is all of this coming from? Why are you attacking me?"

"Because I just don't know how to make you happy anymore. You have this void inside of you, Lana, and trying to fill it is like trying to fill up an empty well with an eyedropper. I just don't know if I can give you what you want."

Her gaze fell as she refolded her napkin. "Everything will be fine once we get to California—"

"Will it?"

"Of course it will."

"Because I don't think it will. I think there'll just be something else you need or want once we get there." He shoveled a morsel of meatloaf into his mouth and chewed so hard he bit his tongue, which only fueled his anger. "You idolize everything you don't have."

"What?" she spat, her eyes squinting into livid slits. "You really think that?"

"Yes I do."

Lana plonked her elbow onto the table, dropping her forehead into her raised right hand.

"I think you worship status and money and prestige."

"Well, who doesn't?"

"I'd like to think I don't." He could feel the heat from her glare all the way across the table.

"You know what, Tyler? I think you should take a good, hard look at yourself. You're not that perfect either. I've seen the history on your computer. I know about the sites you surf at night once I've gone to bed. I've seen the pictures of the naked girls you gawk at…just like your son does."

Tyler stopped chewing.

"What? Are you going to deny that you look at porn?"

Tyler had hoped Lana hadn't figured it out. But now, there was little reason to deny it. "No. I've looked at porn."

"So, obviously, I'm not enough for you. Just like Christina wasn't enough for you…or maybe she was too much for you, I don't know." Her words were biting, her tone purposed to wound him.

"I know I'm not perfect," he said, deflated.

She snorted. Sitting back in her chair, she crossed her arms.

Tyler put down his fork and moved to sit in the chair closest to her, where he tried, unsuccessfully, to make eye contact. "Look, honey. I think maybe we need to slow down here. There's a lot going on right now. For one, we've got this whole debacle with Brandon, and until that's resolved, I'm just not myself. I'm worn out from thinking about it every minute of every day. And then we have Micah and Celia to think about. I don't know how you'd feel about this, but I really think we should consider getting some counseling. Maybe from Pastor Simmons or someone else on staff at the church."

"Ha!" Her mouth turned into a tight, furious frown. "You'd love that, wouldn't you? You'd love telling them what a beast I am and what a saint you are."

"I've just admitted to you that I need some help as well."

"What you're saying is that you don't want to move to California."

"Well, there's something else I haven't told you," he tried to speak with a bright, upbeat tone. "I just found out this week, but I'm being offered a promotion to Program Manager. It would mean a salary increase and more responsibility, and…we could live more like you want. This could mean a lot for our future. Whereas, if we pack up and move, who knows what kind of job I could get out there."

She slammed her hands on the table as tears welled in her eyes. "Why have we been talking and planning for the past few weeks? Why did you even get my hopes up? Why did you tell me to go out to California and chase my dream and see what happens?" Her words trailed off as she burst into loud, frantic sobs, flailing her arms as he pulled her into a forced embrace.

"Lana, honey. Calm down. *Shh*. Listen to me."

But she was inconsolable. Her cries were loud

keens of sorrow and loss that clawed at his heart. He'd crushed her dream, and there was no use talking anymore. Tonight, he would pray things between them could somehow heal. Even so, fear struck at his heart, radiating the message through his entire body that things between them would never be the same again.

18

Kaki
Tuesday, December 20

Kaki stared out the window. She was in her Algebra 2 class, and her skin was crawling. Mrs. Moss was up at the Smartboard, pointing out how to calculate some complicated problem. She was so far behind in the class that she no longer knew what they were doing. And her skin was *crawling*. She was out of the little blue pills. This must be withdrawal. Chewing at her nails, she checked her phone again. No text messages from Damien. He'd been quiet since the weekend. Since after Brandon came home. She'd received one text from him on Sunday evening.

Remember to keep ur mouth shut.

But she hadn't been able to remember why she was supposed to keep her mouth shut. What was she not supposed to tell? A wave of nausea swept over her, and a sheen of sweat broke out over her skin. She couldn't remember the last time she'd gone this long without the little blue pill. She needed Damien to get her some more, but that meant she'd have to work for it.

She focused her eyes on the woods next to the school. In the midst of the trees, color and movement caught her attention. Three kids were filing into the woods. This wasn't unusual when the weather was decent. Kids often sneaked into the woods. It was a spot they used for cutting class, smoking dope, and making out. But it was unusual to see kids hanging out there during the dead of winter. Especially when it was only twenty degrees outside.

A few moments later, the three kids streaked out of the woods and toward the school—two boys and a girl—all pushing each other to move faster and ducking their heads to avoid tree limbs. A few minutes after that, another group of four went into the woods. What was going on?

The scene sparked a flash of memory in her brain. She had been in those woods recently. She couldn't remember the details, but she had been there. An image of walking over frozen ground, tripping and falling over branches...in the pitch dark...with someone...with...Damien. Helping to carry something—something heavy. Getting sick...

She bolted out of her seat suddenly, shoving the plastic chair backward into the desk behind hers as vomit rose in her throat. Clutching her cell phone and clamping her hand over her mouth, she slammed her way out of the classroom, barely making it to one of the over-sized trashcans in the hall before spewing yellow bile and the granola bar she'd eaten for breakfast.

She fell to her knees, holding on to the side of the bin. Another image. She had been holding a shovel when she was in the woods.

"Dig!" Damien's voice reverberated through her head.

What had she been digging? Something deep—too deep. The ground had been too cold, too frozen. "I can't." She remembered that she was on her knees then too...sobbing. She was sobbing now.

"Katherine?" An arm around her shoulders. Someone was crouching beside her. "Katherine, come on. Let's get you to the clinic."

Kaki turned her head to look into Molly Wolf's familiar face.

She helped Katherine to her feet and down the hall. The whole way she talked to her, but her voice sounded far away. "When did you start feeling sick? The flu's been going around...lie down in the clinic...they can call your mom...go home..."

More flashes of memory. Cold, cold ground. Leaves, twigs. Damien's hands on her. Someone else's hands on her.

She had to get out of here. She had to get something—take something—to stop this pain and the swirling thoughts in her head.

She slumped onto the pleather bench in the clinic while Molly talked to the nurse. An instrument was rubbed across her forehead, taking her temperature. She heard words exchanged between Molly and the nurse as though she were listening under water.

"...high fever."

"Call her mom..."

Then Molly was standing in front of her. "Katherine, I have to get back to my class. The nurse is going to take care of you and call your mom, OK?"

Kaki nodded. But her mom couldn't help her. No one could help her but Damien. He had the little blue pills. She fumbled her cell phone in her hand, managing to type in a text with fingers that shook violently.

I need pills. Blue ones. Please come.

"OK," the nurse said after a few minutes. "I

haven't reached your mom yet. But you can lie down in one of the back rooms and wait. I'll send someone to get your things from the classroom."

But if her mom picked her up, she wouldn't be able to get the pills from Damien. Her mom would take her to the doctor and then they would all know…

While the nurse called for a student runner to go and gather Kaki's things, Kaki slipped out of the clinic and down the hall, exiting the building through one of the back doors of the school. Collapsing against the brick wall of an alcove behind the school, she looked down at her phone. No message from Damien. She sent another text.

Pls help me.

She sank down the length of the wall, pulling her knees to her chest and shivering violently against the cold. Three kids walked past her. One of them did a double-take when he saw her form. He looked vaguely familiar, but she couldn't remember his name.

"Hey."

Another tidal wave of nausea lifted her to her hands and knees. She retched on the ground.

"You OK?" one of the other kids asked.

But the familiar-looking kid pulled him along. "Come on. Let's go." And they were gone.

*…there's a body in the woods…Saturday, December the tenth…*the date echoed in her mind as though it had been spoken aloud. *December the tenth…*

Now she remembered.

~*~

Gio George was shouting with a face full of panic. "Look, I didn't do this. You get her out of here! My father'll kill me if he finds out about this. You've got to get her out of here!"

A lot of people were gathered around something on the floor, looking down, snapping photos and video footage with their phones.

Kaki moved forward into the crowd.

Sydney's long, straight, black ponytail snaked down her back. She was face down on the floor, her black T-shirt was on backward. The motorcycle logo was visible on her back when it should have been on her front.

"She just went down," the spaced-out girl next to her said. "Like, she was standing one minute, and then all of a sudden she just fell like a tree. I mean, she's dead."

"What?" Kaki shrieked, and then immediately covered her mouth. It was best not to call attention to herself. Not to cause a scene or any trouble.

They all stood around Sydney, looking down at her as if she were a dead dog in the road. No one attempted CPR or called 9-1-1. No one turned her over. No one even touched her.

Kaki's tongue no longer worked. Her mind ran in slow motion. It was hard to feel anything. Even fear. She stared at Sydney's lifeless body. A rivulet of blood streamed out from her head.

In the background, Gio's voice repeated, "You gotta get her out of here. She's bleeding all over the floor! My dad'll kill me. My dad's on the town council, man. No one can find out about this."

The scene rolled as though it happened in a movie. Damien reached down and grabbed the back of Sydney's T-shirt. As he pulled her from the ground, her arms fell in front of her, limp and swinging. Her head hung and her black ponytail dropped forward and swung in pendulum fashion.

Kaki had never seen anything so horrible. A gasp escaped her throat, but she really wanted to scream. She wanted to yell at the top of her lungs, "Someone call 9-1-1!" But she didn't. No one did.

Someone was taking pictures with a phone.

"Hey! Put that away!" Damien bellowed, pointing his finger at the guy. A struggle ensued as several others pounced in an attempt to get the phone from him.

"No one can ever know about this!" Gio called out over and over again.

Hubby and Damien carried Sydney's body out of the room as they all stood around, and Gio screamed a bunch of curse words at them.

"What happened?" Kaki heard herself ask.

Mattie moved to stand next to her. Her voice was low, her words slurred. "I think she'd had a lot of drugs. And she was with several of the guys. I heard somebody say she came out of that room over there." She pointed to an open door in the basement. "And then she just did a face-plant on the ground. Boom. Dead."

The drugs and shock mixed together and confused Kaki's mind. She stood like a statue.

Damien was back, his eyes wide and wild. Grabbing her arm, he dragged her across the room, his fingers biting into her skin as he growled, "You better never tell anyone about this."

Kaki's next conscious memory involved sitting in the backseat of a truck while Hubby drove and Damien talked about where to drop Sydney's body.

"The high school," Damien suggested. "They'll

just figure somebody did her in the woods and killed her there."

Kaki only wanted to live long enough to see her parents again. To go home. Her lips moved almost involuntarily. She prayed. *Please God...don't let them kill me, too.*

Hubby pulled the vehicle into the school parking lot without any headlights and drove all the way around to the back of the building. The lot had recently been cleared of snow, and Damien directed Hubby away from areas of slush that might leave tire tracks.

"I'm just gonna pull up on the field right by the woods," Hubby said.

"Are you crazy, man? They'll see your tire treads in the mud or something. No, you never pull through ice or snow or anything that leaves tire treads. Are you stupid or something?"

Through drug fuzz in her mind, Kaki registered Damien's words. He'd probably done this before. He'd probably killed women or disposed of their bodies. For all she knew, Damien may have killed Sydney.

"Come on," Damien said to her. "You're gonna help." She followed them, her hands numb with cold. Hubby and Damien carried Sydney's limp, uncovered body into the woods. In a dream-like state, Kaki glanced over at the school—only the tip of the roof was visible from her viewpoint. Monday morning, she'd sit in Algebra and stare out a window to where they'd buried Sydney. And she'd never, ever be able to tell anyone.

Once they'd reached a point in the middle of some pine trees, Hubby and Damien flopped Sydney's body onto the ground with a thud. Damien stood over her and looked down. "Well, my best girl's dead," he said with an almost nostalgic lilt to his voice. "Saturday, December the tenth. December the tenth and I lost my best girl."

"Come on." Hubby slapped Damien in the arm. "Let's go. It's freezing out here."

Damien turned to Kaki. "Dig." He handed her a shovel.

The ground was frozen. It was like trying to dig through rock. The handle kept slipping against her bare hands, giving her painful splinters. "Harder!" Damien yelled. "Dig harder! Dig like you're digging your own grave."

She started to cry. It was useless. She only chipped small pieces of dirt from the ground. A sharp pain radiated up the back of her right leg and she realized Damien had kicked her behind the knee, knocking her to her knees.

He grabbed the shovel and started to hack at the ground angrily. "I outta just bury you with her. If you tell anyone about this, you and your whole family are dead."

~*~

Kaki's phone buzzed with a text, startling her out of the memory.

I'm out front of the school. Where r u?

Damien.

Relief flooded her even as she was wracked with another fit of retching. Scrambling to her feet, she made her way around the side of the school, barely able to remain upright as she spotted his car. He could have driven to meet her, but he didn't. He made her walk, stagger all the way to the door of the car.

Kaki fell into the passenger seat, and he sped away before she even had the chance to close the door. "Where are they?" she gasped. "Give 'em to me."

Damien's eyes were hidden behind sunglasses. "Yeah, we gotta make a stop first."

"Please, Damien," she begged. Her insides were blowing apart. "Please, I can't stand it. I can't stand it." She slumped over her legs, sobs wrenching her body.

"See what happens when you mess up?" he growled.

"I didn't mess up." She spoke to the floor. If she hadn't wanted to die from the pain, she would have been terrified that she had done something wrong. "What did I do?"

Damien paused before he answered. "You told someone."

"No, I didn't. I didn't tell anyone." Her heart pounded. She had just now remembered what happened, so how could she have told anyone?

He was just finding a reason to toy with her head.

"Now you gotta make it up to me. You got a lot of work to do today, baby. A lot of people to see."

Kaki sat up. She didn't care anymore. Gritting her teeth and jutting out her jaw, she responded—barely recognizing her own voice. "I'll do anything you say. Just give me the pills."

19

Tyler
Saturday, December 31

New Year's Eve, Josh and Molly came to Tyler and Lana's for a pre-celebration, which was to be followed by dinner out at a local restaurant—some pre-fixe affair that Lana had organized.

Lana was in rare form. She'd had a good bit to drink tonight—Tyler wasn't sure exactly how much.

"Good heavens, it was like a funeral parlor when I came home from the grocery," Lana told Molly and Josh as they all sat in the living room, slipping chunks of cheese and ham into their mouths. "You should have seen it. All the shades were pulled and the lights were off. I was half expecting one of the kids to jump out of the shadows covered in a sheet, but no. Katherine had everyone down in the basement, hiding out like they were waiting for the apocalypse."

The living room was lit with candlelight, and light jazz music filled the room with a festive, relaxed mood.

Tyler spotted Katherine hovering by the door, her face drawn and pale as she peered out of the windows on either side of it. What was wrong with her?

"Katherine!" Lana called out to her. "What are you looking for? Who's out there?"

Katherine moved from the window. "No one."

"Why do you keep looking outside?" Tyler asked. "What's going on?"

"Nothing," her voice echoed from the hallway.

Tyler looked out. The street was lit with Christmas lights and decorations. "I don't see anything. No one out there."

Lana whispered to Molly and Josh. "I don't know what's up with her. It's like living with a ghost. She floats around the house silent as the grave, peering out of the windows all the time. Weird."

Tyler hated that Lana talked about his daughter as if she wasn't standing right there. But it was true. Katherine only spoke when the Wolfs had arrived, when she'd talked to Molly about their dog and the puppies that had just been born. Otherwise, she was a zombie.

"So, you've got a bunch of puppies in your house now, right?" Tyler prompted the change of subject as he returned to the living room.

Molly beamed. "Yes. We have five of them. Katherine, you'll have to come see them."

Katherine smiled. "Yeah, I'd love that."

"We are now experts at puppy delivery," said Josh. "Space heater blaring to keep the room a toasty eighty-three degrees. We sat by her side all night until this bloody, membranous sac came out."

"Wow. That must have been amazing to watch," Lana said.

"It was," Molly affirmed. "Trixie birthed each puppy one by one, and then she licked the little body until the sac was removed, chewed the umbilical cord to sever it. She knew instinctively what to do."

"They looked like little chipmunks," Josh added. "We could have watched them for hours."

Molly turned to Katherine. "You'll have to come over and pick one out. Or two if you want."

"Well, hold on." Lana gurgled her drink. "Katherine, you'll have to check with your mom about that. Especially if we're moving."

Tyler's neck muscles tensed.

"So, is California still on the table?" Molly asked. She placed a block of cheese on the end of her tongue.

Tyler stood and moved toward the wet bar. "Who needs a refill?"

Josh held up his hand. "I'm good, thanks. I'll get something else at the restaurant."

"Everyone has something to drink, Tyler. Come sit down," Lana instructed.

Tyler ignored her and wiped a cloth over the countertop.

Lana turned back to Molly and Josh. "Well, I'm ready to go tomorrow. I've got the job, contacted the realtor."

Tyler carried a bowl of nuts back to the table. "It's hard right now to think about going to California with Brandon and everything going on with him." His eyes grazed Lana's nervously. "I mean, we just started counseling at the church, and the kid really needs it. He's really, really angry. And as you know, Josh, we may still have a court case pending."

"You haven't received a summons or anything yet?" Josh asked.

"No, nothing yet."

"So...you've definitely decided not to go?" Lana asked accusingly.

"Maybe," Tyler said. "But there's also a little more to it," he added, turning his gaze back to Molly and Josh. "I've been offered a really good position at work.

One that could be hard to turn down."

"Oh?" Josh asked.

"Yeah, it would be a lot more money and a more prestigious position. It's an offer that...you know, suggests they really believe in me and my abilities as a manager. It could change our lives." Part of him was speaking to Josh and Molly, the other part was directing his argument at Lana.

"How?" she asked. "How is it going to change our lives? Is it going to change the weather? Is it going to change the traffic and the rat-race that we live through every day—that you live through every day? No. It's not, Tyler. It massages your ego, that's all."

"Lana." Tyler cringed. "I think this is something you and I need to talk about one on one—not in front of our friends." Embarrassment crept over him.

Molly and Josh squirmed with discomfort.

"It's OK," Josh said, shaking his head and smiling awkwardly. "Really, it's fine. These are all big decisions you're making."

"Yes," Molly said, rising from her perch upon the couch and beginning to collect glasses. "Why don't we head over to the restaurant? Maybe we can get seated early."

Lana's eyes continued to shoot daggers at Tyler from across the room.

~*~

It was a relief when dinner was finally over.

It was evident Lana wasn't enjoying any part of it. She'd ordered another drink once they arrived at the restaurant and barely ate any of the expensive four-course dinner.

Tyler talked, laughed, ordered dessert and lingered over coffee.

Lana remained silent, glaring at them.

On the way home, Tyler tried to convince her how good their life would be with his new job. And he assured her he was going to change. "I'm not viewing porn anymore, Lana. I've come to realize how disrespectful to you that is. I'm starting counseling, too."

"Mm-hm," Lana murmured, but otherwise, she didn't respond.

Whatever. Maybe she was tired or drunk or both. Anyway, he'd done his part. He'd committed to being a better husband. It might take a little time to prove himself, but he meant it. From here on out, things would change. They would be like a regular, suburban family.

Maybe he'd even agree to let Katherine have one of those dogs she wanted so much.

20

Kaki
Sunday, January 1

Lana and her dad came home just after midnight. But then she'd heard Lana milling around downstairs for ages. She really needed to meet Damien, she had already texted him once that she wouldn't be able to get out of the house until around 2:00 AM, but she was beginning to worry about that time frame, too. Lana never stayed up this late.

When she felt pretty sure that everyone was asleep, Kaki moved down the stairs, her fingers trailing the banister for support. She still had a few minutes to kill before Damien would get there, so she went into the kitchen and felt around for Lana's stash of vodka. She swilled deeply from the bottle, and then carried it to the island where she poured more into a glass. She sat on one of the stools and sipped at it.

Her eye caught a slip of paper peeking out from under a coffee mug. Absently, she pulled it out.

Dear Tyler,

I'm sorry, but I can't possibly stay here. You are a good dad to the kids, and I know they will be much better off with you. I'll forward you the address of where I'm living once I get settled in case you change your mind.

Love,
Lana

Kaki swallowed the vodka she held in her mouth, and re-read the letter. She never had any idea that Lana would consider going to California without her father.

Should she wake her dad and tell him? If she did that, Damien would show up and she wouldn't be out there. He'd be furious. No, if Lana was really that unhappy and wanted to leave, who was she to mess with that?

Kaki slipped the paper back, downed the rest of the vodka, and slid off the stool. As she made her way to the front door, the high heels she wore caused her ankle to collapse. "Ow!" She whispered, fighting the urge to cry out.

She limped the rest of the way and slipped out.

Lana was sitting on the front stoop. Her head whipped around, and her eyes met with Kaki's.

With a sense of dread and a flash of fear that she'd been caught, Kaki froze. But then she saw the exact same emotion reflected in her stepmother's eyes.

Lana's mouth opened as though she might say something. Her suitcase sat next to her.

Kaki figured she was either deciding whether or not to go or waiting on a cab. Kaki simply turned to the door and placed her key in the lock.

Kaki and Lana stared at one another for a few more seconds.

Then Kaki passed Lana's seated form and wordlessly clomped down the cement steps in red heels that suddenly felt too high. She teetered into the street where Damien's car—pounding with rap music—pulled up and stopped. Looking at Lana one last time, Kaki entered the car and stared out the window at her stepmother's still seated form.

This wasn't her life anymore. Her father and Lana weren't her business anymore. As she'd looked into Lana's eyes for those few moments, she'd glimpsed regret, sadness, and fear. But there was also a silent understanding exchanged between them. There was common ground after all.

~*~

Kaki didn't return home until ten that morning. It was so late, in fact, that she figured her father might already be up. If he was, he would have seen the note Lana had left. Kaki couldn't walk through the front door now. He would know she had been out all night. It was better to wait until around noon. Then she could make up some story about having gone out early— over to Molly and Josh's to see the puppies. Yes, that was it!

Kaki assessed her clothing. Leggings and a long sweater. Not too bad today. Only the high heels looked out of place. Maybe her makeup wasn't too smeared. Hopefully Molly would offer her some coffee. She knocked on the door. A dog bark sounded from within. A few seconds later, she heard Molly approaching the door.

"Hi!" Molly held onto Trixie's sparkly pink collar to keep her from rushing out of the door and flinging herself at Kaki's knees.

"Hi," Kaki squatted down, reaching over the threshold to pet Trixie.

The dog squirmed against Molly's handhold on her collar.

"Do you want to come in and see the puppies?"

"Sure."

Once in the entry hall, Kaki squatted once again, focusing her affection on Trixie, stroking her head. The little dog soaked up the attention like a sponge.

"Come on in and sit down," Molly offered. "If I'd known you were coming, I would have baked some cinnamon rolls or something for New Year's Day. Your dad and Lana still asleep?"

"Yeah, I guess so." Kaki's voice shook. Who knew what would happen once her dad read that note?

"Do you want some tea or something?" She wished Molly had offered coffee, but tea was better than nothing.

"OK."

Molly's phone buzzed against the granite of the kitchen countertop. "Oh, it's from Josh. He's on his way home from church. He went alone today. I wasn't feeling all that well. Something I ate last night. Anyway, he says he's stopping off at the store on the way home. If you'd rather have something else to drink, I can ask him to pick up something. Apple juice? Soda?"

Kaki shook her head. "No. Tea is fine. I like tea."

Molly turned on the electric kettle and opened her pantry door where she began dismantling the wall formed with boxes of assorted teas. "Well, let's see. I've got herbal tea, black tea, chai tea...which kind do you like?"

"Chai tea's good," Kaki ran her fingers nervously over the granite countertop.

Molly pulled one from the packaging. "Do you

prefer a tall mug, a glass mug, a short mug? Mugs with pictures or plain?"

Kaki laughed. "It doesn't matter. Whatever."

Molly handed her a Christmas mug with a red ribbon emblazoned across the ceramic.

Kaki flattened her hand against the black, sparkling granite. "Lana wants to replace our countertops. She says butcher block countertops are in now."

"Well, I have seen designers on TV using that type of countertop recently. Trends change, I guess."

Trixie trotted through the kitchen and over to the area sectioned off with baby gates. Newspapers lined the floor, and a pink dog bed filled with blankets suddenly came to life as little furry bodies squirmed within. Trixie stood, then turned several times before flopping down amongst their mewling mouths.

"Oh, so this is where the puppies are." Kaki moved toward the pen.

The puppies were unseeing and helpless—their mouths open with hunger and want as they wriggled and scooted like miniature seals, attempting to attach to Trixie's food supply.

Kaki's heart squeezed. "Aw…they're so cute!"

Molly looked down at the puppies proudly. "They're hungry. Feeding time."

There were five of them—a white one, a black one, and three fawn-colored ones. Their funny little chirping noises and the way they crawled up to Trixie in their innocent need made her ache to hold one. But she was content to watch them. They were better off where they were. Safer.

"You going to take one when they're weaned?" Molly asked.

Something inside of Kaki wrenched. She wanted a dog—she really wanted a dog. But not if she endangered them. Damien killed dogs—he'd threatened to kill her whole family, for that matter. Tears sprang to her eyes as she looked down at the tiny puppies. They were safer with Molly and Josh. "Oh, I don't know. I'm not sure what my dad and Lana would say."

"So how's everything going over there now that Brandon's back home?" Molly asked.

Kaki shrugged. "It's OK, I guess." She longed to tell Molly what was really going on, but she'd stick to her original plan. Molly would know soon enough anyway.

"How's your dad coping?"

"Um, I guess he's OK. I don't know. I haven't really been staying there much lately."

Molly moved back to where the electric kettle started to steam and leaned against the countertop. "So how are you doing?" Molly was obviously fishing for information—most likely out of concern.

"I'm OK, I guess. I'm kind of having a hard time keeping up in my classes right now."

"Have you seen your guidance counselor about how you're feeling?"

Kaki cringed.

Molly really had reverted to teacher mode. If a student confessed to a family or an emotional problem, teachers automatically sent them to their guidance counselor.

"No, not really. I'm just handling stuff."

The electric kettle hissed and squealed, and within seconds the click of the button signaled the water was ready. Kaki joined her at the island and looked on as

Molly poured the boiling water over the tea bags.

"Do you want any milk or sugar in your tea?"

"Just sugar." Kaki took the mug along with the packets of sugar.

"So, are you still seeing the guy?"

"Yeah."

"Is that still going OK?"

"Yeah." Kaki would have to be careful what she said about Damien. As much as she wanted to tell someone, Molly Wolf was not the person. She was an adult, her husband was a cop, and she was friends with her dad.

"Does your dad like him?"

"He doesn't really know about him."

"I see."

"He's like…older and stuff. It's just better if they don't know about him." Kaki breathed in the spices of the tea as the steam curled around her face. That was probably enough said now.

Her gaze darted to a collection of photos affixed to the refrigerator with magnets. "Is that one from your wedding?" Kaki slid off the stool and moved in to have a closer look. In one of the photos, Molly and Josh were standing under an arbor decorated with pink and white flowers—Josh in his black tuxedo and Molly in her dress. They were clasping one another, their cheeks pushed together. "You look like a princess in that dress."

Molly laughed. "It was a great day."

Kaki stared at the photo again. "It looks so romantic. How long have you been married?"

"Almost seven years."

"Wow. That's a long time." She couldn't imagine being with Damien for seven years. She'd probably be dead by then.

"Yep. And we married late. I was thirty-two when we got married. By that time, I thought I'd never get married."

Kaki stared intently at the photo as though trying to memorize the scene, the feeling—a memory she'd never experienced. "I was six when Lana married my dad. It was at some really ritzy place. That's all I remember. And I ate ham and cheese crepes." Her heart panged as she remembered again that Lana was gone. She glanced up at the clock on the wall. Ten thirty. Surely her dad was up by now.

"Did your mom ever remarry?" Molly asked.

Kaki returned to the stool. "No. She wants to marry the guy she's with now, but I don't think he wants to."

Molly pulled her dark braid over her shoulder. "Has your mom met your boyfriend?"

Kaki stared down at her nails and used the edge of her thumb to pick at the cuticle on her middle finger. Painted blue, but the paint was coming off. "No. But she knows about him."

"What does she think about you seeing an older guy?"

"She said he's like, a 'bad boy,'" Her fingers curved in the air, symbolizing quotation marks to emphasize the label. "Her last boyfriend was a bad boy, too, and I guess she doesn't want me in that kind of relationship."

"You know, your mom could be right. There are some really good guys out there, and you don't have to settle for someone who doesn't treat you right. My mom took up with bad boys. And it didn't end well for her."

Kaki focused on her nails once again. That was Molly's mother, though—not her. She and Damien had a different relationship. "My boyfriend...he loves me, you know? And I love him. He pays for me to get my nails done and stuff. I don't know...he just buys me a lot of stuff all the time. He bought me this phone," she said, holding up her cell phone covered by a pink and gold glittery shell. "He gives me money sometimes, and he takes me out to eat at nice places." Although, he hadn't been doing that recently. And most people probably wouldn't see forcing your girlfriend to help bury her dead friend as a top boyfriend quality.

And Sydney's body was still there...in the woods. Right where they'd left her. Would she just stay out there? Had no one really started looking for her? Reported her missing or anything?

Silence overtook the room.

Kaki looked over at Trixie, now sleeping in her bed, her furry, spear-like tail tucked around the outside of her legs as her sides rose and fell rhythmically. All of the puppies were cuddled up next to her.

There was a sudden, sharp knock on the door followed by the doorbell ringing.

Kaki's heart jolted. She followed Molly to the door, and as it opened, she glimpsed her father's face—pale with anxiety, looking as though it had aged overnight. The words appeared to stick in his throat when he saw her.

"Katherine? What..."

"I came over to see the puppies," she said quickly.

"OK, fine. Look, something has happened...and I need...well, Lana's not here, too, is she?" His eyes were hopeful.

Molly shook her head. "No."

He sighed and his head drooped. "OK. Well, she's gone. I guess I had hoped she hadn't really done it…"

Molly held out her hands. "Deep breaths. OK. Now what's going on?" Stepping back from the doorway, she motioned for him to come inside, and while the trio stood in the foyer, he inhaled and exhaled, his eyes closed.

"Lana's gone. She left last night or early this morning sometime. I don't know. Left a note on the kitchen counter. She's gone to California."

"What? She just left? With the kids?"

"No." He swallowed. "She didn't take the kids. I don't know. I guess she just had her heart set on going and…" He bowed his head and his hand covered his face. His shoulders shook with silent sobs.

Kaki's heart sank. She'd never seen her dad in such a state.

"Oh, Tyler. I'm so, so sorry. But don't you think she'll come back? I mean, I think she'll realize what a bad decision this was, and—"

"No, I don't think so." He sniffed and ran his hand under his nose. "Anyway, Katherine, I could really use you back over at the house to watch Micah and Celia while I try to make some phone calls and see what's going on."

"OK."

She thanked Molly for the tea and followed her dad back to the house where Celia was screaming and Micah was stoically sitting beside her. Her dad immediately got on his cell phone and began leaving the same message with everyone he knew: "If you hear from her, please call me right away."

Kaki suddenly wished she could just crawl into

her bed.

But she still had two little blue pills stashed away for just such an occasion.

21

Tyler
Thursday, January 5

How had his entire family disintegrated right before his eyes? Tyler saw nothing but devastation. Lana was gone—no one had heard from her, and her cell phone went straight to voice mail. He had left numerous messages. How could she leave her children? But he had to keep going.

Micah and Celia were shuffled between his parents' home in the day and his at night, just as Brandon and Katherine were shuffled between his house and Christina's.

During Brandon's first few counseling sessions, Tyler had remained in the room. There hadn't been a lot of revelation during those meetings. Mainly they had discussed family issues, living arrangements, and family dynamics. Establishing the baseline was what Nick called it.

Nick Melioni, a relatively new member of their church's counseling staff, was a young guy in his early thirties. He was friendly and connected easily with the youth at the church. He often volunteered with their youth groups, and his easy-going, straight-shooting demeanor seemed to put Brandon at ease. Smiling, welcoming, reassuring, dressed in casual jeans, T-shirt, and tennis shoes, Nick opened them in a prayer and asked Brandon questions about his favorite football teams, video games, and music. Then he gently peeled back the shell to reveal the true reasons behind their need for help.

"Let's start out hearing from you, Brandon." Nick leaned forward, his hands locked between his open knees. "You wanna tell me a little about what's going on with you this week?"

Brandon was obviously reluctant to say anything at first. His responses were all "fine" and "OK" and "not much." But this week, they had Lana's absence to add to the mix.

"How are you dealing with that?" Nick asked Brandon.

Brandon shrugged. "OK, I guess."

"We're doing the best we can," Tyler said. "It was completely unexpected. A shock to us all."

Nick sat back, knitting his fingers together. "Hey, Dad? Would you mind stepping outside for a few minutes to let Brandon and I talk alone?"

Tyler was a little surprised. "Sure, sure." He moved outside, shutting the door behind him. But he lingered there, standing close enough to hear their muted voices. He stopped just short of pressing his ear against the closed door, fearful that a member of staff might see him.

Within minutes, Brandon was actually talking— offering information freely. *Well, how about that?* Tyler practically had to threaten his son with starvation and solitary confinement to get him to say anything. Now here he was, answering question after question with hardly any prompting—rolling out his whole life story...for a stranger.

"How long have you been using pornography,

Brandon?" Nick asked.

"Since I was like, eleven."

Brandon revealed the details of a child from a divorced home, shuffled back and forth, never knowing where he was going to be one night to another. Homework at one house, permission slips at another. "And Dad's got his own family. He's got two other kids, Micah and Celia. Katherine and I just don't really count anymore."

Tyler's breath caught in his throat.

"So…you feel you don't matter?"

"Not really. I mean, he never asks us any questions or anything. Only when he's yelling at us for grades or something like that. Otherwise, it's just kind of like we're not even there."

The words hit Tyler like a stone between the eyes. He'd been one of those dads. The kind who neglected their kids because they were too busy with work or the gym or…he cringed at the sudden image of himself, sitting in front of the computer staring at naked women. And then it came to him: he hadn't just neglected his kids, he'd neglected Lana too.

"Why don't we ask your dad to come back in? Could we ask him to join this conversation? Would that be all right with you?"

"I…guess," Brandon answered, his voice halting.

"Jesus," Tyler breathed, "make me worthy of my children. Cleanse my heart. Help me, Lord. Help me." His eyes were wet as Nick called him back into the room.

Brandon looked at him—his expression fractured by fear and dread. Tyler sat in the chair beside Brandon. He hesitated before he slung his arm across his son's shoulders and squeezed him into a side hug.

The triumvirate settled back into their seats, Nick behind his desk, father and son in the comfortable fabric chairs seated across from him.

"So, Brandon and I have talked a little bit, and I think we may have unearthed some things today. I wanted to bring you back in, Tyler, because I think your son may have some things he needs to say to you."

Brandon's head was bowed, and he stared intently at his hands.

"What is it, Bran?" Tyler patted Brandon on the shoulder.

"Just tell him what you told me," Nick prompted.

Brandon swallowed, and several seconds passed before he spoke. "I feel like...I guess I kind of feel like Katherine and I are just sort of like...not part of your life anymore or something."

Tyler tightened his stomach muscles. His eyes welled, and an overwhelming desire to cry made it difficult to talk. When the words finally came, they were thick with emotion. "Brandon, I love you and your sister so much. I know as a dad I've been a sham. And that's my fault. You and Katherine are my world. I love you guys, and I don't ever want you to think that I don't."

Brandon swallowed hard, and he seemed to be having difficulty looking into his father's face.

Tyler reached out to his son again, placing his hand on his shoulder. "I know I haven't done right by you and your sister. And I know we're not going to fix this in one day, Bran, but I am committed to being a father to you and Katherine. OK? Nothing is more important right now." Tyler glanced over at Nick, who gave him a nod of approval.

"Why did Lana leave, Dad?" Brandon asked.

Of course Lana's unexplained departure would hit the kids hard, too. The mere mention of it sent searing pain through Tyler's chest. He looked up at Nick, longing for answers.

Nick's lips pressed together as he inhaled slowly.

"Honestly, Brandon...I really don't know. At least, I don't understand all her reasons for going. But I think I may be partially to blame for why she left. I owe her an apology, just like I owe you, Katherine, Micah, and Celia an apology."

"Do you think she felt like you didn't care about her either?"

Each of these questions was like another arrow in his heart. *Oh, dear Lord. How can I bear my own vile, wicked self? What have I done to my family?* "I think maybe that's right, Brandon. I think maybe she felt neglected, too." He reached up and cleared the wetness from under his eyes.

After a moment, Nick spoke. "Here's the thing, guys. I'm heading up a group here at the church, and it's for all ages, so both you and Brandon would be welcome. It's a men's group for guys dealing with pornography addiction. Because I was addicted to pornography at the same age as Brandon, I struggled with it for years, and I thought it would go away once I married my wife. But it didn't. As a matter of fact, for a while, it got worse."

What? This man who seemed so put-together was once enslaved by porn?

Brandon, too, seemed surprised by the news. He looked up, riveted to what Nick was telling them.

"I was like you, Brandon. My parents were divorced. I was shuttled back and forth between their homes. When my dad remarried, I felt like no one really cared about me. And then I discovered this great high on the Internet. It was really easy to access, and I felt a whole lot better while I was using it. But here's the thing. Porn is a drug. It's like crack for your brain. You've heard of dopamine, right?"

Tyler nodded his head right along with his son.

"Dopamine is this neurotransmitter that kind of steers your brain in terms of pleasure or reward. So, when someone looks at pornography, there's a release of dopamine. Dopamine is triggered during sexual activity of any kind, but even more of it's released during illicit—or forbidden—sexual activity. That's what makes up the addictive nature of this particular drug. And I might even suggest that porn is one of the hardest drugs to kick. Society would have you believe it's harmless, but it is not."

Tyler writhed uncomfortably in his seat. Nick was speaking these words to Brandon, but he might as well have been speaking them to him.

"And do you know what desensitization is, Brandon?"

Brandon shook his head. "No."

"Desensitization means that what you're currently looking at isn't enough. Your brain isn't responding with enough dopamine anymore to make it worth your while to look at whatever images once stimulated a response. That happens when the brain is repeatedly flooded with these dopamine highs, and now you need more extreme and graphic porn, or you need to view it more often. And then you're into hard-core stuff. The stuff you were talking to me about. At this stage, married men sometimes advance into buying prostitutes or having extra-marital affairs."

Tyler's face flamed, images of Tara flashing through his mind.

"And here's the danger," Nick continued. "After years of doing this, the brain gravitates toward this easier route of looking at images online and getting its jollies that way, rather than forming relationships with a partner, which requires hard work and others-centered emotions."

Tyler rubbed his forehead with his fingers.

"You OK over there, Dad?" Nick's smile was understanding.

"Yeah," Tyler exhaled. "Yeah, I'm fine."

"This is tough stuff, I know. And Brandon—just so you know—teens are particularly in danger of addiction, since their brains are producing dopamine at the highest rate they'll ever have. I believe this is one of many reasons we're seeing a spike in social anxiety, depression, and neurological disorders amongst teens. The brain is changed by pornography. And neuroplasticity changes to the brain can be permanent. As I found out, if you keep this up in your married life, your partner can become less desirable than the images viewed because—well, let's face it—the woman on the screen isn't going to challenge or ask anything of you. She's completely there for your pleasure. She's your slave. Not the best way of viewing women, is it?"

"No," Brandon whispered.

"I wanna join your group, too," Tyler blurted, rubbing his forehead furiously. "Brandon's not the only one with this problem." Silence fell over the room, and Tyler couldn't bring himself to look at Brandon's or Nick's face. His heart was pounding so hard he could hardly catch his breath.

"All right. I think that would be great," Nick said

in an even tone.

With some difficulty, Tyler forced himself to make eye contact with Nick.

"In the group, we encourage accountability partners. What better accountability partners than a father and son?"

Brandon's eyes were wide. "Really? You'd join too?"

Tyler nodded. "Yep. I've hidden in the shadows long enough."

"Amen," Nick said, smiling. "It's time to step into the light—that's where God is waiting for us, after all. We just have to walk to Him. Sometimes with baby steps."

Maybe things were reversible, fixable.

Tyler knew what he needed to do. And now that he knew how his son was feeling, he had a better handle on things.

"One more question before you go," Nick said. "Why did you run away last month, Brandon?"

The boy's eyes fixed on a stain at the knee of his jeans as he picked at the fabric. "I was scared, I guess."

"Scared of whom? Your dad? Your mom? Kids at school?"

"Yeah, I guess. My dad and mom a little. But there were other reasons."

"Like what?"

"Like…" His fingers stopped plucking the denim. "I saw something I shouldn't have seen."

"What did you see?"

Tyler held his breath.

Brandon shifted in his seat, his face twisting with discomfort. "I was at this party. This guy I knew invited me. It was at this mansion."

"What happened at the party?" Nick encouraged.

"My sister was there. I knew she was going, and she told me I couldn't go, but I went anyway 'cause Jared told me to come with him. Anyway, when we got there, we had to pay $30 to get in, and that was supposed to cover everything."

"What was everything?" Nick asked.

Tyler was afraid to hear the answer.

"Drinks, drugs…girls."

"What? What do you mean…girls?"

Brandon's face paled before flushing a deep red. "Yeah. I didn't know about that part."

Tyler swept a hand over his face. This was unbelievable. "Did Jared know?"

"I don't know. Yeah, maybe."

Tyler and Nick exchanged glances. Tyler felt as though he were falling from a tall building. *Where, oh where was the bottom of all of this?*

Nick's tone remained calm, coaxing. "So, what happened?"

"I didn't stay for too long. It was kind of weird. It wasn't like the other parties we'd been to. There were a bunch of guys from a gang there. And all these girls were walking around. Some of them were like, really out of it."

"What do you mean they were out of it?" Anger crept into Tyler's voice. He'd have to learn to check that impulse at the door if he wanted answers from his son.

"You know. They were on stuff. Drugs and stuff. And the boys were taking them into rooms and…doing stuff with them."

"Why would you go to a party like that?"

"I don't know, Dad. I guess 'cause a lot of other

guys were going, too."

Tyler had to restrain himself from launching into a lecture. "Don't you know not to... and Katherine was there? At this party?"

"Yeah. That's why I left. I saw her go into a room with this guy."

"What guy?"

"I don't know. Just some guy. I don't know who he was."

Sweat filmed Tyler's brow as tension stiffened his limbs. This couldn't be true. Katherine would never do something like that.

"When did you leave the party that night?" Nick asked.

"Right after that. I told Jared I wanted to go. He was pretty scared, too, so we left. Some of the stuff that happened there was pretty bad. There were a bunch of guys threatening me and stuff. They wanted me to join their gang."

Tyler flashed back to the gang-types showing up at his door. If those were the kind of guys at this party...

"Anyway, I just got scared. And I ran."

"Where were you going, Bran?" Tyler asked.

"I don't know. Anywhere. Just away."

~*~

Nick had warned Tyler not to bombard Brandon with accusations or make him feel as if he was being interrogated. "He'll get enough of that from the police."

In the car, Tyler tried to remain calm, but his head swam with questions. At whose house had this party taken place? Did the parents know? Who was this guy with Katherine? He wanted answers. This involved his daughter, too.

"Dad?" Brandon broke the silence in the car. "How long have you known you couldn't stop looking at that stuff?"

"A long time." It felt good to say the words, to admit his inability to control his need. "Too long."

"Me, too," Brandon said.

He glanced over at Brandon and was surprised to see something other than a scowl on his son's face. "I'm just sorry, Brandon, that you and your sister felt that you couldn't talk to me."

"Dad?"

"Yeah?"

"Since we are talking about this, can I tell you something? Something about Kaki?"

"Sure."

"I think things are really bad with her."

Tyler's heart clenched. "Bad in what way? What do you mean?"

Brandon's voice shook. "Well, I can't really say a lot right now, but I can tell you that you wouldn't like her boyfriend."

A chill ran through him. This was the first Tyler had heard of Katherine having a boyfriend. "Who's her boyfriend?"

Brandon was silent.

Tyler had a momentary urge to pull the car over and force Brandon to tell him about Katherine's boyfriend, but he remembered what Nick said.

"I really think Kaki should tell you about him." Brandon looked out the window. "He's into some bad stuff. But I can't say anything else. I promised her I wouldn't."

Tyler's mind flashed through a multitude of possibilities—all of which required him to have a conversation with his daughter. But she was staying with her mother. The conversation would have to wait.

22

Kaki
Friday, January 6

"Katherine, do you know why you're here?"

"No." Kaki sat in the school's conference room across from Detective Jackson. The woman didn't look the way Kaki would have expected a detective to look. She was really pretty and kind of young. But she was a cop. And Kaki knew that if a cop had pulled her in for questioning, it wasn't good. Every minute she was there was dangerous.

Josh Wolf sat nearby—another reason for embarrassment. Now Molly would know all of this stuff. Kaki didn't want Molly to think badly of her.

Detective Jackson sat back, looking very relaxed as she absently scribbled on a pad of paper with a pencil. "We've received some information about a party that happened about a month ago—a party we were told you may have attended. Do you have any idea what party I'm talking about?"

Kaki shook her head. Damien's warnings echoed through her mind. She wouldn't breathe a word.

Detective Jackson reached for a large envelope. Out of it she pulled some paper and some photographs. She slid the photos across the desk toward Kaki. "Look familiar?"

Kaki saw herself in the photo, standing next to

Mattie. Her stomach lurched at how she was dressed for the purpose of the night. She looked out of it, too. Detective Jackson slid another photo across the table. She was standing in the background with a group of people. Sydney was at the forefront of the photo. The walls of the room pressed in on her.

"Remember this night?"

Kaki clenched her fists together and nodded.

The detective took the photos back. "Here's the thing, Katherine. We're trying to find out some things about that night. First of all, do you know a girl named Sydney Diaz?"

Kaki was glad she'd taken her little blue pill this morning. It was the only thing holding her together right now. Even so, her mind reeled. Should she deny knowing her? It seemed like the best course of action. "No."

Detective Jackson's eyebrow arched. "Really. You don't know Sydney Diaz?"

"Katherine," Josh broke in suddenly. "Actually, we think you do know her. There have a been a lot of reports that you know her—that you guys hung out together…a lot."

They must really know something if they were pushing this hard. Slowly, she nodded her head.

"OK, so you do know her?" Detective Jackson asked.

"Yeah, I knew her." As the words came out of her mouth, Kaki tensed. *Knew*. Past tense.

"OK. Did you see her at the party? I mean, you guys look like you're standing pretty close together here."

Kaki nodded.

"Did you know that she's a member of a gang

known as Masters of Sin?"

A trickle of sweat ran down the back of her neck. She shook her head. She'd said too much already.

"Katherine," Josh broke in again. "I'm sure you know that Sydney hasn't been at school in a few weeks. There's some concern about what happened to her after that night. Do you know anything about where she might be? What might have happened to her?"

Kaki shook her head. She would not answer these questions. Her life—the life of her family members depended on her keeping her mouth shut.

"Are you sure?"

Kaki was done. She just wanted to get out of there. "No, I don't know anything. Can I go back to class now?"

There was a knock on the door.

"Yes?" Josh called out.

A large, African American man, one of the school's security guards, peeked his head in. "You ready for the next one?"

"Send her in."

Jaida Harris. She wasn't one of the gang's girls, but she hung out with them sometimes. Her dark eyes barely grazed Kaki's as she entered.

"Have a seat, Jaida," Detective Jackson said.

Jaida slouched into the chair offered her, opposite Kaki. Jaida was a heavy girl, and today she was wearing a short skirt. When she sat, her hips spilled over the sides of the chair. Her black braids were piled on top of her head in the shape of a beehive.

Detective Jackson nodded at Josh, and he left the room. As soon as he was gone, she typed something into her computer and then turned it around to so that both of the girls could view it.

Kaki's insides lurched. *Oh, this was really bad.*

~*~

The picture was from that night at the party. Kaki suddenly remembered taking it...on Sydney's phone. A group of girls posing as though they were porn stars, completely naked, lips pursed, hands on hips. Jaida Harris was included amongst the girls. Underneath the photo, an array of responses—probably from students at the school:

I always knew she was a ho.

On the lo-down.

Isn't that Ashley?

Detective Jackson turned to Jaida. "Isn't that you?"

Jaida shrugged. "Yeah, maybe."

"You were tagged in this photo too, Miss Jones. Are you in this photo?"

Kaki's eyes were glued to the screen. She waited for Jaida to blurt out that Kaki had been the photographer, but she didn't. Maybe she didn't remember.

The detective turned back to Jaida. "Did you know this picture was being circulated all over social media sites?"

"I don't care who sees it. I don't see anything wrong with it. It's my body, and I'm proud of it."

Detective Jackson appeared curious. "So tell me why you posted these photos."

"'Cause we was havin' fun. We were at a party. You know? We wanted to send it out to the guys we wanted to get with."

"And this seemed like a good idea to you? This

seemed like the best way to get their attention?"

"Sure. Why not? How else you gonna get their attention?" Jaida raised her manicured hands in sync with her manicured eyebrows. Metal bracelets jangled. The glitter on her purple nails sparkled under the fluorescent lighting.

Kaki thought she might throw up. She had to get out of this room. Maybe she could pretend to have a panic attack or something. Lots of kids did that to get out of tests and stuff.

Detective Jackson leaned forward, her fingers tapping on the table top just in front of Jaida's hands. "How many kids you know that do this kind of thing? Send naked pictures of themselves to 'get with' the boys they're interested in?"

Jaida shrugged, visibly surprised at Abbie's question. "Everyone."

"Everyone?" Abbie asked. "I'm sorry, Jaida, but I find that hard to believe."

"Yeah, everyone sexts." Jaida looked to Kaki as though expecting her to concur.

Kaki clenched her lips and her fists tight, dropping her gaze to her lap.

Detective Jackson's mouth pursed, her eyebrows arched. "Everyone you know at this school sends out nude pictures of themselves?"

"Yeah. No one thinks of it as any big deal."

Everyone? Kaki didn't think it was everyone. Her friend Riley never did. Although sometimes it seemed like everyone. Thousands of followers on their social media accounts probably helped play into that delusion.

"All right, girls, let's get down to business," said the detective. "These pictures originated from Sydney

Diaz's social media account on December 10th. She's missing now. We're trying to locate her. I know you were both friends of hers, so this picture aside, I'm hoping you can help me out here. I know you were both at the party. Where did this party take place?"

Kaki would not say another word.

Jaida blurted out, "At a party. Back before Christmas."

"Whose party?"

"Gio George's party."

Now she was going to faint as well as throw up. This was the worst thing that could happen. Damien would probably kill both of them now.

"Does he go to this school?"

"Yeah," Jaida said in a tone that suggested surprise that Detective Jackson didn't already know that. "He's like the star football player, Gio George. You know." She shot another glance at Kaki as if to say, *can you believe this chick doesn't know Gio George?*

Detective Jackson turned her computer back around and typed information into it. "OK. Do you remember if Sydney took this photo?" she asked.

"Nah, that was a guy named Damien."

"What?" Kaki shrieked. Defending Damien was instinctive. "No, he didn't!" As soon as the protest rolled off of her tongue, Kaki slapped her hand over her mouth. Damien hadn't taken that picture.

"Do you know this Damien?" Detective Jackson now turned her attention to Kaki. "Does he go to this school?"

Jaida sat back in her chair, a smug expression on her face. "Damien? No, he's like, old."

Kaki wanted to scream at her, *you don't know what you've done!*

"How old?"

Jaida crossed her arms over her body. "I don't know. Twenty-five or something."

"What's his last name?"

"I don't know his last name."

"How do you know him?"

"He's a friend of Gio's. He had a bunch of girls with him," Jaida glanced over at Kaki as if to say, *you know you were one of them.*

Chills ran over Kaki's arms even as sweat formulated at her brow.

"But...you know, like everybody be takin' photos that night."

"Who else was taking photos?" The detective asked.

Jaida threw up her hands again. "How am I supposed to know that? There were like, a thousand people there that night."

"Really. A thousand people?"

"Yeah. You seen Gio's house? He lives in a mansion."

Detective Jackson turned her gaze back to Kaki.

Kaki looked away.

"And how about you? You know this Damien guy?

Kaki shook her head. "No. No, I don't."

~*~

When Kaki got home to her dad's house that afternoon, she pulled all the blinds and double-checked the locks on all the doors. Her dad had taken Brandon out to dinner, and then they were supposed to go to some men's group meeting at the church, and she was supposed to keep Micah and Celia. He had texted her earlier in the day. *Don't go anywhere tonight. We need to talk.*

He probably wanted to talk about what had happened at school that day. But she couldn't talk about that. She'd already spent thirty minutes on the phone with her mother evading questions and trying to make it sound as if this was all a big misunderstanding.

Every few minutes she checked her phone—waiting for a text from Damien, but other than her mom and dad sending her text messages and leaving voice mails, her phone had been silent. That was not a good sign.

Every time a car drove down her street, she rushed to the windows to make sure it wasn't Damien's electric-blue Mustang or Hubby's black pick-up. And she was out of her little blue pills. She could already feel the beginning of the sweats starting. She didn't know how long she could hold off before she sent a text—too desperate for a fix to worry about her safety. The only thing that was keeping her from doing it was Micah and Celia.

Kaki moved into the bathroom and looked out the window to see if Josh's car was in the driveway. She was thinking about taking Micah and Celia next door, but not if she had to face Josh. Not after what happened today.

Molly's car was the only one in the driveway. If Molly would let them hang out there, they'd all be safer for a little while. None of the members of MOS would come looking for them there. "Come on guys," she said to Micah and Celia, trying to sound excited. "We're going next door to see the puppies."

"Yay!" Celia jumped up. "I want to see the puppies!"

"OK, but you can't touch them or hold them or anything," Micah warned her. "They're too little."

Celia pouted. "But I want to hold them."

"You can't right now." Kaki pulled Celia's arms into her coat. "In another week or so. When they get a little bigger."

"Kaki, when is Mommy coming home?" Celia asked as Kaki zipped up her coat.

Kaki felt sorry for them. Even though her mother was crazy, she'd still had her around while she was growing up. "I don't know. Soon, hopefully."

Celia's blue eyes filled with tears. "But I want her to come back."

As though he sensed an emotional explosion coming, Micah rushed forward and took his sister's hand. "Come on, Celia. Let's go look at the puppies."

Less than ten minutes later, Kaki was standing in the kitchen watching Molly spill Oreo cookies onto a platter.

Celia buried her head in Kaki's shoulder, screaming. "I want my mommy!" She was so distraught her breath was catching, and her mouth yawned open in the shape of an O as she shook out a silent wail. Finally gasping in air, she let out a shriek that rattled Kaki's ear drums.

"Look, Celia," Kaki said, wrenching Celia from her neck and forcibly turning her so she could see Trixie sitting in her gated area surrounded by squirming puppies. The dog's brown, soulful eyes rolled from Kaki to Celia and finally to Micah, who sat down on the other side of the gate and looked in at her. "Look, Celia, look. See the doggie there? That's Trixie."

As the dog came into focus for the little girl, her face changed, softening from the red, bunched-up mask. Hiccupping and sniffing, her face blotchy and slick with tears, Celia climbed off of Kaki and joined Micah in watching the dogs.

Kaki slumped with exhaustion.

Molly rushed over and pulled her into a side hug.

How much did she know?

"How are you doing?"

"I'm fine," Kaki said quietly. She wished she could tell her the truth. Her chest ached. The pressure of holding in all of these secrets…

Molly nodded and returned to the counter.

Celia's crying quieted, and she and Micah talked about each of the puppies—their coloring, the names Celia thought they should have, which ones she wanted.

Kaki sighed. "I saw her, you know." The words were out of her mouth before she even had a chance to contemplate them.

"Who?"

"Lana. I saw her out on the stoop that night—with her suitcase. She was just sitting there."

"Did you say anything to her?"

"No."

"Did she say anything to you?"

"No."

"What time was that?"

"Like, around one in the morning or something. I don't really know."

"What were you doing out there?"

Kaki was risking everything. She was in so much trouble. Damien would probably kill her anyway. At least this way, if she did end up dead, someone would know something. "I was…I was uh…sneaking out to meet Damien."

Molly shot her a disapproving glare. "Katherine."

"I know. I shouldn't do that."

"No, you shouldn't. And please don't do it anymore. I don't think your dad can take another thing. He looks like he's going to collapse."

"Yeah, I know."

"Promise me you won't sneak out any more. It would really, really upset him."

"I don't know if it really would." Kaki looked down at her feet. "I don't know if Dad really cares about me that much, you know?"

Molly's eyebrows raised. "Why do you feel that way? *I* know your dad loves you and cares deeply, but you're obviously feeling that he doesn't. Why?"

Kaki looked up at the ceiling, trying not to cry. "I don't know. I've felt like that for years."

"Since when?"

"Since I was like, thirteen. My dad used to talk to me all the time. We played games and had dates together and stuff. He used to call me Kaki. It was his pet name for me." Pain radiated through her at the memory.

Molly smiled. "I've heard some people call you that."

"Yeah. I always liked it. Some of my good friends still call me that. Some of my aunts and uncles, too. But not my dad."

"Why do you think he stopped?"

"I don't know," she said. "He just stopped. I haven't heard him call me that in years."

"What about your boyfriend? Does he call you Kaki?"

Damien called her *baby*...but she didn't think he'd ever used her name. The realization drove a cold, panicky feeling through her. "No, he doesn't call me Kaki either."

Micah and Celia suddenly laughed loudly at something the dogs did.

Kaki turned, momentarily distracted, but Molly continued her questions.

"So what is that you like so much about Damien?"

Kaki gritted her teeth. Today it was hard to remember. "I don't know. He's nice to me sometimes. I don't know."

"How is he nice to you?"

"He's just like...he gives me a lot of gifts and stuff. He tells me I'm pretty. He takes care of me."

"You've told me that stuff before. I want to know what Damien is really like. Does he ever hit you?"

Incidents flashed through Kaki's mind—images of bruises and cuts—sensations of searing pain in her cheek from the back of his hand. "Not really."

"Not really? I don't like that answer. Does he hit you in any way? Because, Katherine, if he does, that's abuse—"

"No, he doesn't. He doesn't," she said quickly.

"And why does he make you wait outside for him in the freezing cold? And why does he make you sneak out? And why can't your parents know about him? I'm sorry, but this just doesn't sound like a healthy relationship to me." She pulled her toward the table in the kitchen and motioned for her to sit. Molly sat in the chair beside her. Her voice was low as she spoke. "I have to be honest with you, too. Josh has told me about the photos...and about the party."

A wave of emotion swept over Kaki. Like a rag

255

doll, her head flopped onto the table. Her shoulders heaved with sobs.

Molly's arm draped over her shoulders. "It's OK. I'm sorry. I didn't mean to upset you."

All the fear and terror and sorrow erupted inside Kaki like a volcanic blast. But she still didn't think she could confide her deepest concerns—that Damien was coming for her whole family. She straightened and looked into Molly's face.

Molly reached out and smoothed the hair from Kaki's face. "Is there anything you want to tell me?"

Oh, yes, how she wanted to. But she couldn't endanger Molly, too. Despair overwhelmed her again. She couldn't share her secrets with anyone. "There are just some things I can't talk about." Her phone vibrated and she looked down at the screen.

Damien.

Her heart jerked.

Be ready at 11. Im picking u up.

23

Tyler
Saturday, January 7

Tyler still needed to have *the talk* with Katherine. But when he and Brandon had arrived home last night, the house had been quiet. The kids were in bed and Katherine's bedroom door was closed, the lights off, so he'd figured she was sleeping, too. It could wait until morning.

After feeding the younger ones bowls of cereal and packing them off to watch cartoons, Tyler planned to wake Katherine and get to the bottom of this. He glanced at his phone sitting on the kitchen counter. There were messages on his voice mail.

Christina, Christina, Christina. He scrolled past them to the next message. His heart jolted. *Lana.* According to his call log, she had called around 4:00 AM, which meant it would have been 1:00 AM her time. "Hi, Tyler, it's me. I know I haven't called all week. I've just been…I don't know…trying to get set up here—starting the new job and all. I was busy and…well, I just needed to think without talking to you or the kids. Anyway, I'm here. I'm safe. All is well. I don't know if you'll want to talk to me or not, but if you do, you can call me at this number. I'm staying with Erin until I find a place. OK…I guess I'll talk to you later…maybe?"

No questions about him or the kids. All about her. As usual.

Clenching his teeth together, Tyler slammed his phone down on the counter. He still couldn't believe she had done this. Grasping at his hair, a sound of anger and frustration bubbled up and out of his throat.

"What's wrong, Dad?" Micah called from the family room.

Tyler repressed more outbursts. "Nothing. Everything's fine."

He would have to look into some kind of child care for the kids. He couldn't keep relying on his parents, the neighbors, or his older kids. *What a mess.* He was suddenly furious with Lana.

A knock at the door roused him from his angry musings. Dread raised its ugly head as he approached it. Through the beveled glass of the door, he could see a female form. Abbie Jackson.

He opened the door. Her thin smile was eclipsed by the lines on her forehead.

"Hi, Tyler. I'm sorry to bother you on a Saturday morning."

"That's OK. What's up?"

"Can I come in for a sec?"

Tyler stood back from the door. He sensed a different vibe from her than their polite coffee shop chit-chat. She was here for something serious. His heart caught in his throat. *God, help me. Whatever it is, give me the strength to bear it.*

"I spoke with your ex-wife this morning, and she told me that Katherine was at your house. Is she here? I need to speak to her as well."

"She's sleeping, but I'll go get her." Tyler moved upstairs, his chest heavy. Katherine was in trouble now. It was as though a vortex of misfortune swirled over his house.

Opening the door, Tyler couldn't remember the last time he had been in his daughter's room. The first thought that swept through his mind was how clean and neat everything looked—almost as if no one lived there. *Or like a room used for sleeping and nothing else—a temporary crash pad.* The second thought was that the bed was made. He stared at Katherine's empty bed.

Tyler went back downstairs and peered out the front door. Katherine's car was still there. "Her car's here but she's not. One of her friends may have picked her up, or she may be over with the neighbors."

He quickly called Molly. Katherine was not over there. Scratching his head, he sat down across from Abbie. "She may have had some school thing this morning or shopping with her mom or something. Who knows? Teenagers, you know."

He hadn't even known she'd had a boyfriend—and he didn't know what she was involved in nowadays. There had simply been too many other things going on.

Abbie looked at him, her gaze somber and all business. "I really need to speak with her. I already talked to your ex-wife. Katherine's not with her. And I need to speak with you, too."

The messages from Christina on his phone. A familiar falling sensation assaulted him. Brandon's words about Katherine's boyfriend simultaneously returned to him. His mouth felt dry. "What's going on?"

"We think your daughter may be involved with a guy named Damien Rosas-Diego. Know him?"

Tyler shook his head.

Abbie removed a photograph from her bag and held it up for Tyler to see. "This is him."

Tyler's skin pimpled with chills. He stared directly into the face of evil. Black hair and black eyes—like those of a viper. A black T-shirt with the emblem of a dragon matched the tattoo on his neck.

"Ever seen him before?"

"No." Tyler was barely able to breathe the word. "I don't think so."

Abbie put the photo back in the folder. "He's not someone you want your daughter entangled with. He has quite an impressive rap sheet. Drugs, assault, a list of gang-related crimes."

"He's in a gang?"

"Yes. He's a ring-leader in the Masters of Sin."

Tyler nodded his head. Was he having a heart attack? He couldn't breathe. Something pressed in on his chest.

"They're local. Wreaking havoc all over this area and in the area schools as well."

"I didn't even know she had a boyfriend."

"Tyler, he's not her boyfriend. He's her pimp. This is all about teen sex trafficking. That's their game."

"What?" His heart might explode any moment. *No. No, this could not be happening.* Brandon had tried to tell him.

Abbie removed another picture from her file. "Ever seen this girl?"

A girl about Kaki's age with long, black hair and a nose piercing frowned in the photo.

"Never seen her before."

"Her name is Sydney Diaz. Also a member of Masters of Sin. One of their bottom girls. You know what that means?"

Tyler shook his head.

"It means she recruited other girls for the gang—for purposes of prostitution."

Each word Abbie spoke entered Tyler's brain like the stab of a knife. He thought he might die from the agony. His little girl, his Kaki...a prostitute?

"Sydney Diaz is missing. From what we understand, Sydney and Katherine were friends. Close friends. We think Katherine might know something about Sydney's disappearance."

"What would make you think that?" His voice didn't even sound like his own.

"Because they were both at the party the night Sydney disappeared."

"What party?"

Abbie lifted more photographs from her file. "Saturday, December the tenth. Both your daughter and your son were in photos from that night. All taken on various kids' cell phones."

She handed him the print outs of the photographs, and he sifted through them, his insides flinching with each sighting of his children. This was the party Brandon had talked about. *Oh, God. Please. How can this be happening?*

"This wasn't just any party, Tyler. This was a prostitution party where kids come in by paying a $20 or $30 cover charge. This covers their booze, their drugs, and it covers their access to the girls—if you understand my meaning."

He understood all too well. Brandon had talked about it. It was why he had run away.

"Despite what you might think, these kinds of parties are not all together uncommon. We're seeing them more and more, especially in circles where gang-activity is involved."

Tyler struggled to understand how his children had become involved. "How did this happen?"

"I wish I could tell you. These gang members are smart, and they know how to manipulate young people. You've got infiltration within the schools—recruiters—often times their own peers—are very savvy to the girls who will fall for the lure of acceptance, the coolness factor."

"Katherine has never been involved with anything bad. She grew up knowing right from wrong. She's always been a great student." Tyler wasn't sure if he was telling Abbie or himself.

Abbie's face dripped with sympathy. "This spans all demographics, all socio-economic groups, and all upbringings. These people are good at what they do. Deception and manipulation are their specialties."

"What do you need me to do?"

"We need to talk to Katherine. We've paid a visit to the boy's parents whose house was used for the party. He's being questioned as we speak. The problem is that several weeks have passed. The kids who were there that night have been really good about keeping tight-lipped. Even if they saw something, it'll be dangerous for them to say anything. MOS members don't mess around. They're murderers as well as pimps, make no mistake."

His daughter was in danger. Tyler shuddered, his heart breaking into a million pieces. Some protective father he'd proved to be.

"Sydney's mother didn't report her daughter as missing until she'd already been gone for two weeks. That's not uncommon for parents of prostituted girls. If they've been running the streets for a while, the parents are used to them running away. They stop reporting it. But Katherine's been living in your house all this time. She's been able to hide her activities—which in some ways, is almost more insidious. At any rate, something bad happened in that house that night. I think Katherine might know what it was."

"But if it's dangerous for her to talk—"

"Our goal is to get these guys and put them in jail. Drugs, prostitution...murder—whatever charge we can get them on."

The main thing was to protect his kids. Nothing else mattered. "OK. You tell me what to do, and I'll do it."

"Let's start by finding Katherine."

24

Kaki
Saturday, January 7

Kaki could never go home again. Too many people knew about that night, and now there were too many people looking for her.

Damien had picked her up on Friday night and had taken her straight to The Diggs. He hadn't spoken to her on their drive there, and as they had approached the place, she got a sick feeling in the pit of her stomach.

Batman and two other gang members had turned the shed that once stored lawn mowers into a party pad. There were curtains with cartoon characters on them hanging in the window, and someone had spray-painted one whole wall of the cinderblock structure to look like a Rubik's cube. The walls were covered with graffiti, and there were a bunch of old, dirty beds and some tables with ashtrays. Pornography covered some of the graffiti.

A lot of the new girls were brought to The Diggs first.

Kaki dreaded seeing them—girls who'd come to this country thinking they were to work as a waitress or a nanny, and then they ended up here. Most of them didn't speak any English and they were really, really young. Those girls were treated the worst. They were beaten, abused, repeatedly raped.

That night, Kaki was treated like one of those girls. Damien didn't even supply her with the little blue pill. She didn't remember how many men came through the doors. After a while she'd passed out anyway. That night, something inside of her died.

The next morning, sick, in pain, and in the throes of withdrawal, she practiced her mental mantras. *Numb, numb, you are nothing; you don't exist.*

"If you behave yourself and do everything I tell you, then I'll give you your stuff. Maybe I'll even give you a little whiskey to wash them down."

Some other guy was talking…something about packing up.

"We leave tomorrow for Pennsylvania," said Damien.

"You taking her with you?" asked the other voice.

"Have to. Either that or I have to kill her."

Kill me. Please kill me. I'd rather die.

"She won't talk now. I can still use her. We'll see how it goes."

Saturday passed in a hazy shade of pain and sickness. As she lay in that dirty bed in The Diggs, she traveled in her mind. She went back to the time when she was a little girl, when her dad used to take her to the movies or out to dinner. Just the two of them.

Once Micah and Celia came along, that hardly ever happened, but she still remembered those times as some of the best. There were other times of family vacations at the beach, eating fries on the board walk in Ocean City, and taking selfies with the figures in the wax museum at Virginia Beach. Holding Celia when she was born, and dressing her dolls with her old baby clothes. That was back when her dad used to call her

"Kaki." He didn't call her that anymore. She didn't even think that person existed anymore.

~*~

Damien dragged her out of bed early the next morning. "Come on. Get up. We're leaving."

As he pulled her into a sitting position, she groaned. Her jaw hurt from where one of the guys had hit her. There was a stinging sensation on her arm as well—at the juncture of her wrist and hand. She looked down and tried to make her eyes focus. It was a brand. A tattoo of a dragon. And just under it the letters—M-O-S. The skin around it was red and puffy. She vaguely remembered now. Someone—maybe it was Damien?—had done that last night. She recalled a scratching sensation, a stinging. Now she really was property of the gang.

Her stomach roiled with nausea. She wished she could be sick somewhere, but there wasn't time.

Damien grabbed her sore wrist and pulled her off of the bed. They seemed to be in a hurry as they moved outside where Hubby and one of his new girls waited.

"Let's go," Damien instructed. "Get in the car."

Damien pushed her, and she fell against the passenger door of the car. Grasping her arm, he jerked her back while he opened the car door and ratcheted the seat forward. Then he pushed her again so that she fell into the backseat, banging her shin.

The other girl climbed in beside her. Like Kaki, the girl had long, blonde hair, and she was tall and skinny. She didn't look or speak to Kaki.

Damien and Hubby climbed into the car and revved the motor.

"Where are we going?" the girl beside her asked.

"We're making a stop at the grocery store, then we've got an appointment at the motel. Then we're off to Pittsburgh. Don't worry about the rest."

Kaki stared out the window, imagining ways she could die before ever reaching the motel. If only she could jump out of the car, but she was trapped in the backseat. Maybe they'd be hit by a semi. Maybe the end of the world would come.

They pulled into the grocery store parking lot and stopped.

"Come on. Get out." Damien pulled the seat forward and grabbed her arm.

Like drones, the two girls followed the guys into the store where they bought miscellaneous food items, sodas, toothbrushes, and shampoo.

Before they reached the check out, Hubby turned to Damien. "Oh, yeah, we should get some stuff to wash our clothes. Think that place in Pittsburgh has a washer-dryer?"

"I don't know, man," Damien said, irritation creeping into his tone. "Hurry up, though. We're supposed to meet Antoine at the motel in ten minutes."

Panic flooded over Kaki in a tidal wave. Something told her that if she went with them to Pittsburgh, she would never see her family again. For that matter, she didn't think she'd live much longer. Maybe that was a good thing.

They trailed through the line behind people who paid no attention to them, checked out by a cashier who never looked up. She was being kidnapped and no one cared.

As they made their way across the parking lot, Kaki heard someone say her name.

"Katherine?"

The blood drained from her face as she locked eyes with Molly Wolf. Suddenly, any thought of escaping dissipated. If she spoke to Molly, Molly would be in danger, too.

Kaki waved at Molly and forced a tight smile. The frosty wall of resistance was her only hope. *Don't talk to her.* The others moved quickly toward the car.

Molly seemed to be assessing Kaki's companions. She stopped a few feet away from the car, her gaze on Kaki. "How have you been? Josh and I keep hoping you'll stop by."

Kaki shrank back and forced the words. "I'm fine."

"A lot of people are looking for you—wondering where you are. I know your dad is worried."

Kaki tensed. "I've had a lot going on."

"Where are you staying now?"

"At a friend's."

"I see," Molly said.

Damien moved up beside her, his feet apart, his arms crossed.

A shiver ran through her.

"Who are you?" he asked, his tone deceptively calm.

"I'm just a friend," Molly said.

"Yeah, well, she doesn't have any friends anymore. Come on. Let's go." He turned to Kaki and grabbed her elbow.

A rush of shame surged through her. Molly was smart. She could probably see what was happening. She might even go home and tell Josh...or her dad.

"You don't scare me." Molly's tone was confident.

"Yeah, well, you should be scared," he said over his shoulder as he pushed Kaki against the car.

"Hey, wait a minute," Molly insisted. "Wait a minute. Katherine…"

Damien opened the door of the car and pushed Kaki. "Get in."

Kaki pushed back, fighting him. She looked up at Molly in desperation.

"I said get in!" Damien shoved Kaki into the backseat.

Her hands clutched the side of the door, as she looked up at Molly. "I can't. I'm sorry, but I can't." She didn't have the strength. There was no fighting Damien. Anywhere she ran, he would find her. She would just go with him. Less people got hurt that way.

Kaki collapsed in the backseat helplessly, distress flooding her heart as the other girl climbed into the backseat as well. Hubby plopped into the passenger side of the car.

Damien shot Molly one last warning before he climbed into the driver's seat. "Look lady, if I were you, I'd get out of here. Now."

As they drove away, Kaki looked out the back window.

Molly got into her car.

Memories—random and disconnected—entered her brain these days. Sometimes they were from childhood; others were scenes she'd watched in television shows or movies. This one was from something she had read in English class. She couldn't remember the title. One line stuck with her, and as they drove down Elden Street and turned off and away from the town center, it replayed in her mind. "Abandon hope, all ye who enter here."

25

Tyler
Sunday, January 8

Tyler looked in the cabinet for a juice glass. Most were in the dishwasher, so he reached further in and pulled a bottle from the shelf. Vodka. Why would Lana have stored it at the back of the glasses? Throughout the morning, he mulled it over. He sensed this was something to which he should pay attention.

Celia climbed up on the stool, rubbing her eyes, still half asleep. Her red curls were a tangled mess. He'd have to ask Katherine to brush…

The pain in his stomach followed. He didn't know where Katherine was. She hadn't come home, and Christina hadn't heard from her either. Never in a million years had Tyler ever thought he would have to file missing reports on two of his children. Within one month's time, no less.

"When is Mommy coming home?" Celia whined.

"Your mommy… your mommy needed some time away, Celia. She'll be home soon," he said the words mechanically.

"From us?" Celia's big, blue eyes peered out from under her too-long bangs.

"No, not from you, honey. She loves you guys a lot. She's just not in a place where she can call right now." Even as he spoke the words, fear assailed him.

What if she never calls? What if we never hear from her again? What will I tell the kids then?

His cell phone rang.

Molly.

"Hello?"

"I just saw Katherine."

"What? Where?"

"On Elden Street. I'm following the car right now. It's a blue Camaro with the license plate M-O-S-D-E-M-O-N."

Tyler's heart stopped. "Molly, no. What are you doing?"

"I'm following them right now, Tyler. Katherine was practically forced into the car."

"I—I need to...well, I mean, I'm not even dressed!" Carrying the phone, Tyler rushed upstairs to throw on a sweatshirt and jeans as he listened to Molly.

"They just turned down Grace Street!"

Tyler let an expletive fly as he pulled on his shoes. "Have—have you called the police? Have you called Josh?"

"Yes, I've called both."

"I'll stay on the line with you, but I've got the kids and..." Suzanne. He would ask Suzanne if she could watch the kids.

Dashing across the street, he knocked on Suzanne's door, quickly blurting out his emergency situation and need for a temporary place for the kids. All the while, Molly's voice echoed on the speaker phone. "I'm on Locust Street. They're turning right onto Lynn Street."

Suzanne seemed confused by his stammering explanation, but she agreed at once. "Of course, I'll do it, sweetie. Just bring 'em on over."

It seemed to take forever for Tyler to get the kids up and out of the house and over to Suzanne's, but some ten minutes later, he was finally behind the wheel of his car. "OK, Molly. Where are you?"

"I'm on Pearl Street. They're turning into The Pearl Street Motel. I'm going to park at the back of the lot."

Tyler dodged traffic, weaving in and out of cars, praying to hear the peal of sirens in the distance. *Please Lord, please save my daughter…I'll do anything you ask. I just…can't bear the idea of something happening to her.* He heard the sirens before he reached the motel, and tears sprang to his eyes in response. "Thank You, God. Thank You, thank You."

Tyler had never noticed the motel on the corner before. It was a non-descript, respectable-looking place. It was an independently run establishment, but from the outside it looked clean and appealing. He took a sharp turn into the parking lot, his tires skidding slightly on an icy patch. Dodging mounds of shoveled snow, he found Molly's car at the back of the lot. Josh's car appeared moments later, followed by several police cars.

Tyler bounded from his car and moved toward Molly, who stood outside her car hugging herself to stay warm. "They were dropped off at the front of the building."

"How many?" Tyler asked.

"Katherine and two others."

Tyler's heart quaked. He was surrounded by police and their cruisers.

Josh stepped out of his car.

"Josh, the driver just dropped them off. Then he took off again," Molly explained.

Josh nodded and hurried over to the police

cruisers. From the third cruiser, a familiar face appeared. Abbie Jackson.

Tyler moved toward Abbie.

"Are they inside?" Abbie called out.

"Only three of them. The driver of the blue car, license plate M-O-S-D-E-M-O-N—he sped off that way toward Elden." Molly pointed.

Abbie nodded and spoke directives into her walkie-talkie. "Suspect on the move...driver of blue Camaro, license M-O-S-D-E-M-O-N...headed east on Herndon Parkway toward Elden." She turned back to Tyler. "With a license plate like that, he shouldn't be hard to find. And you saw the other three go inside?"

"I did."

"OK, let's go," Abbie motioned the patrol officers toward the building.

Tyler followed.

"No, no, Tyler. You have to stay here with us," Josh instructed.

Tyler longed to rush into the place with the rest of the officers, find Katherine and tear her abductors limb from limb.

"You have to stay back, man. That's the only way you're helping her. Let the police do their job."

With something between a sigh and sob, Tyler slumped over and placed his hands on the hood of his car, breathing hard.

"Come on," Josh suggested. "Let's all wait in one car. It's freezing out here."

All three climbed back into Molly's car and silently watched as the police entered the motel. Tyler could feel his heartbeat in his temples. Adrenaline stimulated every nerve in his body. *God, please protect her.*

"Let's pray. Right now," said Molly.

The trio joined hands, and Josh began to pray for Katherine's protection, for God to lead the police straight to her, for the entire operation to go smoothly and without incident.

Tears burned Tyler's eyes. "Oh, please God!" he wailed. "Please help her!"

Josh and Molly squeezed his hands.

It was up to God now. There was nothing he could do. He had to trust the Lord with his daughter's life.

He caught sight of his own face in the rearview mirror. His skin was a pale shade of winter—his eyes heavily lidded with lack of sleep and worry.

The three of them sat motionless, barely breathing.

Tyler shivered with cold, fear, and anticipation, while silently watching the doors of the motel.

Molly turned the vehicle on and cranked the heat.

Time ticked by with only the sounds of cars moving up and down Herndon Parkway, distant sirens, the sound of their breathing, and the rustling of their coats.

Flashes of blue moved around the side of the motel—two officers who had been investigating the back entrance and now made their way to the front.

"Look," Josh said. "Here they come."

Tyler, Molly, and Josh scrambled out of the car as Abbie marched through the front door of the motel flanked by officers holding onto three handcuffed kids and leading them toward the police cruisers. One of them was unmistakably Katherine.

Tyler gasped, his heart pounding. "There she is."

What a terrible and wonderful sight. Tyler moved toward his daughter but was stopped by Josh's arm.

"Wait. We'll meet them at the station."

Tyler's hands shot through his hair, pain and

anguish assaulting him. He longed to snatch his Kaki up in his arms, keep her safe from any more harm. "She...she looks cold," he whispered.

His little Kaki, dressed in skinny jeans, a T-shirt, and a lightweight jacket. Elevated on heels that were too high for her slight frame, Katherine tripped and leaned into the officers escorting her. She looked scared.

Tyler climbed into Josh's car, and they rode silently up the street to the Herndon Police Station.

"Will they charge her with anything?" Tyler finally asked as they turned into the parking lot.

"Not if I can help it," Josh said.

They all climbed out of the police cruiser and entered the station.

Tyler spotted Katherine right away, sitting on the bench beside Abbie.

"Katherine!" He rushed to her.

She was still handcuffed. Her facial expression was hard and angry, her mouth a solid, frowning line, and her eyes dark and emotionless. She would not look at any of them.

Tyler squeezed her, holding her head just under his chin as he kissed her head. After a few moments, he pulled back from her and touched her hair, which looked and smelled like it needed washing.

She jerked her head away, refusing to make eye contact.

"I love you, honey," he said. She stiffened at the words.

Abbie motioned for Tyler to speak with her a few feet away.

Molly moved in and took his place.

"Hey, could you take the cuffs off of her at least? I

mean, why is she cuffed?"

Abbie motioned to one of the other officers to remove Katherine's cuffs. "We had to handcuff all three of the kids. When we arrived at the door of the motel room, the male suspect who was with them pulled a gun on us. The girls tried to run out the sliding glass doors and out back, but we already had officers on that side of the building. They caught the girls pretty quick. Another officer came in through the glass doors and got the boy, too. The driver—we think that's probably your daughter's pimp, Damien Rosas-Diego—he got away."

Tyler groaned. "Who is the other boy?"

"His driver's license says he's nineteen. Name's James Hubbell. He goes by Hubby, apparently. He has a few drug charges on his record from a couple of years ago. Spent a little time in juvie. I'd say once we pick a little more, we'll find he's up to his eyeballs in gang activity."

"What about the other guy—Damien?" Tyler couldn't stand the idea of that guy getting away. When he thought of what he had done to his daughter…he wanted to kill him.

"Don't worry. We'll get him. He's very engaged in this area with gang activity. He's got a long list of drug possession and violent assault charges on his record, and maybe now we'll have cause to go after him for human trafficking."

Tyler looked at his daughter with watery eyes. Why hadn't he protected his child? His head was reeling…he didn't know what to do. Where did one begin with a girl who was probably so damaged, so angry?

"Mr. Jones," Abbie said, turning to him. "I'm sorry

to do this, but we need to question Katherine. Afterwards, we'll release her to you. You should take her to the hospital right after. Have her checked out. There are no charges against her at this time, but we need to try and get information if we can. There's still a missing girl."

"I understand." Anything to catch that monster.

"But I'll be honest with you," Abbie continued. "These girls coming out of traumatic sex-trafficking situations don't talk, so I don't have high expectations of her giving us names or much information. And the other thing is, once you get her home. You can't just settle back into *normal*…like nothing's happened. These girls have been programmed. Police are bad, parents are bad, and anyone trying to help them is bad. Yeah, they may be scared of their pimps, but I can't even tell you how many girls end up back with their traffickers because they think they're in love…or they're better off with them."

"How could they even think…" Tyler broke off. He was over trying to figure all of this out. Now, he just needed to get help for his family.

"She'll need intensive help and rehabilitation. And she's high risk for running away again. Especially with her trafficker still out there." Abbie tucked a card into Tyler's shaking hand. "Here's the number of a local group who works with girls coming out of trafficking and prostitution. Call them today. Don't wait."

Tyler swallowed hard and nodded. "OK."

Molly approached slowly from the side and put her hand on Tyler's arm. "Tyler, Josh, and I will take Celia, and Micah for a few days—as long as you need them to stay with us. You take care of Kaki and Brandon."

26

Kaki
Tuesday, January 10

Kaki slept for twenty-four hours straight. Lana's hidden bottle of vodka under the bathroom sink was still there—right next to the container of cleanser. She drank it all down in one go behind a closed bathroom door. She still had a couple of sleeping pills, too. She'd taken those as well. And blissful, all-consuming sleep had taken her from Sunday night into Tuesday morning.

There had been arrests. She had been one of them. Then they'd questioned her for over an hour. They'd asked her about Damien—they knew all about him, it seemed. Then they'd questioned her about Sydney. Her heart hurt with the memory of her friend. They were still looking for her. Still wondering if she was alive. *And I know where she is.* She couldn't tell them. Damien had sworn he would kill her. Maybe he still would. But nothing mattered anymore.

Kaki stumbled from her bedroom into the hallway.

Brandon was there, sitting on the floor by her door. He slid his back up the wall and his eyes looked like a startled animal. "Dad!" he called out. "Dad! She's awake!"

"Shh," Kaki's head hurt. "You don't have to shout it out to everybody."

Her dad's footsteps clumped up the staircase, and he seemed out of breath when he reached the top. He grasped at his chest. "You're awake. Oh, thank God."

"It would be better for everyone if I'd just died." She turned away and closed the bathroom door. She filled a disposable cup with water and gulped it. She met her own eyes in the mirror. *Disgusting. Disgusting. Ugly, nasty ho. You are the most hideous thing that ever lived.* She swilled a mouthful of water and spit it at her reflection. *I hate you.*

Opening the cupboard, she looked for anything—aspirin, ibuprofen, anything she could swallow in large quantities. Anything that might kill her. But everything had been removed. With a scream of anguish, she sank onto the toilet, pulling at her hair. She could feel the sweats coming on. Could she text Damien? She couldn't remember what had happened to him...

Her skin was crawling...and itching. She looked at the inside of her forearm. Blue and black ink. Scabbed over. *No. No! No!* She turned on the faucet, immersing her hand in the running water, scrubbing the image and the words—MOS.

You're a Masters of Sin girl now. You belong to us. You belong to me. You're my slave.

"No!" she shrieked long and hard, her voice echoing in the tile of the customized bathroom.

Someone was knocking on the door.

She had to remove this tattoo. She scrubbed and scratched until the skin burned, stung, and then broke open and bled. Only then did she sink to the floor with a sense of relief, her head dropping to rest on the tops of her knees, her tangled, dirty hair falling over her face. The blood would wash away the pain and the stain. But that wasn't just any blood. That was something about the blood of Jesus...

"Hey, Kaki."

She gasped.

"Hey, what's there to do around here...you know, like, for fun?"

Shaking uncontrollably, Kaki raised her head, peering at the source of the voice through a veil of blonde strands. A girl with a long, black ponytail and cat-eye makeup shimmered before her. The image was blurry, but the voice was unmistakable. "Sydney?"

"What are you doing? Why haven't you told them where I am? Do you know how cold it is out here in the woods? Do you know how gross it is being buried under a bunch of dirt and leaves and stuff?"

She reached out to touch Sydney's form. She couldn't feel anything. The image disappeared. "Sydney!" she screamed.

"Girl, you'd better tell them where I am. I'm gonna come mess you up if you don't. You'd better..."

Kaki choked. She gasped, clutching at her throat, and crawled toward the door...

"Kaki! Unlock the door! Kaki! Come on, let us in!" The voices of her brother and father eclipsed that of Sydney's familiar, scolding tone.

She flipped the lock and flung the door open. Then her dad was sitting on the floor with her, holding her in his arms. "It's OK," he breathed against her ear. "You're OK. You're safe. No one is going to hurt you."

"I need to tell someone—I need..." she screamed.

"What do you need to tell me? I'm here, baby. I'm listening."

At first the words wouldn't come, they were stuck at the back of her throat, constricted behind a sob like Celia's breath-defying shrieks. When the words came, it was as though they were shot out of a cannon. "I know where Sydney's body is. I know where she is!"

27

Tyler
Tuesday, January 9

Every day, Tyler prayed Psalm 51. "Have mercy on me, O God, according to Your unfailing love and Your great compassion...blot out my transgressions...and cleanse me from my sin. Against You, You only, have I sinned and done what is evil in Your sight ... wash me, and I will be whiter than snow. Let me hear joy and gladness...Create in me a pure heart, O God, and renew a steadfast spirit within me. Restore to me the joy of Your salvation and grant me a willing spirit, to sustain me."

It was the same prayer King David prayed after the prophet Nathan told him the parable of the man whose pet lamb was ruthlessly sacrificed. When King David reacted in rage to the story, Nathan revealed that the parable was about David himself. He'd committed adultery with Bathsheba and had her husband murdered. David was devastated by his own sin just as Tyler was devastated by his own.

Tyler had not entered this twilight zone of impossibility by accident. This was his own doing. As he stood at the precipice of the woods across the street from Runnymede Secondary School, he was all too aware of the fact that they were there for one reason: his daughter knew where a body was buried, and they were there to find it.

Tyler, Kaki, Josh, Detective Jackson, and several officers advanced through the weeds and into the thick woods that spanned the space between the school and a housing subdivision. The forest was deep, crowded with trees, brambles, and deadwood. As they entered, Tyler heard the sound of the bell releasing the students for the day.

Officer Mendoza unleashed an expletive as he stepped into a particularly icy area and nearly fell over, catching himself with his right arm and rappelling against the mud and ice into an upright position. He wiped his wet hand on his pants, leaving a trail of dirt and bits of twig.

"Whoa—watch out," Josh warned. "This is kind of like a frozen swamp back here."

Mendoza, an older, stocky, muscular guy, wore no coat even in these freezing temperatures. His police uniform and the flak jacket over it was his only protection against the cold. He breathed heavily and pointed up ahead. "Is it up here, Katherine?"

Kaki's face was pale, her lips a strange color. Her equilibrium appeared off, and she seemed weirdly sedated. Almost as though she were drunk. "Yeah," she said, her hand limply signaling in a pointing gesture. "Yeah, it's up here."

Their shoes crunched and sloshed through the slushy, melted areas.

Detective Jackson's winter coat was pulled tightly around her, a purple scarf poking out of the top as her breath made frosty phantoms against the waning light behind them. "You don't believe in coats or something?" she asked Officer Mendoza, a smile spreading over her face as she motioned to his bare arms.

He laughed. "I've gotten used to going without one."

"That's a good way to get pneumonia, you know."

"Yeah, that's what my wife says. But I haven't been sick in ten years."

"Well, OK," Abbie chuckled. "Can't argue with that."

The group made their way over the frozen ground. Abbie nearly fell as her foot skimmed an ice-laden trap. Josh caught her arm and held her upright, as rigid branches and leaves slick with crystallized water crunched under their feet. There was a pain to the silence pulsating all around them.

The day was gray with only the sun's pink and gold rays beaming in the distance, visible through spaces between the tightly-wedged tree branches.

"Look," Abbie exhaled softly, pointing some thirty feet in front of them toward a coyote, it's long, lean body slinking past them. It kept its eye on them until it could safely run farther into the woods.

Tyler hadn't seen a coyote in a while in the densely-populated suburbia.

"Was that a wolf or a coyote?" Abbie asked.

"Coyote," Josh confirmed. "We see them around here in the winter sometimes looking for food. That's usually what they do when they see a person, though—they run."

"And that's a good thing," Officer Mendoza said.

"Well, I know you weren't going to try and pet it," Abbie joked.

"Uh, no, ma'am. No way, no how. They leave me alone, and I leave them alone."

Farther into the woods, the shade grew darker,

and the temperature dropped.

Tyler began to have a sick feeling in his stomach. How far into these trees would they have to go?

They maneuvered over fallen tree trunks, kicking aside trash bags and cans and drug paraphernalia left behind by truant kids.

Maintenance tried keeping the woods next to the school clear of all of the trash, but the kids still found ways to use the grounds—at night, on the weekends, and on days when there were too many things going on inside the school to man the woods outside. Over the past few years, the county had mandated exterior cameras, security doors, and extra security guards. But at the end of the day, if the kids wanted to do drugs, skip school, or steal something, they'd find a way to do it surreptitiously. They were clever and ingenious in their methods.

"I don't see anything out here," Officer Mendoza said. "Are you sure this is where it is?"

"You gettin' cold, Mendoza?" Abbie asked, pointing at the goosebumps on his arm.

"No," Mendoza shook his head. "I'm good. I'm tough. The cold don't bother me."

"Uh-huh. That's why you want to give up so easily."

"I didn't say I was giving up," Mendoza said, forging on.

Tyler was beginning to hope they didn't find anything either. The dread he felt at unearthing a body—one his daughter claimed that she helped to bury—was more than he could process. He had to consciously shut down his emotions. The only way he could get through this was with constant prayer.

A shoe. Just one—a white tiger pattern with a red

platform sole resting heel-down in the brambles. Katherine pointed.

They gathered around the pump and stared at it.

Abbie pulled a pair of gloves and a plastic bag out of her pocket. As she snapped the gloves over her hands, the air vibrated with the sound of cars passing on Dranesville Road and the rattle of the bag as Abbie placed the shoe within it.

"It's up here," Katherine said, pointing straight ahead.

Wordlessly, they continued, crunching over the branches and the ice, their breaths panting rhythmically, forcing clouds of dew into the air.

Tyler stopped short.

An outstretched hand connected to the frozen, mutilated body of a young woman was just ahead.

He quickly looked away, simultaneously grasping the back of Katherine's coat and pulling her back. He didn't want her to see that. That image would be burned into her brain forever. As if it wasn't already.

Somehow, he thought this would be a neater scene—more of a dirt mound in the woods, not the exposed body of a young woman, partially buried, partially eaten, sprawled in the woods behind the secondary school. He hadn't expected to taste the acidic bile rising to the back of his throat.

Abbie's phone was instantly against her ear. "Yes, we're going to need the coroner over here. And homicide."

Tyler continued to back away, pulling Katherine with him.

Her gaze remained glued to the area where the police stood, but she showed no emotion.

"Animals have already been at her. Probably been

dead a couple of weeks," Mendoza said.

"Saturday, December tenth," Katherine said, her eyes fixed, trance-like. "She died on December tenth."

Officer Mendoza was in full investigative mode, seemingly unaware of Katherine's role. He pointed. "They dragged her from here to here."

"Yep," Abbie said, stuffing her phone into her back pocket. She paused and looked around before directing the other officers. "We need to get this whole area cordoned off." Her gaze shifted to Tyler and Katherine. "Tyler, you want to get her out of here? Wait for me back at the car."

Tyler tried to pull Katherine away, but her gaze was still on the officers stretching out their caution tape. "Come on, honey. Let's get back to the car where it's warm." Her body was stiff, but he finally turned her away, and they made their way back to the parking lot.

Standing by the passenger side of the car, Tyler fumbled his keys with shaking hands.

Katherine collapsed.

~*~

For the second time in two days, Tyler sat in the lobby of Reston Hospital. He should've called Christina, but he just didn't want her frantic, crazy energy adding to the chaos. Katherine's collapse and non-responsiveness was terrifying. He assumed it had been due to viewing her dead friend's body. He shouldn't have let the police take her out there. He should have told them to check the woods themselves. But he hadn't thought the girl...Sydney...would be unburied and so *out there*—for all to see.

Rubbing his forehead, Tyler absently gazed at the television. He snapped to attention. A local reporter was interviewing the principal of Runnymede, Penelope Miller.

"Do we know why the girl wasn't attending school? Did anyone contact her parents?"

"Initially we called her house, but her mother had moved, and her aunt said Sydney claimed she was living elsewhere."

"According to her mother and aunt, Sydney's disappearance wasn't unusual, and they didn't want to involve the police. From the school's perspective, after two weeks of no attendance, students are automatically dropped from the roster. We don't generally pursue it, since it usually means they were pulled to go to an alternative school, or their family moved away without telling us. It's not all that unusual."

"So this girl just fell through the cracks?" the reporter asked.

Penelope held up her hands. "We have twenty-five hundred students in our school. We do the best we can."

With voiceover in play, the camera cut to images of Runnymede Secondary and the woods where yellow caution tape stretched across the entrance. Then there was a shot of Josh speaking, his voice finally came up in the audio. "Right now, the police are conducting a full investigation. We don't have a lot of information other than the body was positively IDed by the family. If anyone in the community knows anything, let the county police know."

The reporters voice came on again as more images of the school, kids boarding buses flashed across the screen. "...was positively identified as Sydney Diaz, a seventeen-year-old sophomore formerly attending Runnymede Secondary School. Diaz was found partially buried in the woods adjacent to the school, leaving the neighborhood shocked and fearful. The cause of death is yet to be announced, but foul play and gang activity is suspected."

Local resident interviews followed, the first of which was a middle-aged housewife—a parent Tyler had seen frequently jogging around the neighborhood. She looked as though the reporters had caught her in the midst of a morning jog, dressed in her black, spandex pants and heavy fleece sweater. Her face was reddened with the cold, and tufts of condensation puffed from her mouth as she spoke. "It's really frightening. I mean, I have two kids who go to Runnymede, and...I just...I just don't know what to think about what happened. I mean, you wonder—was this another student who did this, or an adult, or what? Who should we be watching for when we're walking around our neighborhood?"

"Mr. Jones?" The doctor's voice drew him away from the television screen. Dr. Branigan was a young, petite woman with dark, messy hair that she had pinned flat against her head.

Tyler stood immediately. "Yes, how is she?"

"She's in shock...and she's in withdrawal."

"Withdrawal?"

"From drugs."

"Drugs?"

"Yes, her system is full of narcotics. We don't know what kind, we'd have to do further testing to determine that. But I think the most important thing right now is to get her into a treatment program. Like tonight."

Tyler didn't think he could take another thing, or he would end up in a treatment facility.

"I've called ahead to one in Winchester. They have availability there...or if you have another place in mind. We also have some people on staff who can help you find an appropriate place, one that will take your insurance if this one doesn't."

"Yes, I understand." How much more could his heart break? How had he not realized that his daughter was addicted to drugs? *Because you weren't paying attention.* The voice rang in his head as clear as a bell. *Because you were too consumed with your own problems, your own desires...Oh, God.* His heart gave a wordless cry for mercy. If ever he needed God's supernatural peace it was now. He needed it like a lifeline.

"OK," Tyler said, surprised by how resolute his tone sounded. "I'll call her mother, and we'll get her where she needs to go."

Taking a deep breath, he hit Christina's speed-dial. No matter how much she drove him crazy or how much he didn't want to involve her, she was Katherine's mother. Katherine needed both of them now.

28

Tyler
Thursday, January 19

The entire task upon which Tara Pickard worked was moved to an office in Crystal City.

If Tyler had been a singer, he would have been belting out an aria. Relief. That was one problem solved.

There were still other problems. He kept finding vodka bottles hidden all over the house—at the back of a drawer in the bedroom, another behind some books in the living room. How had he missed what was really going on? Easy. Just like he'd missed Katherine's double-life, his son's addiction, he should have seen Lana's problem.

Some days he didn't know how he managed everything. Learning a new job, taking care of two little kids, attending counseling with Brandon, and figuring out who would watch Micah and Celia in the afternoons when they got home after school consumed him.

When Molly and Josh offered to help watch the kids, Tyler nearly cried with gratitude. One more problem solved. He could never repay them for opening their home and their hearts to his kids— especially when they had none of their own.

Tyler kept in constant contact with Christina.

Neither of them were allowed to visit Katherine at her treatment facility, but they both checked in frequently with the clinic and each other. She had even been supportive of Brandon's counseling, the men's group, and Tyler's educational plan for the kids.

"I want Brandon on homebound until the end of the school year. Next year, we can talk about alternative education plans for both of the kids. I don't want either of them going back to Runnymede."

He braced himself for Christina's tirade, waiting for a stream of expletives, accusations, and threats delivered in a glass-shattering decibel. Instead, she remained quiet. Finally, she sniffed. "Whatever. I guess it's about time you started acting like their father."

As offended as he wanted to be, as much as he wanted to throw her remark back in her face and accuse her of being a sorry mother, he stopped himself. Humility. Taking responsibility for his actions. No escapism. All things he was learning in his men's group. He hadn't been much of a father. He'd been self-consumed and absent. It had taken Lana's departure, the near loss of his son, and the ongoing battle to retrieve the soul of his daughter to realize that he was a lousy father.

God had been trying to get his attention for some time. *Well, now You have it, Lord. I hear You loud and clear.* Everything had been ripped out from underneath him, leaving him in a fast free fall.

Tyler and Brandon attended counseling together every week, and on Thursday evenings, they went to a men's group led by Nick. There, they met and prayed with other fathers and sons struggling with the same weakness. There was a difference in Brandon—his eyes were brighter, he smiled more, and his face was beginning to lose that burdened, pained expression. But it would take time—years, perhaps—to completely heal from all that had transpired.

As the meeting ended that Thursday, Nick Melioni suggested they take prayer requests.

Going around the circle of seventeen men ranging in age from thirteen to seventy, the prayer requests varied from needing help to stay off of the Internet to prayers that their wives would take them back.

"I've got one." Tyler's voice shook, and he cleared his throat. "My daughter's in trouble. She's uh...she's at a treatment facility...for drugs and...um, other stuff."

"How's she doing there?" Nick asked.

"Well, they had a hard time with her at first. She was asking them every day to leave, and trying to run away. She had a...a sort of boyfriend...except he wasn't really a boyfriend..." Tyler was too embarrassed to tell them the real story. He couldn't hold back the tears that waited at the rim of his eyes. As soon as they spilled over on to his cheeks, he pawed at them. "Actually, her boyfriend was a gang member who was prostituting her." The words muffled as they stuck in his throat.

The other men stared at him with expressions of horror, sympathy, and anger.

"What?" One of the men asked, his eyes wide. "How old is she?"

"She's sixteen."

A groan resounded from several of the men. Many others shook their heads or gaped with enlarged eyes and furrowed brows.

"Are the police involved?" Nick asked.

"Yes. They arrested at least one of the guys, and

there's a warrant out for the other one. There's a full ongoing investigation."

"The same thing happened to my daughter." Luis was around Tyler's age, although Tyler didn't know him well. Luis had been relatively quiet the last few weeks in the group, doing more listening.

"When?" Tyler asked.

"Three years ago. She ran away with her boyfriend to New Jersey. He was in a gang, too. He was giving her drugs, pimping her out..."

"I didn't know that, Luis," Nick said. "How long was she missing?"

"We looked for her for a year and a half. All over New Jersey."

"Did you find her?" Tyler asked, hopeful.

"We didn't find her," Luis answered simply. "The police did."

"Where did they find her?"

"In New York City. In a dumpster."

The room surged with the men's expressions of horror—slight, chuffing sounds as they processed Luis's words, his matter-of-fact confession. A father's unimaginable grief. Then, a blanket of silence. Bile rose in Tyler's throat. He wanted to say something, but his tongue wouldn't work.

"I'm so, so sorry, Luis," Nick said.

Luis nodded, his facial expression unwavering. "When Karla ran away, that was the last time I ever looked at pornography. Her mother found Karla's pictures online. When I saw it, I thought of how I'd looked at pictures like that for years. When the pictures didn't do it for me anymore, I'd even thought of calling an escort service—just like the one that was advertising my daughter. When we're young, we all think pornography doesn't hurt anyone. But now, we all know that's a lie. Look what it has done to us. Look what it's doing to our children."

Images of Katherine dead in a dumpster flickered in Tyler's mind. He squeezed his eyes shut, desperate to squelch the vision. He couldn't bear to think about it.

"I want to pray for your daughter," Luis said. "I want to pray she does not end up like my Karla. What's her name again?"

"Katherine...Kaki...I used to call her Kaki."

29

Kaki
Monday, March 20

Two months had passed since Kaki had arrived at Whiteway Rehabilitation Center. Her physical need for the drugs was gone. But the emotional noise still flooded her mind at night. The memories of what she'd done were much worse than the symptoms of withdrawal. And she could not shake the fear that someone was looking for her.

Damien was still out there. Would he show up at the facility in the dead of night and make her go with him? Would he kill her family while she was at the rehab facility?

For the first few weeks, she hadn't been allowed any contact with family. She chewed all her fingernails down to the cuticle worrying about what was happening at home. And she struggled with strange, inexplicable desires to contact Damien.

What would make her want to return to a man who drugged her, beat her, and forced her to have sex with other men? But once she received phone privileges, she fought the urge to call him. Insidious thoughts wormed through her brain—*wouldn't it just be better if you went back to him and got it over with? Wouldn't everyone be safer that way? Aren't you worthless to anyone else at this point anyway? Who could ever love you knowing what you've been?*

She stared into the mirror in the communal bathroom. She no longer looked like herself. Her hair was dull—stripped of all its shine from washing it every day since she'd arrived here. She couldn't get clean enough. She looked down and touched a finger to the black tattoo upon her wrist. She might have been removed from Damien's presence, but his brand was still on her body.

"You know, I know someone who can help you take care of that."

Kaki spun around and looked into the face of one of her counselors, Darienne.

In her thirties, Darienne had short, spiky hair and eyes that swirled and sparkled like green marbles. But most importantly, Darienne had once stood in Kaki's shoes.

"You know someone who can remove tattoos?"

Turning on the water at the sink, Darienne stood beside Kaki and began washing her hands. "They'll remove them, or they'll tattoo over them. Either way, they make those brands disappear. See? Here's mine." Darienne pulled up the sleeve of her shirt to reveal a purple butterfly. Underneath it, a verse of scripture. "It used to say Rokk—my pimp's name."

"Romans 6:18?"

"You have been set free from sin and have become slaves to righteousness." Darienne pulled a paper towel out of the dispenser and dried her hands. "God takes what was meant for evil and turns it for good. I figured that I'd been a slave to my pimp for long enough, and that hadn't gotten me anything but a drug addiction, a messed-up head, and a bunch of sexually transmitted diseases. After I got away from him, I chose to become a slave to righteousness—to the One who chose me first. To the One who really loved me. Jesus."

Although Kaki didn't really understand, it was obvious that Darienne really meant what she said.

"Once you're out of here, I'll give you the name of the organization and the contact person. They'll get that brand off of your wrist one way or the other. And you'll feel so much better once they do."

"Isn't it expensive to have a tattoo removed?"

"They do it for free. They're a ministry supported by donations. The woman that started it is like us. She was in the life too. God had a purpose for her life…just like He has for yours, Kaki."

Kaki shook her head. "I just can't imagine ever living a normal life again."

"You'll do it," Darienne assured her. "With the grace of God, you'll do it."

Kaki gazed at Darienne. "How did you do it?"

Darienne smiled almost as though she had been waiting for that question. "I was a runaway. Out of the house at fifteen because my mom's boyfriend kept messing with me. Oldest story in the world. I was already doing some drugs anyway, but once I was on the streets—well, I needed to eat. I needed a place to stay. I met a guy who promised me all that and drugs, too. I was with him for three years—until he nearly killed me at a truck stop one night after a john complained. Another trucker there took pity on me and called 9-1-1. It's the only reason I'm alive today."

"Did you ever want to go back to it?" Kaki asked.

"Sure. My trafficker was the only person I knew anymore. Once I was out and realized how alone I was, I nearly did go back to the life several times. Those are the feelings you have to fight, Kaki. You have to fight them like your life depends on it. Because it does. It's a form of Stockholm Syndrome. You ever heard of that?"

Kaki shook her head. "No."

"Stockholm Syndrome is when the one who's been kidnapped, trafficked, or oppressed falls in love with their victimizer. It's a coping mechanism when you realize you've lost all control. Outside the life, you have to deal with those feelings and recognize them for what they are—a lie from the pit of hell."

It felt so good to hear Darienne talk. Kaki's heart soared with relief, and she soaked in every word of wisdom. She had gotten so used to hearing Sydney's "pep talks"—all lies and propaganda about how normal stripping was or how much money she could make working for Damien—that she'd forgotten how it felt to really connect with and trust another person.

Darienne wasn't in any rush either. She leaned against the sink, talking as though they were side by side on a soft couch with a bowl of popcorn between them. "You have to pray to know that nothing good will come of going back. It's a process, and it doesn't happen overnight. It happens through God's patient, healing hand. You done any praying on your own?"

Kaki shook her head. Other than prayers with Darienne at the facility or nighttime prayers with her dad when she was a little kid, Kaki had never really talked to God before. When she was young, she'd gone to church with her dad and Lana, but God never seemed real to her. "Some of the sermons here during the church services are starting to make a little sense, though." Her voice was shy, unsure.

Darienne smiled. "That's a great start."

Encouraged, Kaki continued. "I've even started

reading the Bible a little. It doesn't all make sense to me, but some of it does."

Darienne's green eyes were kind. They were so alive and fiery.

She hoped one day when she looked in the mirror, her own would stare back with that kind of life.

"God will never give you more than you can handle, Kaki."

Kaki laughed. "He must think I can handle a lot, then."

~*~

Friday, March 24

Going home was hard. Much harder than she'd thought. Kaki had moved from Damien and the gang, to a treatment facility, and now she was going back to her dad's house where she was expected to live a semi-normal life.

When her father picked her up, she was simply relieved that everyone in her family was still alive. "Have they caught him yet?" she asked on the ride home.

"Who?"

"Damien."

"No, honey. They haven't caught him yet. They will, though."

"How do you know?" She noticed her dad's hair had faded to a light gray. She always thought of him with blond hair.

"Because I know that God is good and just. Whether Damien is caught today or twenty years from today, God will bring about justice. I know He will."

Because the words came from her dad, she willed herself to believe them. She needed to believe them. She needed to start having hope again. Damien had stolen six months of her life, and she was determined not to give him anymore. She tensed a little before asking the next question. "What about Lana? Any word from her?"

Her father's face fell and he answered softly. "No. No word." A few moments of silence passed. He reached over and grabbed her hand, squeezing it. "Your mom's anxious to see you."

"She came to visit me last week. Actually, she came every week she was able to visit." It had made her feel good to have her mom around again. Even if she was a little crazy, Kaki was starting to believe that her mother loved her nonetheless.

"That's good. And your brother really wants to see you, too. He's doing a lot better. But...we're all just taking it one day at a time. That's the best we can do. I guess we all have to start new lives." A tight smile pulled at his lips.

Kaki nodded, although her insides trembled with fear. She couldn't envision what a new life looked like. She wondered if her dad felt as scared as she did.

Sydney's death was an ever-present memory, although Kaki had worked hard to put it behind her. Officially, an autopsy ruled Sydney Diaz's death a drug overdose, and not a homicide.

Damien Rosas-Diego was charged for concealing the body and found guilty in absentia, and Kaki felt some comfort in the knowledge that a warrant for his arrest was out there...but Damien was out there, too. No one had found him yet. She still awoke to the nightmarish vision of his black eyes staring down at her, his hands reaching out to wrap around her throat. "Do I have to go back to school?" she asked, dreading the answer.

Tyler cleared his throat. "Well, that's the other thing I wanted to talk to you about. How would you feel about doing homebound until the end of the year? And then, at the start of next year, Molly would teach you and Brandon at home. Almost like homeschooling. How would you feel about that?"

The idea of never having to set foot in that school—with all of its memories and associations that made her physically ill—provided monumental relief. The muscles in her neck and shoulders loosened. "I think it sounds like a great idea."

~*~

Saturday, April 1

The adorable, heavy-footed puppies ran back and forth and all over Josh and Molly's living room floor.

Something inside Kaki sang. For the time she was sitting on the floor with them, running her fingers over their fluffy heads, or holding their warm, furry bodies in her arms, not one thought about Damien, her fear, or the ugly black and blue tattoo on her wrist entered her mind.

Kaki looked down at her wrist. She'd been keeping it covered with a terrycloth tennis wristband. It looked kind of dumb, but it was better than the tattoo. She had called the organization Darienne suggested and had an appointment next week to have a plastic surgeon look at it. She could hardly wait.

One of the puppies grabbed the wristband

between its teeth and tugged at it.

Kaki laughed, extracted the cloth from the puppy's mouth, and held its fuzzy body under her chin. It looked up at her and licked her. She breathed in its sweet puppy breath. The puppies were the purest form of love Kaki had ever known.

Molly said a dog's love was God's way of revealing a small glimpse of His love. "A dog loves unconditionally, no matter who we are or what we do. They never leave us or forsake us. A lot like God."

Kaki couldn't understand how God could ever love or forgive her when she was so dirty and unworthy. But it helped her to believe He might be able to accept her when she held one of those puppies. The furball she was holding licked her face until her cheeks were wet and shining. It wanted nothing more than to be in her company.

"When are you going to pick out one of those puppies and take it home with you?" Molly asked.

Kaki wanted one of the puppies. Her dad had even said she was welcome to bring one home anytime she wanted. But she couldn't. Not with Damien still out there. "I don't know," Kaki said. "I'm not sure."

"What? You can't decide?" Molly laughed. "OK. That's easy. Take two of them. They're small. Your dad won't even notice the second one."

"It's not that. I just...I don't know."

"Well, listen. We can't keep all of these. We already gave away two, and we've got to find homes for these others. Josh said we can only keep one of them, and I've already decided I'll keep whichever one isn't chosen."

Kaki pointed at her two favorites, a little fawn-colored chub and the black and white runt.

"Great!" Molly exclaimed. "You can take them home with you today. Nothing'll take your mind off of your woes like puppies. I don't even think about babies anymore. God used Trixie and these puppies to completely divert my attention to a different type of mothering—one that requires me to feed, water, clean, and care for these furry babies...all because of the gift of a stray, pregnant mutt on the doorstep one freezing January afternoon."

"Really? So, you don't even feel bad about not having any human children?"

"I just know that God's plans are much greater, and much more comprehensive than mine. Maybe, if we'd had those children we so desperately wanted, we would have been too busy, too consumed with them to be of use to anyone else's kids...like to you and your brothers and sisters. Maybe one day we'll look back and say, 'So that's why.' Or maybe we'll just have to continue to trust that the Lord is good."

Kaki looked down at the puppy she held. It's little fawn-colored body blurred as her eyes filled with tears. She wanted to snatch up those puppies and run home with them right then, but something stopped her. Fear for the puppies. "I'm just afraid, Molly." She hated the way her voice sounded.

Molly's large, dark eyes grew serious. "What are you afraid of?"

The tears threatened to spill over. She hadn't cried in ages. The lump in her throat made her voice sound thick. "I'm afraid Damien will kill them," she said, bursting into sobs. "They haven't caught him yet. He said he'd kill my family, my friends, my pets..."

Molly pulled her into a tight hug. She held her until she finished crying, which seemed to take a long time.

Finally, Kaki pulled back and looked at her. An idea suddenly occurred. "Could the puppies stay with you until they catch Damien? Until I know it would be safe to bring them home?"

Molly had tears in her own eyes as she nodded. "Of course, sweetie. They can stay here until you're ready."

"Until he's caught?"

She nodded. "Until he's caught."

30

Tyler
Tuesday, April 5

Tyler watched the moving truck back into the driveway across the street where Suzanne and her husband used to live. New neighbors were moving in—a young couple with two small children. He hoped they would prove to be friends for Micah and Celia. Despite everything, he was glad he hadn't put their house on the market or chosen to move away. He loved their neighborhood.

But Tyler was tired. The past week had been spent with lawyers inside the Fairfax County Courthouse, witnessing several separate trials in a confusing attempt to figure out who was responsible for what crimes.

All sexting charges for Brandon and three other boys his age were dropped, much to Tyler's relief. Several of the older boys at the party ended up with more severe convictions, including obstruction of justice, aiding and abetting a crime, and possession and distribution of child pornography, for which some of them received fines or time in the juvenile detention center.

The most surprising conviction of all went to Gio George in a separate trial regarding the events that had taken place at his house. Despite the expensive defense team his father had hired, Gio was convicted on several counts of contributing to the delinquency of a minor, aiding prostitution, and taking persons for the purposes of prostitution. Although he had not yet been sentenced, as a legal adult Gio was facing up to two years in prison followed by requisite registration as a sex offender. His family was, of course, appealing his conviction.

Moving into the kitchen, Tyler stacked two plastic cups and carried them, along with the pitcher of lemonade, onto the back porch where Katherine sat in the rocking chair, her foot pushing against the wrought iron coffee table as she stared out into the yard.

The weather had been a warm and breezy spring day. It was wonderful to see his daughter so relaxed. She was in no way completely healed, and it would take years for her to feel whole again. Or perhaps she never would. He'd have to pray for God to supernaturally heal those wounds that time and modern medicine couldn't touch.

Tyler and Katherine had never spoken about those horrific months. The weeks following her return home were all about watching and protecting her, making sure she didn't run, and attempting to bring some normalcy back to her life. He hoped she would talk when she was ready. He set the lemonade down on the glass table.

Katherine dropped her feet from the edge of it.

"Molly made this," he admitted.

"I know," Katherine said, sipping.

"It's all natural with no preservatives, no doubt," Tyler said.

A smile tugged at the corner of Katherine's mouth. "No doubt."

There was a slight breeze blowing, and the chimes affixed to the overhang—silvery pipes of different sizes strung from a model of a cathedral—jangled together. Lana had hung those when they'd first moved into the house. They still sounded beautiful, even though the strings were dark and weathered. A pang of regret surged in his chest.

Father and daughter stared off into the empty yard where the grass was nearing an overgrown state and dandelions pushed their way through the green blades. Some of the pollen scattered across the tips of the grass as the breeze blew a little harder. It was so quiet—as though the wind begged Tyler to say what had been on his heart. "You know, Kaki, I've been waiting for the right time to say this."

Kaki swung her head toward her father.

"I feel…that what happened to you…was in some way my fault."

Kaki said nothing, but her eyes were wide.

"And I really feel the need to ask your forgiveness. I've realized I've been a less-than-stellar dad. Absent, neglectful, self-consumed. You and Brandon both needed me to be there for you, and I haven't been there for years." He paused, swallowed, and looked out at the yard. "There are a lot of reasons for that, some of which involve my own selfishness. Maybe your mom and I had our own problems to contend with, but we should never have taken it out on you and Brandon. It wasn't right."

Katherine nodded, and her gaze shifted to her hands. Could she forgive him?

Tyler wasn't sure he could forgive himself. "I get the feeling you and Brandon think I don't love you—and I know I've been abysmal at showing it—but Kaki,

I love you, Brandon, Micah, and Celia more than anything in this world. You kids are the greatest joy I've encountered in this life. I mean that."

Katherine's mouth pressed together, and tears spilled over her cheeks.

His heart clenched. "Do you believe that?" He asked, trying to meet her eyes.

She nodded and gasped a sob.

"I know I haven't been any kind of a father to you, Kaki, but I promise that with the Lord's help—and I really need His help, because I'm just as messed up as the next person—I'm committing myself to becoming the best dad I can possibly be from here on out. How does that sound?"

Kaki's face crumbled as the tears rolled over her cheeks in rivulets.

Tyler's chest tightened as his daughter's silent tears turned into loud, heaving sobs that wracked her whole body. He held her hand while she cried, his own tears streaming from eyes that leaked much too easily these days. He stood in front of her, still squeezing her hand between his own. "Kaki, will you forgive me?" As he spoke, he realized how long it had been since he had called her by the nickname.

"Yes." For the first time since she'd returned, Kaki allowed her father to hug her.

And just that small gesture made his heart soar. "I love you, honey." His phone vibrated and buzzed.

"What now?" he sighed, wiping at his eyes and looking down at the screen. He didn't recognize the number, but he answered it. "Hello?"

"Tyler?"

"Yes?"

"It's Lana."

Tyler's heart and mind simultaneously seized with shock. He looked over at Kaki, still wiping her eyes. "I'm taking this inside," he said, patting her shoulder.

With a pounding in his chest, Tyler moved inside, but where he could still see Kaki from the window. "Hi," he said with a dry mouth. Reaching a shaking hand into the cabinet, he grabbed a glass and filled it with water.

"I know it's been a while."

Anger welled. "Lana, it's been three months."

"Yeah, I-I know," she said, and her voice sounded different, subdued. "How are you?"

"I'm fine." His mind reeled with questions.

"That's good. And the kids? How are they?"

"They're fine. Lana, I'm sorry—but why are you calling? I'm busy right now. Kaki's waiting outside on the porch for me. You can't even imagine what's been going on here."

She didn't have a clue about the pain, the trials they'd all been enduring.

"Oh," she said. "Oh, I don't want to interrupt your day. I just—"

"You just what?" he asked, teeth clenched.

"Tyler, I know I don't deserve one minute of your time, and everything that I've done is...well, inexcusable. And to tell you that I've changed is probably unbelievable to you. But I guess I'm just wondering...if we might be able to talk sometime."

The energy drained out of him. Hearing her voice again twisted something inside of him. He wished he could see her. "Where are you, Lana?" he asked.

"I-I'm in Ohio. I'm staying with my aunt right now."

"You're not in California?"

"No, I left a month ago. It—it wasn't what I thought. And...well, I needed help, Tyler. But you probably knew that."

An image of a vodka bottle hidden behind the bottles of cleaning products flicked through his mind's eye.

"I-I was in bad shape," she continued. "I started going to treatment...for drinking. And for everything else, too."

Tyler had been holding his breath, his hand moving up to pinch his temples. "I'm glad you're getting help. I've been getting help, too. For *my* problem. We're all getting help."

"That's great. Yeah, that's really great, Tyler. And I'm going to church here in town with my aunt. I'm trying to make some big changes in my life."

Tyler didn't want to be manipulated again. He'd gone down this road once before.

"I know I can't expect you to forgive me. All I'm asking is a chance for us to talk. Whenever it's convenient for you. And if it's OK, I'd love to speak to the kids, too. I've missed them."

Tyler had worked so hard to recover, to move on and forget her. But in his mind, he heard the word as though it had been spoken aloud. *Forgive.* He had to forgive Lana. Whether their marriage was salvageable was something only time would tell—but forgiveness was non-negotiable. God had forgiven him, so how could he not forgive?

"Tyler, are you there?"

"I'm here. Let's talk later tonight."

"OK."

"Lana, thank you for calling. I know the kids miss you."

"I miss them. And I miss you."

Tyler sighed, closing his eyes in a silent prayer. "Well, let's just talk later. Maybe we can take it from there."

~*~

Saturday, April 9

Tyler and Kaki were in the kitchen preparing five bacon and egg sandwiches for their car ride to King's Dominion, a theme park located an hour and a half away. Of course, the trip required a wide variety of snacks. Micah hated string cheese, but Celia loved it. Kaki loved chocolate, whereas Brandon was allergic. Water, lemonade, sodas, juice, and the cooler was full to brimming.

"Who's going to carry this thing?" Tyler called out to no one in particular. "This weighs a ton."

"I'll do it," Micah volunteered.

Tyler ruffled his son's hair. His brave boy who had endured so much yet remained generous and giving. Tyler prayed Micah would be blessed one day for his selflessness. "Thanks. But I was just kidding. I'll carry it. It's too heavy for you."

"I can do it," Micah said, as he began to half-carry, half-drag it across the floor toward the front door.

"All right, kids!" Tyler called upstairs. "Everyone come down and grab something. It's time to hit the road!"

His cell phone buzzed against the countertop. Swiping at the phone, he carried it with him into the hallway, ignoring the ring until he'd made sure all the kids were working together to move items out to the car. When he was sure everyone was pitching in, Tyler looked at the incoming number. "Hey, Dad."

"Just checking to see how everything was going over there."

"Just walking out the door. We're on the way to King's Dominion."

"Oh," his father said. "That's great. I just called to see how things were going. It...it's been a few days since we've talked."

Tyler stared out the window as his kids gathered around the car. He recognized the beginnings of dissension. Soon they would be debating about who was sitting up front. "You and Mom OK?"

"Oh, yes. We're fine. Your mom is out in the garden this morning. Everyone here is fine."

Tyler tapped his fingers on the countertop impatiently. "Yeah, Dad, I really need to go. World War III is going to break out if I don't get outside."

"I understand. I understand. I'm just...very proud of you, Tyler. Your mother and I both are. You've really stepped up to the plate."

Tyler wasn't sure he'd heard his father right. Had he just heard Lyman Jones say he was proud of him? No. He was hallucinating. "Thanks, Dad," he said. A warmth rose inside his chest just as a lump swelled in his throat.

The horn honked. Tyler glanced out the window. Kaki was reaching through the driver's side window and pressing down on the steering wheel. There was probably a squabble breaking out between Micah and Celia. He had to get off the phone before something bad happened.

Lyman sniffed and continued gruffly. "Yeah, well, anyway. You should probably get out there to the kids."

"I love you, Dad," Tyler offered.

"Yes, yes. Talk to you later, son."

He smiled as he clicked off the phone. The love part was a little too much for his dad just yet, but he'd told him he was proud of him. That was a great start.

~*~

Tyler put the gas nozzle back in the pump, pulled his receipt from the slot, and opened the car door to climb in.

"Dad...that's him." Kaki's voice was shrill, panicked. Her blue eyes were wide and filled with terror.

"Who?"

"It's Damien. He's right there. That's him!"

Tyler swung his head to look.

It was a black car, and a guy with black hair sat inside. His arm, a sleeve of tattoos, hung out the driver's side window. A young girl came out of the gas station mart holding a bag. She moved toward the car, her long, dark hair falling over her face as her head bent over a cell phone. She appeared to be walking and texting simultaneously.

Tyler couldn't really tell how old she was, but she looked young.

As she moved to the passenger side of the car, the girl pulled at the edges of the short skirt that barely covered her thighs, as if suddenly embarrassed at how little it concealed. She climbed in beside the man Kaki had identified as Damien.

"Hey!" Instinctively, Tyler called out, slamming his door and moving around the front toward the black car.

Instantly, the driver floored the gas and sped out of the gas station, headed for the main road.

Tyler pulled his phone from his pocket and dialed 9-1-1. He climbed into his van just in time to see the black car run the stop sign and T-bone an on-coming car in the right lane. Both vehicles skidded into the ditch on the opposite side of the road in front of a child care center.

"Driver rammed another car on Dranesville Road, just in front of Petunia Child Care." Tyler spoke to the dispatcher on the line.

Kaki began to take quick, loud, desperate breaths. Hyperventilating. He wrapped his arm around her shoulders and pulled her close to him. "It's OK, honey. It'll be OK."

Tyler looked at Brandon sitting wide-eyed in the backseat. "Was that him?"

"Yeah. That was him."

Tyler turned back to the accident. Across the road next to the childcare center, a police vehicle was parked. An officer scrambled out and approached the accident, holding his radio to his lips as he moved toward it.

"Daddy, what's happening?" Celia asked from the backseat. "What's wrong with Kaki?"

"She's fine, honey." He held Kaki tighter against him, not taking his eyes from the cars in the ditch. "There was just a car accident across the road."

"Where?" Micah asked, peering over the backs of the front seat for a better look. "Whoa. Look at that!"

Other cars pulled off the road and people climbed out of them—some just to see what had happened, others to see if they could help. The familiar peal of sirens rang out in the distance. As the officer approached the car on its side in the ditch, the door on the driver's side of the vehicle popped open as if on springs, and a man wearing a T-shirt emblazoned with a wrap-around, elaborate dragon propelled himself out of the car, his arms pumping back and forth as he ran with a distinctive limp. Immediately, the officer broke into chase.

"Whoa! Look at that! He's chasing him!" Micah called out.

Kaki gasped and looked up.

Tyler grabbed her hand. "It's OK. They're gonna get him. Don't worry."

Celia climbed over the front seat, kneeling on the console to see better.

"Celia, move!" Micah squalled. "I can't see."

"Celia, sit down." Brandon directed.

The officer caught up to the injured man within a few seconds and reaching out his hand, grasped the dragon's tail on the back of his shirt. The officer pushed off of his front leg, leaped forward, and tackled him from behind.

Tyler, Brandon, Kaki, Micah, and Celia watched, transfixed, as the officer grasped the man's arms and wrestled them behind his back, managing to hold him down as he cuffed his wrists.

Two police cars quickly flanked the scene, just as the cop yanked the cuffed man to his feet, his black eyes staring straight ahead with all the humanity of a lizard.

Officers stuffed him into the patrol car, while another one approached the black car in the ditch as the young girl crawled through the driver's side—the passenger door inaccessible due to the embankment.

As soon as the girl was free, she too broke into a feeble attempt at a run in her five-inch high heels. Three strides in, she toppled over, falling into the same ditch where the car rested.

"I can't believe we're seeing this, Dad," Brandon breathed.

Tyler couldn't believe it either. They were less than a mile from their house.

The girl fell to her knees. One of the officers caught her upper arm and lifted her to her feet, supporting her weight against his side as she limped toward his police cruiser.

Tyler looked over at Kaki.

Her breathing was slowing, but her vacant expression looked eerily similar to the one he'd seen the night he got her back from the clutches of the traffickers. He started the car. "Kids, I'm sorry. But the amusement park will have to wait for another weekend."

Celia started to cry.

Tyler ignored her and left Micah to explain to her that sometimes circumstances altered things—words that could have been spoken from his own mouth. He backed up the car, turned around, and drove back into their neighborhood, squeezing Kaki's cold hand the whole way.

~*~

Tyler settled the three younger kids in front of the television with bowls of popcorn and a funny family film. Celia loved this movie. She could quote every line. Micah and Brandon tolerated it.

Kaki hadn't spoken a word since they'd gotten

home.

Tyler had made her chamomile tea, something Molly had told him would be soothing. "If that was him, Kaki, they've got him. Right?"

"It was him," she said glumly.

"So that's a good thing, right? You saw him being arrested."

Kaki's eyes were empty of emotion. It was as though she had reverted to that girl he picked up from the police station in January. "You don't know him, Dad. Damien's been arrested tons of times. He always gets off. He knows too many people—friends who'll bail him out."

Shaking her head, she slid off the kitchen stool and returned to the den to sit with the other kids.

The doorbell rang.

Through the beveled glass, he recognized Abbie Jackson.

As he swung the door opened, he tried to get an early read on her face. Was she here with good news or bad news. Her face was blank. Somber. He braced for the worst. *That wasn't Damien. They couldn't hold him. The charges didn't stick.*

Abbie followed Tyler into the kitchen, a safe distance from the kids in the den.

He didn't want Kaki or Brandon to hear the verdict just yet. They'd been through enough disappointment.

"Can I get you anything to drink? I've got lemonade in the fridge."

"No, thanks."

She paused by the island, her eyes dropping to the floor.

Uh-oh. This didn't look good.

A smile spread over her lips as she shot him a look. "We got him."

Tyler felt like he'd just come up to the surface after holding his breath too long underwater. "What?" he whispered.

"We've got charges galore—including one count of murder."

"Murder!"

"Yes. A girl in Pennsylvania. We think that's where he's been the last couple of months. Until now. He was the focus of an FBI sting operation up there. But he got away that time. There was more than one warrant out for his arrest."

Abbie's gaze shifted to something behind him.

His daughter was standing in the doorway—her face ghostly pale. "Was it him? Is he going to jail?

Abbie nodded. "He is. He's behind bars. Without bail."

"So it's over?"

Abbie nodded, her face somber. "We've won this battle. But there's a larger war. The trouble is, there are a lot more out there like him."

"One at a time, right?" It wasn't a smile that graced Kaki's lips—it was more like relief.

"Right."

Kaki's eyes were haunted but bright with tears. She almost looked happy. Slowly, she turned and joined her brothers and sister in the den.

Tyler saw Abbie out to her car. "Thanks, again." he extended his hand.

"This is a labor of love for me." Her expression hardened, her mouth stiffened. "I was one of those girls, too."

"What?"

"Nineteen ninety. I was eighteen years old. His name was Carlos." She stared off into the street. "Took me four years to get away from him. Four years, a broken nose, two black eyes, a knocked-out tooth, and two trips to the hospital for overdoses. I know the Damien Rosas-Diegos of this world all too well."

Tyler stood in stunned silence.

Abbie climbed back in her car and backed out of the driveway. It was hard to believe that such a strong, confident, capable woman had ever been the victim of a trafficker. It gave him hope for his own daughter.

His energy completely spent, Tyler dragged himself back inside. He needed to think about making dinner. Or maybe he'd just order pizza. He called out to them from the hallway. "Hey kids! Wanna order pizza tonight?"

A resounding "Yeah!" from the other room made him chuckle. He stood in front of the refrigerator, his eyes scanning over all of the magnets, looking for Joe's Pizza Place.

The doorbell rang. Tyler's shoulders slumped, his eyes closed. "What now?"

"I'll get it, Dad," Kaki called out.

Still a little wary of who might show up at the door, Tyler attempted to beat her to it. "No, it's fine. I'll get it."

But she was already opening the door.

Josh's left hand held a black and white puppy, it's paws scrabbling in the air. In the right hand, he held a fawn-colored puppy that licked his fingers.

Kaki's face lit up. A smile that he hadn't seen in years dimpled her cheeks.

Josh smiled, too. "Hey, Kaki. These little guys just told me they were tired of hanging out at our house and it was time they went to their new home." He looked up at Tyler and winked. "They're ready for a new beginning. I think they're going to fit in well over here. Don't you?"

Author's Note

A few years ago, the school district where I teach put together a video in conjunction with JustAskVa.org to warn teenagers, parents, and educators about teen sex trafficking. The public service announcement outlined the methods traffickers used, profiled the types of girls they victimized, and discussed where it was happening.

Traffickers often look like the homecoming king or the captain of the football team; the girls they traffic don't have a "type"—they could be the girl next door, or the girl down the street living in a wealthy neighborhood; and the trafficking is happening within the schools. Girls are being recruited by other girls who work for the traffickers. A trafficker (a pimp) might be that straight A student from math class or they might be a gang member.

Although my first novel was about sex trafficking, I focused on international rings or connections between prostitution and pornography. After watching this documentary, I followed up with more research and found many news articles pertaining to teen sexting scandals, high school prostitution rings, and parties sponsored by traffickers for the purpose of sexual exploitation. I couldn't believe how many news stories I found. It seems sexting is epidemic, and in-school trafficking is on an upward trend.

Just this year, a former student of mine—the homecoming princess of the junior class—went to a party where she was given miscellaneous, crushed-up drugs to snort. She later mixed that with anti-anxiety medication. She made it home, climbed into bed, and never woke up. This party took place in a wealthy neighborhood, and the parents were home at the time.

Drug use and sex trafficking go hand-in-hand. As a teacher in the public schools, I have seen and heard far too much to delude myself that these things don't happen. They happen every weekend, in every state around the nation, in every socio-economic demographic. We live in a time where kids are sacrificed on the altar of busy lives, high-powered jobs, and dissolution of the family unit. Many teenagers have no moral code and think everything they do is up to chance; nothing they do matters.

Even so, there are some kids who stay above the fray. They have a sense of right and wrong, a need for God in their lives, and an obligation to serve others. I've had the privilege of knowing some of those wonderful kids. They remind me that God is on the move amongst today's youth.

For more information on teen sex trafficking, sexual exploitation or pornography addictions, check out these resources:

Just Ask Prevention Project
http://justaskprevention.com/

Polaris Project
http://polarisproject.org/

National Center on Sexual Exploitation
http://endsexualexploitation.org

Thank you...

for purchasing this Watershed Books title. For other inspirational stories, please visit our on-line bookstore at www.pelicanbookgroup.com.

For questions or more information, contact us at customer@pelicanbookgroup.com.

Watershed Books
Make a Splash!™
an imprint of Pelican Book Group
www.PelicanBookGroup.com

Connect with Us
www.facebook.com/Pelicanbookgroup
www.twitter.com/pelicanbookgrp

To receive news and specials, subscribe to our bulletin
http://pelink.us/bulletin

May God's glory shine through
this inspirational work of fiction.

AMDG

You Can Help!

At Pelican Book Group it is our mission to entertain readers with fiction that uplifts the Gospel. It is our privilege to spend time with you awhile as you read our stories.

We believe you can help us to bring Christ into the lives of people across the globe. And you don't have to open your wallet or even leave your house!

Here are 3 simple things you can do to help us bring illuminating fiction™ to people everywhere.

1) If you enjoyed this book, write a positive review. Post it at online retailers and websites where readers gather. And share your review with us at reviews@pelicanbookgroup.com (this does give us permission to reprint your review in whole or in part.)

2) If you enjoyed this book, recommend it to a friend in person, at a book club or on social media.

3) If you have suggestions on how we can improve or expand our selection, let us know. We value your opinion. Use the contact form on our web site or e-mail us at customer@pelicanbookgroup.com

God Can Help!

Are you in need? The Almighty can do great things for you. Holy is His Name! He has mercy in every generation. He can lift up the lowly and accomplish all things. Reach out today.

Do not fear: I am with you; do not be anxious: I am your God. I will strengthen you, I will help you, I will uphold you with my victorious right hand.

~Isaiah 41:10 (NAB)

We pray daily, and we especially pray for everyone connected to Pelican Book Group—that includes you! If you have a specific need, we welcome the opportunity to pray for you. Share your needs or praise reports at http://pelink.us/pray4us

Free Book Offer

We're looking for booklovers like you to partner with us! Join our team of influencers today and periodically receive free eBooks!

For more information
Visit http://pelicanbookgroup.com/booklovers